About the

Walter Holder, M.D. is a retired physician and surgical oncologist who also has deep interests in spirituality, religion, human evolution and environmental issues. He has taught medical students and residents lifelong and did extensive biomedical research in tumor biology and tissue engineering for many years at Duke University, Stanford University and the University of North Carolina. He has numerous peer-reviewed publications in the medical and research literature, and has written a number of scientific and medical book chapters in various textbooks for W.B. Saunders, Springer-Verlag, Williams and Wilkins, Academic Press and Aspen Publishers. Over time, he has continually expanded his knowledge base and interest in cutting-edge science and the many, often paranormal, mysteries of life and the universe. This interest has expanded his writing considerably beyond the left-brain, scientific and technical writing to include more complex, right-brain views of science, faith and the future of humanity. He has found that fiction is an excellent medium for developing new ideas and introducing concepts that may be foreign to the reader. This is his first novel.

FUTURE PAST PRESENT

WALTER HOLDER

FUTURE PAST PRESENT

Vanguard Press

VANGUARD PAPERBACK

© Copyright 2022
Walter Holder

A CIP catalogue record for this title is
available from the British Library.

ISBN 978 1 80016 329 4

*Vanguard Press is an imprint of
Pegasus Elliot MacKenzie Publishers Ltd.*
www.pegasuspublishers.com

First Published in 2022

**Vanguard Press
Sheraton House Castle Park
Cambridge England**

Printed & Bound in Great Britain

Dedication

To the beautiful loving woman that is my joy and
inspiration, Fran Holder.

Acknowledgements

I want to thank my friends and family who have encouraged and supported me in all my endeavors and the great staff at Pegasus Publishers who made this book possible.

Foreword by Zoë Abrams

This is my story. I should not be so presumptuous to say this since it is actually your story as well, even though you have no reason to believe this assertion at this point. I realized the importance of what has happened in my life and am only now coming to fully understand the reason and significance for an unimaginable plot in which I was the center. I suppose plot is the correct word to use. How else could one account for what was, for all practical purposes, an elaborate, well-planned manipulation of me, my friends and others over the passage of many years? I think that this scenario should seem to you like an abhorrent terrorist plot. It was actually done out of love for humanity. I was very frightened and unnerved during my first awareness of the situation.

As my fear subsided, I was both increasingly curious and insatiably fascinated as the grand scheme unfolded like a beautifully complex origami structure emerges from a nondescript scrap of paper. To this point the plan has blossomed like a delicate and precious flower, but I sincerely worry that the flower will fade and a dire future lies ahead. Despite my concerns, I stand in awe, being a part of this wonderful series of events that has happened to me for the sake of mankind.

It has now been thirty years since my first remarkable encounter with the architect of the plan that turned my tiny world upside down. I have not seen him in nearly that many years, but know that will change before too long. I spent most of my life believing that I was like the proverbial leaf blowing in the wind and in my disparaging of the human situation, knew in my heart that mankind really did not have a future. He taught me that human beings are basically good but need guidance. Like sheep, we require herding and prodding. However, we continue to learn and evolve and in due time will learn to guide our own evolution and create a bright future. Human beings can ultimately accomplish anything.

Since the birth of my son, I have been busy raising, teaching, protecting him and preparing him for the future. I've been blessed with a dear husband and good friends who love and support me. My needs are few and my life is serene. It seems that I am just waiting for the next step, whatever that may be. Two years ago, three wonderful friends from my past sought me out and insisted on writing my story so that future generations would know the truth about me and my family and how it all came about. They insisted that they thought about this for many years and more recently became obsessed with the idea and suddenly felt compelled to find me. They spent over a month taking notes and recording everything I could remember. Their questions opened the floodgates of memories as I told them everything, including much of what I thought was forgotten. The guys even left a recorder so that if I thought of anything to say I could dictate it for them. They meticulously recorded notes from everyone who was a witness to the story and finally their manuscript came together. They continued to say how compelled they felt to write about all of this. Amazingly some of the information they wrote about should have not been known by anyone but me.

I have now read the manuscript, several times in fact. Those three little boys who are now wonderful grown men are to be congratulated on their creditable accomplishment. They may at times have taken some poetic license, but it is heartfelt and true to the story. Most importantly, they were major witnesses to some of the actual events.

We are beginning a new phase in our history when we can envision a coming time of peace and prosperity for the human beings of the future who will ultimately lead us to the stars. The passage will not be easy and there will be much tribulation before we reach our destiny. This is our story.

Zoë Abrams

Chapter 1
The Final Option

"The dreadful scourge has engulfed us all and our pathway is broken. We know we are facing our eminent extinction. Is there no help for us? Who can we call upon to save our noble race that has evolved on our Mother Earth and survived for millennia until now? There is only one who is powerful and wise who has steered our course through many troubled times. Our salvation is at hand if only he will help us. We will humbly call on him and hope that his care will be upon us. We all agree that we must beseech the man from the distant stars who is the only one who may be able to save us. Therefore, our counsel has decided and it will be done. Our request goes out to him and we pray to our universal soul for help and salvation."

Chapter 2
Nightmare

"Oh my God! That damn wretched dream again!" Zoë Abrams gasped for breath as she was shaken awake from a deeply troubled sleep. She sat up on the edge of the bed and rubbed her eyes. "Why does this keep happening to me?"

She glanced at the clock and the numerals glowed 2.22 a.m. As she sat there in the darkness with her mind in a maddening swirl, she tried to make sense of this recurring phantom dream that had tormented her sleep since she was a teenager. Sighing deeply, she felt exhausted as if the surreal nightmare had actually wrenched her life away. She shuddered as her emotions reached for some semblance of calm and reality. The touch of her warm blanket soothed her mind and she savored the soft velvet of the carpet on her feet as she sought solace in the intimate familiarity of her bedroom.

Her racing heart calmed as she took a sip of cool water from her bedside glass and once again told herself that it was just a bad dream. But why should she repeatedly have the same horrible dream to torment her sleep? It was just so real and she wondered if it really was a dream. The calm of the night filled the room and seeped into her troubled soul, and she once more drifted into a fitful sleep.

Every day she struggled with what would cause her to have this torment. Surely there was something within her or something that happened to her in the past that was roiling within her mind, and this was somehow surfacing in her dreams. She replayed the poignant memories of her life and could think of nothing that would cause her such agony. Zoë remembered the first dream occurred after the death of her mother, Anne. This was a devastating time for her as a young teenager, for she had lost the person she held most dear. Her stern father had left them and she had no one else. For the first time in her life, she felt frightfully alone and abandoned.

She came to believe that the universe was a cold, lonely place and that if God had created everything, he was certainly not involved with anything now. As a youth, she had shared the optimistic hope of her mother's Christian beliefs that God was good, kind and loving, but these beliefs had failed her with her mother's agonizing death. With deeper insight, she considered that maybe it was this terrible loss that contributed to the horrific night terrors. Zoë was a medical student and knew basic aspects of psychology and psychiatry and was concerned sufficiently by her dreams that she had sought counseling through student health. The counselor expressed the opinion that her bad dreams were likely related to the loss of her mother and that this is something that she should try to work through. That was easier said than done. Talking about it did not help her and if anything, made the situation worse. She would just immerse herself in her school and studies and leave the past behind.

The horrid dream was always the same, but completely unpredictable when it would happen. Sleep would come normally and comfortably for several hours and in her usual dreams she often envisioned playing with her current and childhood friends and being with her beloved mother. They were always having a good time and her mother's face would glow with love for her. Then there was the insidious onset of fear and foreboding, and she knew that all would come to a terrible end. Then she seemed snatched into a dark endless void and was suddenly and most terribly alone.

Numbing darkness penetrated everything and she was freezing cold, shivering and feeling the warmth of her life drifting away in the vast, cold emptiness. The unbearable icy darkness gripped her being as her teeth chattered and her body shook uncontrollably. She then realized that not only her death was coming, but the entire life of the world would vanish. As she gave up her struggle, there was one last dreadful thought that there is nothing beyond and no purpose to life. The struggle was lost as she awaited her death and then the dream ended as quickly as it began, and she awakened feeling as if she had actually died.

This is the troubled and enigmatic beginning of Zoë's story and her incredible life's journey. This will be a journey in which she will experience even stranger events, often beyond her capacity to understand, that will continue to confront her and challenge her perspective of the world and herself. Her fragile beliefs have thus far created her worldview but her experiences to come will be her true reality leading to a future beyond imagination.

Chapter 3
Midnight Tryst

As Zoë struggled with her lost faith and the demons in her troubled mind, there were others not far away who she would soon encounter who were also struggling with demons in their own lives. She will find that the lives and experiences of these people are vital in her journey to find redemption and purpose in her life.

A hunched figure, clinging to her walker, moved slowly through the shadows of the long hallway, taking agonizingly slow, painful steps. It was nearly midnight and the lights had been turned down by her caregivers, producing an eerie setting that looked like a night scene from an old black and white Hitchcock movie. A sharp stabbing pain radiated down her legs with each shuffling step and her arthritic back yearned for the comfort of her well-padded chair. Yet, she was drawn to his room like a moth to a light in the darkness. She had thought of him throughout the day and now yearned to be in his presence. He was the only light in her otherwise dark life. She finally reached his room door and knew he was waiting for her inside. Slowly moving her withered hand from the walker, she reached out and turned the doorknob. The silent door opened widely and she moved into the dark room, inching her way to the foot of his bed.

His large dark eyes were open and she heard her name, *"Macey"*. Was it her ears that perceived the subtle sound or was it her mind? It didn't matter because she was with him again and her soul was filled with joy. As she stood there in the dark silence, a wave of warmth and light spread through her mind. She forgot about her decaying body as her thoughts soared in ecstasy through unimagined worlds and undreamed experiences beyond anything she had ever known. Never had she sensed such love, kindness, caring and hope. She wanted to remain there forever but knew she must go soon. She lingered a while more, smiled and reached over the rail and gently touched his hand. She delighted as his small, thin hand almost imperceptibly moved. She left silently as she had come, thinking that this was her last time with him.

As Macey slowly reentered her bedroom, she was aglow with the memory of the wonderful encounter. What she did not know but would soon realize is that a man that lacked every good characteristic of her beloved friend would soon intersect her life.

Chapter 4
Jack's Journey

Not far from Zoë's house is the ancient Hudson River Valley that extends over three hundred miles and has been home to Native Americans and early European settlers who were beneficiaries of its rich, bountiful waters and fertile soil. Evoking a sense of wonder, the river inspires artists, writers, and city-weary travelers. Farms, towns, parks, and old mansions, each with its own unique stories, are scattered on its banks and legends of enchanted woods and strange happenings still fascinate children and adults alike. There is a sense of pervasively hidden mystery in the long shadows of the evening. Driving along the river kindles thoughts of life's basic questions as the river relentlessly flows to the ocean. Drivers often stop, savor the beauty of the moment and contemplate their lives.

Could it be that when the events of life do not go well, a second chance occurs by coincidence? Maybe, as some have said, there are there no coincidences? This day was a perfect day for another chance at life for one troubled man, Dr Jack Adams. The road stretched ahead through the valley as a single cloud drifted in the clear blue sky. The cloud's shadow crossed the river road and momentarily blocked the sun as it floated into the distance. Autumn had swept from south to north across the countryside, transforming the trees into glorious reds and gold oblivious to the warmth of Indian summer. Jack Adams knew that the unseasonably warm weather would last only a few more days and then the cold winds would return. He wondered about his chances for a fresh start. His mind was troubled and bitter. Did he even want to try again?

Jack was finally free after two years of imprisonment and another of rehabilitation. His medical license had just been reinstated with stipulations, of course, but he could once again practice his profession.

He resented the fact that the medical board would still be checking on him like some parolee, which was his true status. The very thought, like the clicking of a switch in his head, caused his pleasure with the beautiful day to rapidly fade. He began to fume as he thought about his situation. Quickly, he felt his old rage coming back like a familiar angry intruder rising from the depths of his mind. The rage slowly fed on itself and spiraled out of control. Jack's pulse pounded as the anger poured over him like an ocean wave. He slammed on his brakes and screeched onto the overlook. The beauty of the day fled as he raged like an injured wild animal, jumping from the car and flailing the trees with his bare hands.

"Damn those bastards!" Jack muttered with fire welling up in his chest, remembering his so-called friends who turned him in and his wife who betrayed him and left him penniless. Joni was his fourth wife. She was a busybody money-grubber just like the others, he thought. He remembered each of his wives with disdain. "Every damn one of those bitches just wanted to rip me off and take everything I had." He got back into his car and continued his journey, still fuming.

As the morning sun flashed through the passing trees, he remembered times past that were often clouded by alcohol or drugs and tried to put it all into perspective. That's what the shrinks in rehab told him he should do: "Keep things in perspective. Every action has consequences. You are responsible for the consequences of what you say and do."

"They really did a number on me; every God damned one of them. They drove me fucking crazy, put me away and took everything I owned." He grumbled to himself as he erratically sped along more quickly, now almost oblivious of where he was going. He knew that his only mistake was getting caught. He had been smart enough to say all of the things they wanted to hear to convince them that he was truly remorseful and that it was the drugs that had been his undoing and not his basic immoral character. However, Jack knew that his downfall came long before the drugs and alcohol.

Jack had started his career as a great success story. He seemed to be a good child and student, and everyone knew that he would succeed in having a wonderful and successful life. Somewhere along the way, Jack underwent an inexplicable change and, in this process truly lost his soul. He had always looked out for himself, but during his medical training he made a conscious decision that if he were to succeed, others must fail and he began to use his friends for his own ends. He found it very easy to do as it became a game with him. The impression of compassion that he once seemed to possess had disappeared from his life. His growing ego overcame him and he was increasingly more disdainful of everyone, and he cared for no one. The only one he loved, if it can be called love, was himself.

He scammed his way into a top training fellowship position by undermining his competition, including his lifelong best friend. His acclaimed research publications contained falsified data, but it got him a faculty position at the university. He learned that people were easy to manipulate. They wanted to believe that he was a good and sincere man, an honest hard-working guy they needed to help. He began supplying drugs to manipulate people to do things for him. He developed a fondness for cocaine and the web of deceit began to ensnare him when his drug habit expanded and got out of hand. The mistakes began. Of course, the mistakes were always someone else's fault. Two nurses lost their jobs, accused of negligence. A colleague was severely reprimanded after two patients' questionable deaths. Jack had changed the medical records to cover his incompetence. But it was more than incompetence. It was a willful desire to do evil. He began forgetting the details of his elaborate web of lies and suddenly his charade became transparent. Four people, including Jack's wife Joni, went to the hospital director and put an end to his career. His license was suspended and criminal charges were filed against him. After two years in prison and a year of rehabilitation, he was ultimately placed on probation.

When he finally calmed and the rage drained from him, there was only the rustle of the leaves and the soft rippling sound of the river coming through the open car window. He stopped once again and looked through the glove compartment and found the prescription his psychiatrist had given him and took two of the pills. An exhausted Jack pulled back onto the road and headed north for several more miles until he saw the sign — Hampton Oaks Nursing Facility.

Chapter 5
Jack's Second Chance

The cut-off to Hampton Oaks was narrow and tunneled through a canopy of old-growth oak and maple trees. Freshly fallen red and yellow leaves covered the pavement at the first sharp turn and Jack swerved to stay on the road sending a flurry of dry leaves into the air. An arrow to the parking lot came into view at the top of the hill and he pulled into the 'Guests' section and parked. Nine other cars were parked at one end of the spacious lot and he presumed they were employees' cars. He took a deep breath as he turned off the ignition, wondering what he was getting into. He sat in the car for a few minutes composing himself.

It had been a struggle for Jack to find work once he had been released from the rehabilitation facility. The story of his crimes, downfall and punishment were well documented in the newspapers and on the Internet. His name was still on a list of physicians who had their licenses revoked, despite the fact that he had been reinstated over a month ago. Of the eighteen letters he had written, he was invited to three interviews, two of which were cancelled at the last minute for unlikely excuses. The interview for the Hampton Oaks job was at the Fairmont Hotel in New York City. Jack's mind flashed back to the interview. Roger Morris, who looked like an elderly Albert Einstein, conducted the interview in an elegantly tailored suit. As Jack sat in his car, he remembered the details of the interview that occurred two weeks earlier:

"I see you have had some problems in the past, Dr Adams."

Morris had done his homework and knew everything in detail. He seemed to know more about Jack than Jack knew about himself. In a rather clinically detached way, Morris was quite matter-of-fact about everything concerning Jack's circumstances. It was almost as if his troubled life did not matter at all to the old man.

"Hampton Oaks has had its problems also. We all have our problems, Doctor. What I am proposing to you is a second chance to turn your life around and get your act together, as the young people like to say. Sometimes things look gloomy and there seems to be no hope, and then an opportunity arises that can change everything for the better. And so here you are. I am glad you came today, and we most definitely would like to offer you an opportunity to get back to work."

Jack who had said nothing up to that point spoke up: "Dr Morris, I need this job. You will not be disappointed with my work. I have made some bad mistakes but…"

"I'm well aware of all of that but I think you will do nicely. You are just the person we were looking for. In fact, we could not ask for anyone who is more ideal."

Jack was completely caught off guard: "Well, fine but I think I need to explain…"

Morris interrupted Jack again, now with superficial chitchat about the weather and road conditions in the winter and about how important it was to maintain Hampton Oaks' image. He casually asked Jack how he managed diabetes and heart failure in geriatric patients and completely disagreed with most of his answers.

"Hampton Oaks needs a competent, reliable physician to take care of approximately one hundred residents who are primarily aged or infirm and have multiple debilitating medical problems. Quality of life and keeping the residents and families happy is what it is all about. Do you understand what I mean, Dr Adams?"

"Yes, sir, I do. I certainly have the training and ability and would like…" Jack was again cut off in mid-sentence and it was beginning to irk him.

Morris droned on: "Based on your past record, I think you would probably like to let all these seemingly hopeless people die from their chronic diseases, but you can't. I know what you are thinking, but they need to be kept happy, comfortable and have dignity at the end of their lives. Almost all of them are here until the end. Hampton Oaks has a long and proud reputation, and an important part of that reputation is excellent care and always having a doctor available for every contingency. You don't have to live on the premises, but you certainly may if you like. However, you must be available within fifteen minutes for emergencies. We have some generous families who have kept us funded and competitive over the years. We pride ourselves in being able to continue to care for individuals whose funds have run out. Medicare alone is not enough and we would surely fold if we didn't have other resources. We must continue to maintain our edge."

Jack nodded with feigned interest in Morris' banter.

"Dr Adams, I am aware that you have limited opportunities available and that a job at Hampton Oaks is probably not a choice pick for you. So, I think we have something to offer each other."

To Jack's amazement, they came to a verbal agreement with a decent salary and benefits. Yet Jack couldn't escape the feeling that he had been trapped like a desperate animal searching for food that had fallen into a pit. There was a sinister gleefulness in Morris' eyes, Jack thought as they finalized the agreement. Morris quickly concluded the interview, despite Jack's efforts to get more information.

"Everything will be fine and we will move ahead. Be there two weeks from today, Doctor. We do not look back but are looking ahead with very definite expectations of you. Yes indeed, you will do just fine!"

They shook hands and departed. Morris smiled gleefully as he left the room. This was the first and last time Jack saw Roger Morris.

Jack remembered this interview in vivid detail as he sat in his car and prepared to go into Hampton Oaks to start his new job. He entered the large oak front door as he moved from his thoughts about the strange interview. "What a piece of shit this is!" he mumbled, thinking about his past and how much he had lost. "Look at this — this is real desperation. Something is not right about all of this. What the hell am I getting into?"

Chapter 6
The Trap is Set

Hampton Oaks was much larger than Jack expected. The main building was at least two hundred years old and was one of many Hudson River mansions whose glory days had long faded. He later discovered that a decision was made in the 1930s to convert the well-built, old home into an elite 'Rest Home' for wealthy retirees. With the magnificent views, gardens and ample rooms, this proved to be a financially successful plan. Additional domiciles were built on the property as well as a hospital unit. Several wealthy clients left substantial inheritances to the institution so that very few who came here and then ran out of finances had to leave. Unfortunately, upkeep had lagged behind and there were considerably fewer than the original number of residents.

As Jack entered the huge door, there was a vacuous foyer where two large, solemn portraits peered down at him. These were no doubt the original owners, Josiah and Esther Banting, hovering like gargoyles warding away evil visitors. There was a musty smell of old places on the verge of decay, residues of open fires, cigars, candles, kitchen cooking and mildew. A single black on white sign with the word 'OFFICE' pointed down the oak-paneled hallway. Sconces with yellowed shades lit the way intermingled with old photographs of river mansions, horse-drawn carriages and area scenes from bygone years. In the back, a clean, brightly lit, tiled hallway led to the newer additions. A second sign became apparent to the right and further down a modern-looking hallway. Finally, there before him was a large door with an opaque glass panel imprinted once again with the irritating 'OFFICE' sign in the center of the glass. Jack felt like a rat in a maze following the damn office signs to a snare at the end. He sensed that this place was indeed a trap and he had been lured right into it. Inside, he encountered a plump middle-aged lady, peering at him over the top of her spectacles, who greeted him with a booming voice.

"Dr Adams, we have been waiting for you. I thought you would be here before now. You should not have kept us waiting," she said with a hint of condescension. Jack said nothing and stared at her with derision.

"You are Dr Adams, aren't you? You look just like the Dr Adams I imagined, tall with dark eyes and black hair. You know people say that I am psychic and I really do believe that I am. You look just like the man I was expecting. I have this uncanny ability to foresee the future, and yesterday I saw you just as plain as day riding down here on the river road in your convertible." She chirped away, unable to constrain her free association of thought.

He had not said a word and was standing there with his mouth open, trying to take in this strange loquaciously aggravating woman, then finally forged ahead with his response. "I don't have a convertible and I don't even know who you are."

"Oh, excuse me, I am being so rude. I certainly know that I should have introduced myself. I was really taught better manners than that. My mother was such a proper lady and always said that good manners are the most important thing to teach children. I have always tried to do that even though I don't have children. I have a hormone problem…"

"Look, I am Dr Adams and am supposed to start work here today and I still don't know who you are, Mrs…"

"Oh no, it's not Mrs, it's Miss, Miss Annie Bellington. I have never been married. Although I have not given up on the prospect…"

"Please, I just need to know where I should go." Jack was beginning to think that this woman was some kind of a nut.

"Oh, you don't have to go anywhere. I have everything you need right here. You just sit down and I will give you the documents to sign one at a time. Here, sit there and take this pen. First, sign your contract. It's a three-year contract. That is about right — not too long."

Jack had never seen the contract. "I need to read this over first."

"No, that won't be necessary. Dr Morris went over all of this with you in New York. He said that you would sign and not give me any trouble or I should just show you to the door. He was actually very specific about that. I know he has explained all this to you. Now after you have signed that, you will need to sign for your parking permit, health insurance, dental insurance, IRS withholdings and retirement account. Dr Morris must think very highly of you to offer you retirement benefits so soon. That's quite impressive. So here are the forms. Sign away!"

With that, Jack looked up at Miss Bellington's determined face, took a deep breath and began signing the papers. He was trapped. There was no choice.

"Now I will take you to see Miss Harrison," Annie said as she escorted him to the door.

"Miss Harrison?" Jack said, now wondering how strange she might be.

"Yes, Frieda Harrison is the nursing supervisor. Miss Harrison knows more about Hampton Oaks than anyone on the staff. The place couldn't run without her. She was an army nurse and came here after the Vietnam War."

"Who is her supervisor?" Jack queried, thinking it might be him.

"She doesn't have one. She is the supervisor. She meets with the Board of Directors twice a year and they do what she tells them to do."

Jack was taken aback by this impressive account as he was escorted into her rather mundane office. Frieda Harrison sat at her desk signing a stack of papers and placing them in the out box to her left. She was short and stocky and wore a white nursing uniform. She wore no make-up and her sanguine face was tired and lined with years of small wrinkles. She presented a grandmotherly appearance as she peered over her reading glasses. Jack pictured her sitting in a rocking chair by the fire with her knitting, sipping a cup of tea with a cat at her feet. This was a fleeting image as she instructed him with her commanding voice to sit down across from her.

"Dr Adams, I have been at Hampton Oaks for over forty years and I know how to run this place. Doctors like you come and go. You are not here because you want to be here, but are here because you have no other

28

choice. If you do a good job and don't cause any trouble, you will eventually move along to something better. If you cause trouble, this will be the last job you will ever have. I don't think they would even consider you for dog catcher if you screwed up this opportunity. You will not jeopardize the reputation of Hampton Oaks. I expect to be informed of all your activities regarding patient and staff issues. I will be your best advocate or your worst enemy. The choice is yours."

He sat dumbfounded as the grandmotherly image of Frieda Harrison melted away. Frieda sat patiently waiting for a response as Jack breathed deeply and swallowed his anger.

"I want this to work out and will do whatever it takes," Jack blurted out, feeling he had to say something positive.

"Good. Now that we have that over, I would like to welcome you to your new job at Hampton Oaks. Your scheduled clinic days are Monday and Thursday. Fridays are open for special procedures. Tuesday and Wednesdays are for semi-annual patient evaluations. These are done in the office or at the bedside and will be scheduled for you. Your nurses are Barbara Mattson and Meg Vandever. There are additional nurses in the hospital unit but there is a shortage and we are overly relying on nursing aides which is a potential problem. They need to be watched and supervised. Most are good but I have concerns about some. As she escorted him down the hall to his office, she gave him a pager and Dictaphone.

"This is your office. It's really more than you need." The room was sparse but well-lit with a desk, bookcase, file cabinets and a coat rack. A large window provided an excellent view of the gardens. A door led to two exam rooms, a room with four cubicles for nurses and a large medical records room. Jack was introduced to Nancy Petty who kept the medical records files.

"Nice to meet you, Dr Adams. I'm looking forward to working with you."

"Likewise, I'm sure," Jack answered half-heartedly. "Where are my nurses?" Jack snapped at Frieda.

"There is a patient management conference every Monday from eight until ten a.m. which of course, you missed today by being late. I will introduce you later. Now, let's get through the tour." Frieda was ready to get back to work.

The tour was long and interspersed with numerous introductions to staff and 'charming' patients. Jack was bored and saw this all as an unnecessary formality. He didn't bother to try remembering any names. He noted that the staff seemed to be doing a reasonable job despite being short-handed. However, he truly hated being with all these old and infirm patients.

Back at his office, Frieda handed him his keys. Annie had already put a schedule on his desk for the week. "Get settled in. I will meet with you again at lunch and cover more details. By the way, your student is coming next Monday and will be using one of the cubicles."

"Student! What student? I do not want a student," Jack snapped. That was all he needed; someone else to irritate him. Frieda looked at him and didn't answer.

Zoë Abrams was soon to encounter this troubled man, Jack Adams.

Chapter 7
The Bold & The Beautiful

The houses on Maple Street showed the wear and tear of many families over the years. The lower middle-class neighborhood was now filled with rental property that was popular with students. Some of the larger houses had multiple bedrooms and often six or more students living together. This was the neighborhood where Zoë lived.

"Hey, somebody give me a hand with the pizza!" Patrick David yelled as he kicked the screen door.

Zoë appeared, opened the door and gave him a kiss on the cheek. "You are such a dear, but please don't break the door. It's about to fall off its hinges as it is and I really need my deposit back when I move."

"Move! You can't move! I keep you in pizza and beer and I'm such a handyman, fixing everything that's broken down in this dump. What more do you need?" Patrick said as he grinned at her.

Zoë retorted, "Yeah, I will miss the man with the tools but there is life beyond medical school. By the way, the doorbell needs to be fixed if you haven't noticed and this light socket is out. I wouldn't advise sticking your tool in it though."

"You really know how to hurt a guy. Just using me for my innate talents, aren't you?" Patrick sighed.

"Hey, somebody give me a hand with the beer!" Scott Larson grunted as he kicked the ailing screen door.

"Don't break the door. I'm coming," Zoë yelled.

Scott lumbered in with enough beer for a week-long party. "If we run out, it won't be my fault. I've got real beer for the real men, and pussy-lite for the rest of you weenies," he smirked. "And there is more in the Jeep."

"Hey, somebody give me a hand with the wine," Erin O'Donald pleaded as she kicked the screen door.

"Don't kick the door!" Zoë shouted with exasperation as Scott went to let her in.

"Hey, babe, you are looking hot tonight. Those are fine jugs… of wine you have there," Scott crooned. Scott was infatuated with Erin from the first time they met but despite being a tall, dark and handsome jock, he was shy.

"Scott, you're so full of shit. Here, take the wine and cool it." Erin smiled, obviously enjoying his flirtation.

Scott obliged and took the wine to the kitchen and began loading the beverages into a cooler.

"You people are a damn bunch of boozers." Zoë laughed. "I have never seen so much alcohol. I hope you brought sleeping bags because I'm not letting any of you drive home."

"Hey, somebody give me a hand with the ice," Martine yelled as she kicked the dying screen door. The hinge gave way and the old door splintered and fell apart leaving a pile of shredded screen wire and kindling.

"Oh, no. There goes my deposit," Zoë moaned.

"Looks like we have wood for a fire tonight," Patrick said as he cleared away the rubble.

Preparations began for dinner. Erin and Martine made a salad. Scott put the drinks on ice. Zoë set the table. Patrick announced that there were three kinds of pizza: the Carnivore for the real man, the Triple Cheese with extra cheese for the real man wannabe and his cheesy friends, and the Very Veggie for Zoë, the lone vegetarian, and malnourished friends.

"Where are Twiddle Dum and Twiddle Dee?" Scott asked.

"Deirdre and Jenna will be here in a bit. They had a late meeting with their professor," Zoë said.

Deirdre Lindquist and Jenna Yelton finally arrived and the group was once again complete. Their classmates called the group of seven 'The Bold and The Beautiful', a take-off from a soap opera, but a name that they liked and readily adopted. The B&B, as they were usually called, had been close friends and allies throughout medical school and had come to rely on each other like a close, extended family. They had met and bonded during orientation and gross anatomy and quickly became inseparable. There was an immediate chemistry between them that was almost mystical — like long-separated friends suddenly and joyfully together again. Privately they dreaded breaking up when they graduated but vowed to remain friends forever.

Patrick was the exception. He had started with the group but near the end of his first year decided medicine wasn't for him. He always seemed to be searching for something that continued to elude him and he continued turning aside to try to pursue new goals. Everyone considered him a 90-percenter, since he worked hard at everything he tried, but always fell short. He was exceptionally smart and aced everything he tried and was always planning for something new and different, but when he almost achieved his aspirations, he would retreat from his goal. Some thought he wanted to fail. As a result, Patrick had become a jack of all trades and master of none. It took him six years to complete his anthropology degree, only after threats of bodily harm from his father. Painting, drawing and artistic endeavors were the only things that consistently gave him joy but he even retreated from this when he was offered a job in a well-known art studio working at the very things he loved — drawing and painting. His excuse was that it would be too confining and he would not have the artistic freedom he needed. Speaking of love, Zoë was always on his mind, but he couldn't see their relationship lasting. Zoë was very popular and had definite, big plans for the future while Patrick had none. She was always smarter, brighter and more outgoing, while he was much more introverted and felt outclassed by her.

Zoë was a goal-oriented go-getter, to state it succinctly. She only had to be told that she couldn't do something for her to pursue it with a vengeance. She was always filled with questions and was never quite satisfied until her questions were fully answered. In any group Zoë quickly became the leader. She had been the unofficial head and social coordinator of the B&B group since they first met. This was always difficult since they were rarely on the same clinical rotations together. E-mail and cell phones held them together and she knew if their parties lasted long enough, they would eventually all show up. She was fortunate to live with Erin and Jenna in this quaint, old house with space to accommodate a crowd.

As the meal progressed, Zoë spoke over the clatter of the plates and silverware. "Everyone be sure to let me know your schedules for the next rotation so we can plan our fall event."

"Hey, we get real plates and silverware for a change," Scott noted. "What's the occasion?"

"Well first, it is Deirdre's and Jenna's birthdays this month and, of course, there will be birthday cupcakes later," Zoë noted, "but most importantly, Patrick fixed the dishwasher." This comment brought an immediate round of applause and cheers.

"OK, where will everyone be on your rotations?" Zoë queried, taking her pen and notebook in hand. Each rotation was usually six weeks in duration and could be at several different sites. The majority of their rotations were at the university and affiliated hospitals.

"I'll be in Thorgood's lab," Martine said. "Where else would I be? Just me and the DNA from three hundred Alzheimer's patients. Testing, testing, and more testing. By the way, I want to thank all of you for donating blood for me to use as controls for the genetic tests. I assume that you are all normal, although I have some doubts about Scott. Hopefully, I will be finished with the bulk of the work and back on clinical rotations by April." Martine Baier had taken the tough path of getting a combined M.D.-Ph.D. degree in genetics and would graduate a year after the others.

"I'll be breaking bones on orthopedics for the next two months," Scott chimed in. "I'm thinking about doing orthopedics and sports medicine when I finish. That will make me one hot commodity. The NFL will be recruiting me like a hot quarterback to fix up those players' injuries."

"You're supposed to set bones, not break them," Erin quipped. "But knowing you, you will probably break some old lady's arm just examining her hand. At least you won't be able to do too much damage to the football players. Zoë, I'll be doing gastroenterology at the university and will get to participate in a lot of colonoscopies. Here's to looking up yours, Scott." She smiled and toasted him with a glass of wine.

"Pediatrics at the university," Deirdre said. "They see tons of kids and a lot of endocrine and genetic disorders so it should be interesting. I better get my flu shot now since I always catch something from those kids. I've heard it is a great rotation despite the snotty noses. Those kids are just little cesspools of infection."

"Jenna, what about you?" Zoë asked. Everyone looked at Jenna for her answer but her mouth was full of pizza.

After a lot of chewing and a big gulp she smiled and said, "I will be doing internal medicine at the Davis Clinic. It's supposed to be the best rotation in a private practice setting with good teaching and lots of neat stuff that I'm sure to see in practice later in my career. I really need a lot more hands-on experience. I still feel like such a klutz and completely clueless about so much. This should be an excellent rotation for me."

There was a long pause as everyone then looked at Patrick, not knowing what to expect of him but hoping he would move beyond home repairs and Poppa Petrelli's Pizza delivery.

Patrick smiled and said, "Well, looks like I'm in the hot seat now! First let me say, I have decided to put my pizza delivery career on the back burner. You are on your own for Poppa Petrelli's Pizza from now on."

"Hey, don't leave us hanging," Martine demanded. "No more pizza? Well, we might be able to live without pizza but must have Chinese delivery. I know you can do that. It's Chinese, isn't it? So please tell us, what are you really up to?"

"He's so good at delivery, he got a job at UPS. He'll be all brown now," Scott quipped.

"Hardly! Besides, I don't look good in brown. See how good I look in this nice green sweater?" Patrick was enjoying their increasing curiosity as he continued. "My old anthropology professor, Jacob

Horowitz, has offered me a job assisting him with some really neat archeology research. He got a big grant last week from the National Science Foundation and called me right away. He said he knew he could trust me and offered the job. Well, I decided to take it and I'm committed to him for at least a year and maybe longer."

"Does this mean that you might be going back to school?" Zoë said, feeling that this turn of events could be a great opportunity for him and a chance to give him a goal he might even finish.

Patrick thought a moment and said, "You never know. The more I think about it, this is some hot stuff he is doing and could be the basis for a Ph.D. thesis. That's a real possibility. In fact, I kind of like that idea."

"A Ph.D.? I'm impressed. That would be great for you to do, Patrick, and I'm sure it will work out well for you if you just put your mind to it. So, it looks like you will be leaving here, eh?" Jenna asked.

Zoë hadn't considered that he might have to leave and suddenly felt an unwanted apprehension. Her feelings truly surprised her since it seemed that she was more attached to him than she thought.

"I'll be in central America for about a week or two at a time cataloging artifacts, bundling up the good ones, and doing some photography and drawings to bring back here for study. The real significant work will be done in Horowitz's lab at the university," Patrick replied.

Zoë was relieved that Patrick would still be close by. She realized that she was gradually becoming quite attached to this handsome dark-haired enigma.

"OK, Zoë, it's your turn to tell us where you are going. What's your deal?" Deirdre asked, interrupting her thoughts of Patrick.

"You probably will think I'm crazy, but I really want to do a geriatrics rotation to see if this is something I might like to do long term. The population is getting older and I enjoy working with older patients and think I could make a positive difference in their lives. People are living much longer than before and can have good and productive lives for many years. It's amazing the number of people who are living to be one hundred or older. I just need to check it out."

"So, let's try it again — where are you going?" Deirdre asked once more.

Zoë paused once again, considering if she had made the correct choice and then answered: "It is an old but previously well-known nursing facility that has been updated and now has an attending medical staff and the medical school has set up a two-month-long rotation there. It is about a two-hour drive up the Hudson River and is called Hampton Oaks."

Chapter 8
Zoë

Zoë had been driving a while along the river up from New York City to Hampton Oaks. Above the Hudson Highlands, the river once again widened and the landscape was covered with farms and orchards. She always wanted to stop at one of the wineries but would never allow herself the pleasure. Someday, perhaps, she thought. There is just too much to do and too little time. Zoë loved being with Patrick and all of her friends, but she also cherished her time alone. The drive up from the city was a perfect time for her. The haunting dream had been pushed to the back of her mind.

She turned off the radio and watching the scenery flow by, and contemplated her life. She had always taken charge of every situation and was goal-oriented since she was a child. Her father, Joe, when he was around, had insisted that she have a plan for each day. Her mother, Anne, enjoyed watching her as a five-year-old supervise her friends' tea parties and games in their yard. Her mother was loving and compassionate and they were close friends. Zoë always sensed what was the right or best approach to any situation and was compelled to make things happen as she thought they should. She sincerely believed that she was exceptionally fortunate to have the resources to live her comfortable life freely and take it in whatever direction she wished. Indeed, she was very thankful for her good fortune although she didn't know who or what to thank.

Zoë had no siblings and was without family since the deaths of her mother when she was thirteen and her father when she was eighteen. Her father took care of her physical needs but always seemed deep in thought, aloof and uncaring. She missed the bond that her friends seemed to have with their fathers. As a child she was very secure in her mother's love and her counsel that God would always take care of her. Her mother encouraged her to pray and to know that God would answer her prayers. However, her most sincere and desperate prayers in her youth for the life of her mother went unanswered and she came to feel that if God existed, he was remote from her. For her it seemed that if God exists, he only watches and waits and does very little if anything. She realized if anyone takes care of Zoë, it has to be Zoë herself. The ancient river relentlessly flowed down to the city and out to the sea as she continued to drive along and contemplated her life.

The end of four years of medical school was approaching and Zoë would be graduated with honors. She would not be first in her class because of one bad evaluation to come. She knew she wanted a good residency in internal medicine but could not envision a future beyond that. She enjoyed the regimented life of medical school and knew that residency would be similar with daily routines planned for her. "I want to take care of sick people but there has to be more to life than this," she thought aloud.

Her thoughts flowed within her mind and she continued talking to herself as she frequently liked to do. It was as if she had another person within her head with whom she could talk and be open and frank, much like a psychiatrist who would sit, take notes, and occasionally say, "How do you feel about that?"

"I guess I would like to get married and have kids at some point. It would be a good life to have a nice home in the country with a great husband and wonderful children. I can picture myself there now, sitting in my garden, having a glass of wine. I could have a good practice, with excellent partners of course, and really be in control of my life. Maybe some horses and a nice Mercedes. An English sheepdog would be good. In fact, that would be fantastic. And a swimming pool. Definitely a swimming pool. I would have to have good neighbors that I could have parties for and we could do charitable things together. This could be my life, picture perfect in every way."

She thought of articles that she had read in *House Beautiful* and other magazines of wonderfully idyllic homes and a beautiful, charming family. This is the kind of life her friends aspire to. Her father had always insisted with hard work she could make anything happen. She knew that this was everyone's ideal — the carefree, beautiful life.

The psychiatrist in her head then spoke up. "Do you really want all of that, tying yourself down to a superficial existence and just accumulate things? You don't think of yourself as a material girl. You want to experience things, meet people, make good friends and see things you've never before seen — experience life beyond yourself. The journey is more important than the destination. Where are you going anyway? There is this yearning inside for something you can't explain and it is not for a cushy life."

Zoë once again spoke aloud. "There is something important out there that seems to be beyond my reach. My life has to have significance. When I die, at my funeral, I don't want them to say about me, here lies Zoë; she was a good doctor but she's dead and gone now, so much for her. I know that my life is just a blink in time, but I want my blink to be significant and somehow my existence here on this tiny planet lost in a universe of stars will be important. Can anyone do anything significant or make a difference in their brief life? I don't know. Eat, drink and be merry for tomorrow you die. Is that all there is? God, I hope not."

The psychiatrist in her head then pushed out more words to say. "So, is there a reason, a plan, or purpose for your life, girly? You know you're not the first one to ask that question. This is probably the oldest question in the universe that began when some ancient beings realized for the first time that there was more to themselves than that which meets the eye. It's a journey. Listen to your heart and make it happen. Become God."

"Okay, I'm going to say that there is a reason and a plan for my life and I'm going to forge ahead on this journey, listening to my heart, and trying to have faith in my path to God whatever He or She might be, on to my destiny whatever that might be." The struggle in Zoë's mind somehow seemed to be momentarily at rest. It certainly was not completely gone, but she did have a sense of acceptance that something good would come of her life despite her horrid dreams and misgivings about her existence. Her thoughts turned to her friends and the people that she loved and the internal struggle seemed to fade away.

She remembered yesterday to be a great day, a free day with no classes and nothing that had to be done. She certainly did not want to stay at home on such a beautiful day. Zoë went to dinner and a movie with Scott and Deirdre. The movie was ridiculously funny and the dinner delectable, and they laughed until their sides ached, kidding, joking and savoring their time together. There was entirely too much wine and Scotch. Scott was determined to have them taste several different Scotches and Zoë, aware of a dull ache in the center of her head, was certain now that she didn't like Scotch. Mixing it with wine probably didn't help either. It was one of those rare halcyon days, kind of like some of her best times in college, just enjoying experiences with no expectations and just going with the flow of friends and events. They were all happy, content and felt fulfilled being with each other and not concerning themselves with anything but the day.

Zoë's mind then jolted back to reality and her attention turned to the destination and rotation that lay ahead. She was excited and positive about the new experience but no one she knew had been to Hampton Oaks before and much was unknown except for the excellent reputation of the place for good patient care. She had no clue about the unusual events that had happened there previously and continued to unfold even now, that would set the stage for one of the greatest events in human history. A role would be presented to her that only she could play and no one else.

***

Zoë had never before been to Hampton Oaks and on her arrival was surprised at the size and beauty of the complex. It was in a lovely setting with beautiful gardens and vistas and she knew the patients should be very happy here considering the view and the amenities of the place. She checked in with Annie Bellington and got a quick tour, meeting the nurses and Frieda Harrison.

Annie delighted in her role as public liaison and quickly took a liking to Zoë. She had arranged for her to have a better than dormitory type room for her to stay during her rotation within the Hampton Oaks complex.

"Zoë, we are really glad to have you here at Hampton Oaks. We want this to be an excellent rotation for you and will do our best to make it a pleasant experience. We had medical students come here in the past, you know. They were primarily interested in orthopedics and were here because of the rehabilitation center. They go to the center at the university now because it is much bigger and well-staffed and has newer equipment. I'm afraid we can't compete with them now. We love to have students and quite frankly, the patients enjoy the attention directed to them by new visitors. Dr Morris earlier this year spoke to the dean at your medical school and was able to set up this rotation that will primarily be geriatric medicine. We have other patients as well that you will see, but geriatrics will be your focus. Your dean was somewhat reluctant to do it until we got Dr Adams on board. He is a certified internist, you know. Dr Morris was quite determined to set up this rotation for you."

"What do you mean, set up this rotation for me?" Zoë asked, genuinely puzzled.

"Dr Morris said that he knew a student who would love a rotation like this and would be an excellent prospect to come here. We really only want the best students and I'm sure Dr Morris thinks you are the best. He was really excited to hear that you were coming today," Annie said with a smile.

"Well, I would be very interested in talking to him because I had no idea this was arranged just for me. The dean told me he thought this would be a great rotation because of my interest in geriatrics but I had no idea there was some sort of arrangement made without my knowing it. I need to talk to Dr Morris about this. This is quite strange. I don't understand this at all," Zoë said.

"Oh, that's not strange at all. Dr Morris would not let just anyone come here, only the best. Your school recommended you highly and you have outstanding credentials. I can tell you are going to fit in here very well and do an excellent job. You are such a nice, young lady too," Annie retorted.

"Well, thank you very much, Miss Bellington, but I still want to talk to Dr Morris," Zoë said emphatically.

"You should call me Annie. I wish I could do that for you, but he is away and I have no idea when he will be back. Sometimes he is gone for months at a time and who knows how long this time. And as far as phoning him is concerned, he doesn't even own one. I don't know how he gets by. If I didn't have my phone, I would never get anything done. I have a new cell phone that is really nice that I will show you. I just love technology. Who knows what they will think of next?" Annie finally completed her prolonged discourse on cell phones, but Zoë remained puzzled and concerned about the arrangements that had been made without her knowledge.

"Let's take a break down in the dining room and then I will introduce you to Dr Adams."

Zoë knew that she would have a mentor at Hampton Oaks but knew nothing about Jack Adams. If she had known about his sordid background, she would have cancelled her rotation. She would eventually come to know that keeping this hidden secret was essential for someone's plan that was now quietly evolving without her knowledge. Her meeting with Jack Adams was to be one of the most consequential and intimidating occurrences of her life.

Chapter 9
Coercion

Annie had been considerably restrained, and that was most unlike her, in talking to Zoë about Jack Adams. She was well aware of all the sordid details of his recent life that she was not permitted to disclose. Also, she had gotten along reasonably well with him, although most of the other staff had come to mistrust and dislike him. Many were actually fearful and went out of their way to avoid encountering the abrasive man. Everyone loved and had the greatest respect for Roger Morris but could not fathom why he had ever hired Adams. He simply would not discuss this issue with anyone.

Morris remained extremely pleased that Jack had agreed to come, but had admonished Frieda Harrison to let him know if there were any indiscretions or other problems and he would personally handle the situation. Frieda, being the workhorse that she was, hardly noticed Jack after he was hired. She did not put up with anything from him that was not by the book. Hampton Oaks was Frieda's show, and he was just one of many people that she had to deal with. She was a stickler that he accomplish his daily assignments, that she posted on his desk each morning.

"Zoë, Dr Adams can be difficult to get along with for some people. He seems rather brusque at times, but I think he is basically a good doctor. He is very smart and often seems absorbed in his thoughts. There's a lot of negative talk among the staff and you should just disregard it. People will always talk and be judgmental. Just remember that you are here for your education and not gossip. We should deal with people at face value," Annie counseled.

Zoë knew for certain that she was going to find out more about this guy who was supposed to be her teacher and mentor. She was becoming increasingly uneasy and suspicious about the entire situation, despite Annie's encouragement. Annie knocked on Jack Adams's office door and they went in together.

"Dr Adams, this is Zoë Abrams, our new medical student. Zoë, this is Dr Adams."

Annie did the introductions before he could say anything and explained that he would be her mentor and write her evaluation when she completed her rotation. Jack scowled and shot daggers at Annie, obviously more than annoyed at the intrusion.

"I will leave you two and get back to work. Zoë, let me know if there is anything I can do to help. Come back to the office when you finish here."

Annie left and Jack didn't look up but motioned for Zoë to sit in the chair across from his desk. Zoë was perplexed and definitely unprepared for what to expect after Annie's comments. In front of him was a disarrayed pile of charts and papers that flowed from his desk onto the floor. She noticed a lack of books, journals or educational materials on his bookshelves. The office was dead quiet and she sensed his anger as he gazed at a blank piece of paper on his desk. She waited for him to speak yet he said nothing. She was becoming unnerved and considered she should leave now and perhaps try to speak to him later.

Jack appeared to be in his mid-forties and could be considered rather handsome with Mediterranean skin and dark eyes. There was stress and anger in his expression and a definite heavy negativity about him. She sensed for a moment that he was like a black hole that seemed to be pulling the energy from her body. This creepy sensation worsened and became very uncomfortable. Then finally Jack began to fidget with his pen, moved his eyes quickly back and forth, looking across his desk and seemed increasingly irritated. Zoë wondered if he would ever speak and at this point, pulled together her strength and determined to get the conversation going.

"I'm pleased to meet you, Dr Adams. I'm looking forward to this rotation," she said somewhat reluctantly, again wondering what she had gotten into with this worrisome mentor.

"Okay, I wasn't expecting this! Nobody prepared me for this. This is supposed to be my show and now I've got to deal with students like you. Students are a ball and chain to me, hanging onto you like a leech day and night with a million inane questions," Jack snapped as he glared at Zoë.

Zoë retorted, "I'm afraid I don't know what you mean. This is a student rotation approved by my medical school and arranged for here at Hampton Oaks. I didn't realize that this was going to present a problem. I'm here for an education and not a lecture on why I should not be here."

"Well, all these arrangements were made before I came here and this is not something I knew about or wanted, and just another little surprise to make my life even more difficult. But here you are and I guess I will have to live with it."

Jack's tone of utter disgust seemed not just directed at Zoë, but against the entire world. Jack had considered running her off but knew that would be a strategy certain to backfire on him and God knows, he would not want to do anything to detract from Hampton Oaks' wonderful reputation. He thought if he heard of Hampton Oaks' 'wonderful reputation' again he would puke.

"Dr Adams, I want to be perfectly honest with you. When I heard about this rotation, it sounded very appealing but quite honestly, I need the rotation to graduate. I don't want to be any trouble. I will work hard and do a good job and do more than my share of the work. When I finish, I can tell the dean that you really don't want to teach because of all your responsibilities and ask him to work out some other rotation, but right now I need to be here and get credit for this. You can depend on me to do what is right. Would you please try to work this out?" Zoë pleaded.

Jack thought about her proposal and relished the idea of no more students, but with all the crap Frieda was giving him to do, she might be able to help him. In the meantime, he could get her to do all the frustrating grunt work and dump her on the nurses and staff to herd around every day. If he put together a good plan, he would hardly have to deal with her at all. He began to finalize a scheme in his mind that in a strange way would ultimately work out favorably for Zoë. For the first time that day, Jack's scowl began to soften and slowly turned into a wry smile.

"That sounds like a reasonable arrangement. That just might work out very well," Jack said after contemplating the situation a few more moments. "Here's the way it's going to be," he said emphatically.

Jack went to the file cabinet and pulled out a folder and tossed it into Zoë's lap, then sat on the edge of his desk glaring down at her. He enjoyed seeing her cower before him. Zoë could hardly breathe as his intimidating shadow loomed over her like some fierce raptor about to devour its prey.

"That's a list of all the patients. Each patient has to have a periodic examination. You're going to do it and that's not all. There is documentation — pages of damned documentation required by those assholes in Washington. You are going to do that and when you are finished with each one, you will give me your notes to sign. When one of these old farts has problems, you will go check it out with the nurses and write it up. Got it?"

"I can do that but I'm just a student and will need some help and guidance because there is a lot I don't know and that is why I am here to learn. I have got to have some supervision and help and really want to get an education in the process," Zoë said, feeling that she was getting set up to be abused.

"Read a damn book! Go to the weekly conference and ask your questions there. Never talk to me unless you have talked to the nurses and you have no recourse. Meg is a physician's assistant and can help you with physical exams. Stay out of my office unless I call for you but don't expect to be called. Your cubicle has a computer, so use it. As you well know, you are responsible for your own education," Jack snapped. "Remember our deal. You want to pass, don't you?"

"I need to pass the rotation, Dr Adams, and I will do what you asked," Zoë said feeling that she had just made a pact with the Devil. Maybe she had.

"Get out of here!" Jack snapped.

Zoë felt in a daze, having not anticipated this strange course of events that would ultimately lead to her life's destiny. How could she know that this was planned?

Chapter 10
Path to Perdition

After Zoë left the office, Jack remained at his desk, seething in his venom. A shot of whisky washed down a handful of pills. His starting again as a reformed physician was a ruse. He didn't want to be at Hampton Oaks and didn't want to be anywhere, but just left alone to stew in his outrage, the personal hell he had ordained. He fumed and bellowed, "Why is my life such a pile of crap?" as he slammed his fist on the desk. As the roaring anger in his head gradually subsided, long-suppressed thoughts of his youth slowly surfaced as he slipped into a dreamlike trance.

Jack had everything as a child; at least he and his parents thought this. His mother and father were each considerably more than independently wealthy. He was an only child and in retrospect, was more like a pet than a son; a cute, little thing to be cuddled and shown off at appropriate occasions. His every need was catered for by multiple servants and nannies who were aloof and constantly changing because they were frequently fired for inane reasons. Despite this, he could somewhat bond with the transient help much more than his parents. It was difficult to love someone who never interacts with you. His parents lived on a separate side of the house that was off limits to him, but he could do anything he wanted with the rest of the vast house and grounds.

He was rarely allowed friends, and only those who were considered appropriate for someone of his elite class. Even then he did not have the social skills to maintain a friendship. Although he literally had anything available to him, he usually played alone with his toys. He was desperate for attention and once, he hadn't seen either parent in days, so he decided to smash a rare Venetian sculpture. Maybe his parents would come to scold him. Maybe he could see them, but they didn't come and cared less about what he did. Where were they and what were they doing? He began to sneak into their side of the house just to catch a glimpse of them, but he was afraid to be caught and they would send him away to boarding school or worse and he would never see them again. After several days of searching, he found a number of good hiding places where he could watch them incognito.

As he hid and watched his beautiful, young mother for several hours one day, he longed to be held and touched by her. He imagined her soft hands and arms around him and her silky black hair touching his face. He visualized the gentle curves of her tall, thin body and recalled her wonderful smell. He remembered the divine bouquet of jasmine and rose in her perfume, but it was years before he found the name of this haunting fragrance. He wanted her to kiss him, to kiss him all over his face and hands and leave the imprint of her bright red lipstick for others to see how much she loved him. He yearned for her and could bear it no longer as he burst from the closet and rushed to her, proclaiming his love as he clutched her tightly around the waist.

"What are you doing here? Get away from me! Get away, you little pervert! Can't you see I'm in my gown? I told you to never come in here. You do not belong here. Never! You are a bad boy!" she yelled as she slapped him. "You will never come here again!" She looked at him with anger and disgust. The frightened child stood before his beloved mother, quietly crying with his spirit crushed.

There was a knock at the door and a young man came in, an impressive, muscular fellow wearing nothing but a towel. He looked at Jack's mom and asked if she was okay.

"It's just him. He was hiding in here. He didn't see anything," she snapped.

"Is this Jackie? Hi, Jackie, I'm Dan. I'm a friend of your mother's."

Jack quickly ran from the room with the realization that his mother had a boyfriend. Afterward, his dreams were filled with vivid images of her anger and her slapping him and pushing him away, and there was no comfort for him, not even in his tears.

Jack's father was more aloof than his mother. Nearly a month later, he suddenly showed up after a long absence and his mother and the boyfriend disappeared, avoiding being in the house at the same time with him. For years afterwards, his parents and their lovers would come and go. His father always had a different woman, other than his mother, whenever Jack saw him. The vixens were always very young, sexy, and astonishingly beautiful. His father always got what he wanted. When Jack was sixteen, he found himself alone with one of his father's girls who happily seduced him. It was his first time and he later learned that his father had arranged the affair, one of several rites of passage. His father was fond of giving him exacting lessons of his view of life. He remembered the lessons well, particularly one near his twenty-first birthday.

"Jack, you are becoming a man and you've got to be tough. No one gets anywhere in life being a wimp. Do you know what a wimp is?"

"No, Dad, I don't."

"A wimp has no balls, no guts, spineless, like a slug. The world is full of wimps. They are afraid of their own shadows and will follow anybody with money and power. That's the first judgment you make about anyone you meet. Are they a wimp? If you find a wimp, you have found someone you can use. They are so fucking worthless, they have no life. So you must use them and they will give you money and anything you want because they are spineless and willing to do anything for you because of your power over them. They believe in the stupid Good Samaritan thing and are looking for pie in the sky. They will be your scapegoats and you can fuck them. Damn, they're fun to fuck! Jack, you got to be tough as steel, hard-nosed and uncompromising. It is a damn harsh world and you can't trust anyone but yourself. Nobody is looking out after you and it's sure as hell I'm not looking after you. You are on your own and you are your own keeper."

"Dad, we will always have each other. Don't talk like that. I don't want to be alone. We have each other and can always get together at holidays and do things. I need some people I love in my life," Jack pleaded.

"You don't get it, do you? I'm taking care of myself and you're taking care of yourself. I bought you into a good Ivy League school and it's time for you to look out for number one and stop being a forlorn juvenile creep. Your mother wants no part of you and frankly, I've got other things to do and I don't need any baggage like you to tie me down or hold me back. Another important lesson, get rid of the fucking baggage."

Jack was dumbfounded as his father handed him a huge check and ostensibly said get out of his life. He was standing alone again with a piece of paper that was his legacy. That was the last time Jack cried and he promised himself he would never ever cry again. Within several days, he moved out of the mansion, got an apartment and started college. No one said goodbye to him and he never saw his parents again.

The daydream ended and Jack's mind was again in his office. He opened the desk and the false bottom and replaced his bottle of Jack Daniels amid his pills, drug paraphernalia and a small pack of white powder. So, this is what it will take to work here, he thought.

There was a knock at the door and Jack quickly closed the drawer. The unwelcome intruders on his space were endless. Who the hell is it this time?

"Yeah, come in," Jack said, expecting to see Zoë again.

"Hi, Jack. I just had to come see you when I learned you were here." The voice was very familiar from his past.

"What the hell are you doing here? You're the last person I wanted to see," Jack said with exasperation in his voice.

It was Joni Adams, Jack's third wife. She was tall and thin with jet black hair and wore her familiar bright red lipstick. She had always looked like a *Vogue* fashion model, but now was even more beautiful as she had matured and gained a little weight.

"Jack, I just wanted to see you and make sure you are okay. I do care for you and feel so bad about what happened."

"You damn well should. You screwed me; you and my so-called friends!"

"Jack, you screwed yourself. Everyone finally caught on to what was happening. You couldn't hide it any longer. Everyone knew. You had to be helped or you would destroy yourself. It could have been a lot worse."

"But you led the pack, didn't you? Right to the hospital director."

"I knew they were coming down on you and I was trying get a deal from him. I told him I would get you to resign and into rehab if he wouldn't press charges. I was not trying to con you or hurt you. Jack, they were going to send you to prison for a very long time. You made a mistake. Everybody makes mistakes. You deserved another chance," Joni said with her most sincere voice.

Joni and Jack had lasted three years, the longest of his three marriages. She was blindly in love with the handsome, young doctor. They were a captivating couple and made a glamorous photograph for the society page of the newspaper. She knew that he was a bit wild, but was confident that he would settle down and give her the life and family that she dearly wanted. What really shook her up was when she found that he led a Jekyll and Hyde life. He was very good to her and whenever he came home, he would hold her and kiss her like he would never see her again. He liked her bright red lipstick on his face and the haunting smell of the *Odalisque* perfume he insisted she wear.

"Another chance? To hell with another chance. I lost everything in this deal except my miserable life and look what I've got now; this lousy job taking care of these worthless dying old farts. I don't even know how I got it. It makes no sense. Nobody else would even give me a chance to talk to them, Joni. Look up my name and there is my whole miserable damn life for everyone to see. I've got to get out of here but I have no place to go. This is it! This is the best I'll ever do," Jack bemoaned.

"Jack, you are really doing okay and I'm proud of you for getting this job, even if it is not so good. I'm sure it will work out for you. When you re-establish your reputation, you can get something better. I know you can do it," Joni said trying to cheer him.

Jack sat there in silence with the now familiar scowl on his face. He knew she was probably right, but he was certain he deserved better than this menial job and could never forgive her for betraying him. She had turned on him like everyone else. Why did she come here to torment him even further?

Joni pulled her chair over and sat beside him, putting her hand on his arm. She looked at him and remembered their lives together when she loved him more than anything else. She thought she still loved him despite all that had happened, and she still wanted a family and a home, and for a fleeting moment wondered if they could try it again. She would take him back if he would come to her. Jack's arm was unmoving and felt cold. Her warmth seemed to be pulled from her body. She had never known him to feel so cold.

Jack looked up at her with a bone-chilling stare. His eyes looked vacant and dead as if he were not even there. She felt as if she had seen a ghost as Jack pulled his arm from her hand and rasped, "It's time for you to go. You are nothing but a bad memory I want to forget."

Joni stood and pursed her lips as tears welled up in her eyes. She knew that it was over. In her sorrow, she feared the worst for him.

"Goodbye, Jack."

As Joni walked away down the long hallway, she felt as if she were walking out of a tomb, some cold dark place of the dead. She breathed in the fresh air outside and received the vital warmth of the sun on her chilled body. She was alive and Jack was not. She remembered hearing that prisoners awaiting execution were called dead men walking. Jack was a dead man walking.

Chapter 11
Dead and Dying

Jack had been at Hampton Oaks for about a month, and the more he got into the daily routine, the more he hated it. From his view, everyone there was just waiting to die and he was beginning to think he was also on the list. Frieda had insisted that he review every chart and make an initial contact and do an evaluation with every patient during the first six weeks and that this would provide the appropriate basis and continuity of care that the residents of Hampton Oaks so 'richly deserved'. Jack had to admit that Zoë came along at the right time to take care of much of this loathsome work. He could see already that Frieda was going to be a taskmaster as he picked up a list of chores that she had put on his desk. Frieda was frequently there very early and often left work late at night and always knew what was happening with the patients, or rather 'the residents', as she preferred calling them. Jack was smart enough to know that Frieda could be his undoing if he crossed her.

On the list were a number of problem patients that he had to see this morning and he needed to stop by the morgue and sign a death certificate on a newly departed one. Jack swallowed a few pills he had found that he thought he would like and walked over to the Extended Care Unit.

Most of the acutely ill patients there had some degree of heart failure requiring a constant juggling of diuretics, cardiac drugs and fluids while keeping them out of kidney failure. The nurses were quite caring and possessive of these patients and were persistent in getting appropriate medications and treatment orders. Jack couldn't slough off here without getting caught. He would not let that happen. He noted that there was a good supply of narcotics, but this was much too closely watched. To get at them would take considerable creativity but he had the time, patience and the skill.

He looked around the unit, disgusted with the number of near-death patients and the total waste of time and money being spent on them. He considered if there was something he could do to hurry along the process. Henrietta Jackson had tried to die at least eight times in the last month. Oh, but she wanted to be kept alive to see those grandchildren on weekends, so the nurses would work with her for hours to keep her going for one more week. If Jack had his way, this would be her last day. Yes, the last day for all of them, leeches that they are, taking up resources with their worthless lives. Like old suffering dogs, they need to be put down, and Jack didn't have much interest in keeping anyone alive, including himself. He did what he was expected to do, signing the orders, co-signing Zoë's notes in their charts and trying to act like he cared.

Jack had not previously been to the morgue and had to ask one of the aides for directions. Frieda's note said that Wanda Zelig had died as expected last night of complications of diabetes. She wanted the death certificate signed before the funeral directors picked up the body.

Jack finally found the east elevator to go down to the basement. The elevator door opened noisily after a loud chime announced its arrival. At the end of a short hallway was a door with translucent glass marked 'MORGUE' in large block letters. As Jack arrived, he noticed a light in the morgue and could see the shadow of a person moving quickly around, accompanied by considerable noise and shuffling. Opening the door, Jack encountered a small pipsqueak of a man who reminded him of the old movie actor, Peter Lorre, with inflamed-looking beady eyes. He was wearing one of the institution's maroon tunics that were issued to the nurses' aides. The man was obviously surprised and appeared worried as he hustled around the cramped space, hurriedly putting things away.

"I'm Dr Adams. What's going on in here? Who are you?" Jack said as he looked around the room.

The room was small with a tile floor and sink. A large fluorescent light hung down over a stainless-steel examination table in the center of the room. The area had apparently been used for autopsies in the past but was now mostly used as a distribution center for the dead bodies that passed through its doors. The refrigeration unit on the side contained four spaces for bodies and Jack noted that one of the doors was partially opened. On the other side of the room were shelves containing several large boxes, one of which was on the floor and was opened showing a pair of old shoes. Several pieces of women's clothing were lying on the floor. It appeared that the strange, little man had been going through someone's belongings.

"I am Reen, Draco Reen," he said with a heavy Eastern European accent. "I work here and I check morgue. New body. I have to check."

"Just what are you checking, Mr. Reen?" Jack asked.

"I check for body and I check for belongings," Reen answered.

"Well, what did you find, Mr. Reen?" Jack queried as he continued to look around the room where he saw other pieces of clothing lying around.

"I found body and belongings. I put everything in order," Reen said as he began to put the garments back into the box.

"You look for death certificate? It on desk," Reen said in a halting cadence, pointing to the desk on the other side of the room.

Jack walked to the desk, watching Reen from the corner of his eye. Reen bent over and put what looked like a pair of panties into his pocket and the remaining clothes into the box and placed it on the shelf.

"I go now. Finished," Reen said.

"Where is she?'

"She is dead."

"I know she is dead. Which unit is she in?"

"Three unit. She in three unit," Reen said as he quickly left.

"They don't get any stranger than that," Jack said aloud when Reen was out of the room.

Jack noticed that the number three unit was open as he initially thought. He opened the door widely and pulled out the tray containing Wanda Zelig's naked corpse. Right away, Jack noticed that something was not right as Wanda's body was partially on its side and her legs and arms were spread apart like some macabre porno pose. The body was cold and becoming stiff but still somewhat pliable. Rigor mortis was beginning.

"Damn, this is not good. The morticians may have something to say if they suspect what I suspect," Jack said to himself as he put on a lab coat and gloves.

Rigor mortis is caused by stiffening of the muscles after death and usually begins about three hours after death, depending on the temperature. Wanda's death occurred about four hours ago and the muscles would gradually become more rigid, locking her joints into place over the next several hours. Jack knew that he must bend her body back into a suitable position for family viewing while time permitted. It would not be good for the institution or his job if anyone thought that Wanda had a sexual fling after her death.

"Frieda's not going to like this," Jack said as he put Wanda back into her cooler and then signed her death certificate.

Jack was right. Frieda was furious. She had been suspicious of Reen for several months but never had any hard evidence. Even now, it was all somewhat circumstantial. To make things worse there was a real dearth of qualified people who did the many jobs that Reen was able to do, including being a nurse's aide.

Frieda told Jack, "He is supposed to take bodies to the morgue and box up the immediate belongings and arrange for transportation to a funeral home. That is definitely one of his jobs. We certainly cannot fire him without due process or the union would be all over us. You won't get anything talking to him and I would guess that you picked up on that already. At least he has not harmed any of the residents and there have been no complaints about him. We will just have to keep a closer eye on him. If you catch him doing anything that is not on the up and up that can be well documented, fire him on the spot and let's get him out of here. I will deal with the consequences and the union."

"Something tells me we haven't heard the last of Draco Reen," Jack cautioned.

Chapter 12
Predator and Prey

Jack could barely tolerate Hampton Oaks' do-gooder staff with their smiling facades. Every day he remembered that this was the only job he could get — that was the only reason he was here. Why were these people so anxious to hire him when they knew all the sordid details of his life? It made no sense. There were certainly others who would love this glitzy, crap job with a big salary and nothing of importance to do. The staff ran the place and all he did was examine patients and sign forms. Why had they chosen him? It was as if he had been singled out and given the position because of something beyond his knowing.

Frieda Harrison had acted as if she expected him to be trouble from the start and continued to cut him no slack. He knew that she was monitoring his work daily. Frieda was all business and expected him to do exactly what she told him to do. He could not skirt her assignment of methodically reviewing and examining every patient in the facility and today there were five more for him to review — Room Checks, as she liked to call the doctor visits. Jack preferred the room checks because he usually did them alone and there were no eyes to keep him from very short visits in which he did nothing. Zoë was tied up in another part of the facility today and he couldn't dump this job on her. The nurses liked Zoë a lot and it was obvious that they were keeping her busy and away from Jack as much as possible. However, Jack was still able to dump quite a bit of work on her. Jack continued to be obsessed with disdain for the old and weak ones and the efforts to keep them alive. They needed to die and stop sapping everyone's energy and resources. He often thought that an overdose of pain medications would correct the problem and he would do it if he could get away with it.

Jack had quickly seen two of the patients on his list, scribbling short and inconsequential notes in their charts and then moving along. He walked down a long hallway, going to the next patient on his list when he passed an open door. This was the room for a patient he did not know that he later would determine belonged to John Asterman. An eerie chill passed through his body as if a blast of cold air had caused his hair to stand on end. He stopped, looked around and saw nothing. The air was pleasantly warm and there was no draft, yet he felt something strange. For years, Jack had shut out emotions and feelings that most people consider basic to their existence. Love, compassion, caring, humor and all of these were weaknesses he had eliminated from his life, but suddenly he could feel these emotions coming to him once again. As he stood in the hallway, he felt threatened as he protected the anger, hatred and darkness within him. The goodness that he felt radiating towards him was abhorrent and he sensed a threat to the evil that had become him. Yet mysteriously and irresistibly he was drawn to the open door, like a moth to a candle, and the fascination for what was inside overcame his fear. Breathing deeply and with his heart pounding, he turned and cautiously walked through the doorway. The room was filled with glaring bright light from the sun bursting through the unshuttered window. He squinted in the brilliance and just barely saw the foot of a single bed. As his eyes slowly began to accommodate, he heard:

"Come in. Come in."

Jack sensed the greeting but did not truly hear the words. Although he felt like running from the room, he fought the urge as his curiosity continued to rise. What could this be and why do I feel compelled to enter here? What fearful goodness lies here? I don't want to go but I must see what is here, he thought.

Jack then suddenly remembered a Christmas long ago. He awoke and knew that good things awaited him: happiness, joy, and wonderful presents. This was one of the few times that his family was together. He also remembered fear. His fear was that his parents would not be there, fear of finding something else evil coming into his life. Fear that he would never have the experience again.

Jack walked into the center of the room and was startled back into the present, seeing two large, dark eyes staring directly at him. There was a man-like figure in the bed, but all he could discern were the large penetrating, vacuous eyes. Jack was empty and hollow and knew with certainty that whatever goodness had ever been within him had long gone. Now he felt like a deer must feel when caught in the hunter's trap with the cross hairs of the gun site in the center of his chest and he was the prey, now aware of the predator about to destroy his existence.

Jack shuddered with fear and gasping for breath, fled from the room with his heart galloping in his chest. He sprinted down the corridor and slammed his back against the wall at an open window. His head reeled and he gasped again for breath as black spots moved over the image before his eyes as he stared into a mirror. He was aghast at his own visage and knowing he was passing out, slid to the floor and put his head between his legs. The floor seemed to move like waves of the ocean and his head throbbed and spun. A wave of nausea came over him and he clambered up the wall to the open window and vomited on the trees below. As he clung to the windowsill, his malady improved as his mind began to slowly calm and reclaim reality. Jack had seen himself dead in his own horrible image in the mirror, his pathetic, empty shell. It seemed as if he was already dead. Those terrible, abhorrent eyes had pierced his very being and showed the emptiness of his existence. Jack also realized that the horrid being he had beheld was more alive than Jack had ever been. The fear was complete. Jack would never enter that room again, but this would not be his last encounter with the stranger.

Chapter 13 A Friendly Note

Zoë's concerns about her rotation at Hampton Oaks rapidly faded as she began her consuming work. The nurses and staff were great to her, supporting and teaching her a wealth of information, even more than she expected. She found the care conferences to be very useful and a good forum to voice her questions and concerns. She also got to sit in on two continuing medical education teleconferences so that she didn't feel so far removed from the university. All of the nurses liked her and were grateful that she was around helping out. She found the best way to get information from Jack was definitely at the conferences when everyone was present and he seemed to give fairly straight answers. She avoided being alone with him because she was still quite intimidated by his demeanor and she believed that he would try to harm her or coerce her into doing something she didn't want to do. She learned through personal experiences and many sources that he was definitely one who couldn't be trusted and she decided there would be no more bargaining with Jack. If he tried anything with her, she would report everything and leave and would just have to graduate late.

Hampton Oaks had a quite diverse and interesting group of residents. Some of them were younger, requiring chronic care but at least eighty percent were senior citizens. Zoë found most of the elderly patients to be very pleasant and often quite funny. She was very shocked to find several of them 'sleeping around' as they liked to say. Several little, old ladies who were over ninety were determined to find themselves another husband and were quite jealous of each other in their exploits.

Most of the exams for the ambulatory residents were done in the clinic area. Some patients, who for various reasons could not go to the clinic, were evaluated in their rooms which were less than optimal but this worked okay. Today there were two people who Jack wanted Zoë to evaluate in their rooms. The first patient, Margaret Peterson, had recently become quite dizzy and had difficulty walking. Zoë quickly determined that her heart rate and blood pressure were low as a result of newly prescribed medications that had produced her dizziness.

The second patient, Harry Burns, had begun to have leg pain and was unable to walk. Zoë checked his chart and found that he had a history of atherosclerosis that was continuing to narrow his arteries despite medications. On examination, his left foot was quite cool and purplish in appearance, and she could not feel any pulses in his leg below his groin. She immediately knew that he had occluded an artery to his leg and likely needed immediate surgery or at least an arterial stent. She finished her exam and quickly reported her findings to Jack's nurse, Meg Vandever, who confirmed what Zoë had found. Zoë later learned that Harry Burns was transported to the medical center for vascular surgery and Margaret Peterson had her medications adjusted and were both doing well. Zoë was very pleased that she had made the correct diagnoses that immediately benefited the patients. She was never able to determine if Jack had actually seen the patients or not. His signature eventually appeared after hers in the chart notes.

During her first week, Zoë was having lunch in the dining room and overheard two aides discussing a patient about whom they were quite concerned. Her interest was piqued when she heard them say that no one had been able to figure out what was wrong with the patient and that he continued to decline and they thought he would die soon.

"Excuse me. I couldn't help overhearing your conversation. I'm Zoë Abrams, a medical student doing a rotation here. Is this a patient I should know about?" Zoë asked.

"We don't think so. He has been here a long time and everyone is expecting him to die soon. You probably wouldn't learn very much," one of them replied.

"What is his name?" Zoë asked, being definitely interested since this sounded like a challenge for her.

"It's John Asterman on 2-West but I also agree you probably shouldn't waste your time," the other responded.

"Well, I do like mysteries. I believe I will drop by and see him. Thanks," Zoë said, wishing them a good afternoon.

Zoë discussed several patients with the nursing staff and asked them about John Asterman. She told them about her conversation with the aides and that she thought this would be an interesting case to look into.

Meg Vandever was the first to speak. "He is not a geriatrics patient and you certainly have enough to do without taking him on. He is just an enigma. Everyone has worked with him for years and recently he just continues to get worse. He's got some kind of birth defect and injury and there is just no hope for him. You probably shouldn't waste your time."

"What do you think, Barbara?" Zoë asked Barbara Matson who had done physical therapy with him for several months in the past.

"You know, he is a very strange man and some of the staff are uncomfortable working with him. Others, me included, just love to be around him. He is uplifting in a strange way, but he looks so bizarre and I think that unnerves a lot of people. No one has ever seen him fully functional. I heard that he was able to sit and feed himself at one time, but now he can't eat and has to have tube feedings. You might want to meet him just because he is probably one of the strangest people you will ever meet. However, I agree with Meg and think that you shouldn't spend the short time you have here trying to figure him out."

After talking to the nurses and exchanging information with them about the patients she had seen, Zoë stopped by her cubicle to finish her notes. On her desk were some journals the nurses had passed along to her and a note from Frieda Harrison commending her for her good help with Margaret Peterson and Harry Burns. Zoë put this note safely away as documentation in case Jack gave her any grief about her rotation. She then saw a small sealed envelope with her name written in elegant calligraphy on the front. Was this an invitation to some institution soirée? No, but inside was a cryptic note written in the same handwriting:

John Asterman is the key to all you seek.
— A Friend

Chapter 14
John Asterman

Zoë had first heard of John Asterman only an hour before and now this strange note appears out of nowhere. Why is it that everyone sees him as dying yet one person calls him the 'key to what I seek'? What am I seeking anyhow? Zoë had already decided to check out John Asterman after everyone told her it would be a waste of her time, but the note sealed the deal for her and she would definitely study this strange person. She began asking everyone she knew if they had sent her a note and it was uniformly denied. Her story was that someone had sent her a note about doing a good job and she wanted to know who it was to thank them, but she didn't reveal the true contents to anyone.

That evening when many of the staff had left, Zoë went to 2-west and told the attendant that she needed to go over some records. She found Asterman's chart and settled in to review it. Immediately she noticed that the chart contained information for only the last two years. She checked a filing cabinet that usually contained earlier volumes of patients' records but there was nothing there. The first record in the chart from twenty-two months previous was an annual exam. There was the usual checklist and everything was checked as 'normal' and signed by Dr Jason Wallingford. She later found that Dr Wallingford was subsequently fired for incompetence and negligence and addiction problems.

There were subsequent notes about his tube feedings, problems with his tube, and documentation of his continued decline in health. Some blood work had been obtained over a year ago which appeared normal and there was a note that he didn't have diabetes. Zoë thought, how could a chart contain so little information? She was used to seeing an information sheet in the front of the chart with contact and insurance information but there was none in Asterman's chart. A small square of paper was taped in the front of the chart, stating to call Dr Morris for any problems and that the patient was a full code in case of a cardio-respiratory arrest. With chronically ill patients, the nurses always need to know what to do if a patient's heart or breathing stops. This is a decision usually made well in advance by the patient, physician and family so that if someone wishes not to be resuscitated, then everyone is aware of it and will follow the patient's wishes. It was obvious that someone wanted to keep Asterman alive.

Zoë put the chart back into the rack, realizing that it was of no help at all. Over the next several days she searched for additional records and there were none. If there ever were any, they seemed to have disappeared.

At least this evening she could meet Asterman and maybe get some information out of him. She heard that over the past few months, he had not been speaking but she would try. Asterman was in a private room, but she was informed by the nurse that he would be moved to a small ward situation soon for management purposes. Zoë thought of all the gossip about him and the strange note she had received and began having some subtle apprehension about meeting him.

She walked to his room, knocked twice and opened the door and announced herself. "Hi, Mr. Asterman, I'm Zoë Abrams. I am a medical student and they asked me to come and check on you." However, this was not the case but it provided her with a valid introduction.

The room was dark and she could only see his outline in the bed. He did not make a sound as she came closer to him. His features remained indistinct and she bumped the edge of the bed in the darkness.

"Sorry, I didn't mean to bump you. Mr. Asterman, I need to turn on the light so I can see you. You might want to close your eyes since it will be bright for a moment." Zoë moved over to the bedside table and turned on the lamp.

Zoë had seen a lot of unusual patients, but was unprepared for the visage that suddenly appeared from the darkness. His large, piercing eyes were open wide and looking directly at her and it was as if she had unexpectedly encountered a wild animal right in front of her in the forest. She gasped as her heart raced and she had this overwhelming urge to run from the room. She had never felt that way before and it was as if she were facing an unknown terror, something from a childhood nightmare and there was no escape. She stood agape and unable to speak, fixated on his eyes.

"Don't be afraid. Come, sit down."

Almost immediately the fear ceased and she began to feel the most remarkable sense of peace and tranquility. Her mind reeled as this evolution of thought and sensation flowed through her brain. She suddenly felt great compassion and endearment for this very strange man.

"Oh, I am so sorry. I was frightened and I should not have been. I know you were startled by me barging in here in the dark unannounced and that was very rude of me. I can come back some other time if you wish."

"No, sit. Please sit."

Zoë stood there in amazement and as she talked to him, she felt that Asterman understood her every word, even though he said nothing. Once she had finished her apologies, he flashed a weak smile, nodded slightly, and moving only his index finger, slowly pointed to a chair beside his bed. He never took his gaze off of Zoë and she continued to become increasingly more relaxed. There was so much she wanted to know about him, but she felt uncharacteristically compelled to tell him everything about herself and she began talking almost continuously. She described her early life, the death of her parents and the uncertainties and doubts and fears that ensued, her school and friends and her decision finally to go to medical school.

"You know, I just love working with people and helping them, but I worry about the future and what lies ahead for my children, if I ever have any. I really want the world to be a better place and for humans to evolve as excellent beings and survive long into the future. We have not taken very good care of our world and have done so much plundering, pollution and destruction of the environment. People are so greedy and selfishly don't take care of each other. There is so much goodness in life and I want that goodness to prevail against all the bad things that are around us and to have it last forever. We need a world where clean energy is free to everyone and we will be unencumbered by the need to struggle to make money and can focus on a society that will be at peace and eliminate poverty and disease. We must become enlightened to the greater reality of existence and become one with each other and the universe. A much better world where we can experience love and be at peace with each other, that's what I want," Zoë said with her deepest sincerity as she continued to talk for more than an hour surprising herself by her unloading all this information on a total stranger who could not even speak.

Asterman continued to watch her intently and would smile gently at some of the things she said. Finally, he began closing his eyes and seemed very tired.

"I'm sorry I have talked so much about myself. The real reason I came was that I want you to know that I am quite concerned about you. I would like to come back tomorrow if it is okay with you and to examine you and check on you again. I really believe I can do something to help you get better if you will let me."

Asterman briefly opened his eyes once more, smiled at her, nodded slightly and then fell asleep.

Chapter 15
The First Clue

What is this fascination or rather obsession with Asterman? Zoë was surprised at herself. Never had a patient or anyone else for that matter enthralled her in this way. She found herself thinking about him throughout the day and he had even crept into her dreams. Zoë knew that he needed help and somehow, she knew that she was the only one who could help him. But how could this possibly happen? She was a good student and outstanding in her class, but she lacked the years of experience that made for a good clinical physician.

She reviewed everything from his meager medical record and to her irritation, there was almost nothing there to give her any clues. Hampton Oaks did not have an electronic medical record as was the case in most other facilities. It interested her that very few people had written anything substantive in his chart — there was no medical management plan or nutritional plan and it appeared that he was on no medications. Most patients have what are called PRN, or as needed orders for things such as laxatives, medications for pain or fever and a variety of everyday needs. There were no PRN orders in Asterman's chart. Also, he rarely had any blood work, even though there were some abnormalities noted in an earlier study that had been done. It appears that he was intentionally neglected in many ways.

Nancy Petty, the medical records librarian, had searched for Asterman's old records and to her surprise, had been unable to find anything. Zoë asked if they could have been misplaced or accidentally put into storage and an indignant Ms. Petty assured her that was not the case, noting that she had always been in charge of the files and that there had never been a problem before. Her over-reaction to Zoë's questions complicated things even further in that Ms. Petty believed that somehow

Zoë was trying to impeach her job as medical records librarian. This certainly was not Zoë's intent; however, she was denied a request to look through the file storage herself to see if something could be found. This annoying roadblock only increased her determination to search for more information.

Zoë continued to wonder about the mysterious note regarding Asterman. She had questioned more people but there was universal denial. She even wrote a note to Dr Morris, but Annie said she did not know when he would come back to read it. Zoë had also carefully checked, but in vain, the handwriting in the charts and documents to see if someone was using a fancy script. For now, she would just catch up on her notes and reading.

"Are you working late tonight, Zoë?" Meg Vandever asked.

"Yes. I have several more notes to write and some schoolwork I need to finish. It's quiet here and a good place to get things done without any interruptions," Zoë replied. It was also a good time to get into the medical records files and take a first-hand look. The custodian had just emptied the trash bins and was mindlessly pushing the dust bunnies around on the floor, moving them from one part of the room to another. Finishing, he very unobtrusively left, trying not to disturb Zoë and Meg.

Meg locked her desk then put on her coat and gathered her belongings.

"Goodnight. See you in the morning."

"Goodnight, Meg."

Zoë looked down the hallway as Meg left to see if anyone was around, and no one was there except the custodian who moved on to his next room.

Zoë checked Nancy's desk but it was locked. The key to the file room she knew to be in the center drawer, but there was no way to get to it. After looking around to see if there might be a spare key hidden somewhere, Zoë stood at the locked medical records door staring at the doorknob as if that might somehow cause it to open. She jiggled it several times and found it to be quite secure. Beside the knob she could see the catch and then noticed the deadbolt that was just above the knob was not engaged. She again tried wiggling the knob back and forth, but of course it didn't budge.

"Hmm, I wonder," Zoë said aloud as she went to her purse and got out a credit card and metal nail file. She scraped the tip of the file over the catch and found that it would move ever so slightly. Next, she placed the credit card at an angle behind the catch and again used the file to move back the catch. The credit card then slipped into the groove and she pushed the catch completely back and the door popped open.

"All right! My American Express and I didn't leave home without it!" Zoë beamed at her accomplishment.

The files were quite orderly and were arranged by medical record number. She reached into her pocket and pulled out a piece of paper with Asterman's number and began searching. She found charts on both sides of where his records should be located but nothing was there. She then looked in the catalog and found three names similar to Asterman and checked these on the chance that information was misfiled but with no luck. She checked every corner of the chart room and found a stack of charts to be re-filed but none were Asterman's. Then she went back to the place where his chart should have been and took down all of the adjacent charts on the shelf and began looking through each of them page by page in case some of his records had been misfiled. Again, there was no luck, but as she was placing the charts again on the shelf, a single crumpled dusty piece of paper on the back of the shelf came into view. She shook off the dust as she picked up the yellowed document and flattened it out on an empty shelf.

"My oh my, and what do we have we here?" A smile spread over Zoë's face as she read:

Hampton Oaks Nursing and Rehabilitation Center
Admission Data Sheet
Name: John Asterman
MRN: 18-22-963
DOB: Unknown (Est age 25)
Date Admitted: 9/23/1983

Admitting MD: Roger Morris
Facility: Continuous care
Diagnoses:
    Rib fractures
    Burns
    Dehydration
    Malnutrition
    Altered mental status
Code Status: Full Code
Contact: Rachel Devane, Power of Attorney
Pay Status: No Insurance; Rachel Devane, benefactor

Finally, something to work with! Zoë whispered to herself as she folded the paper and put it into her jacket pocket. After another thorough check and replacing the charts and carefully leaving everything in place as she found it, Zoë knew that there was nothing else to be found in the file room. She knew her next step was to have a little talk with Dr Morris, if he ever returned, but more importantly to find the mysterious Rachel Devane who was listed as Asterman's benefactor.

Chapter 16
Abuse

Jack saw possibilities in nurse Barbara Matson from the first day he worked with her. She was short, with sandy blonde hair, trim with a nice figure. She was in her forties, but had a worn and weary expression and demeanor. A series of wrong choices and unhealthy relationships had plagued her all her life and she seemed to continuously gravitate toward abusive men. She had been to multiple physicians for chronic pain in her back and headaches. Frequently missing work, Barbara found her problems compounded by addicting medications and a mentally challenged daughter she could barely care for, even with the help of friends and social services.

Jack detected in her weak and vulnerable personality that she was someone who could easily be manipulated for his benefit. He had already begun giving her pain medications knowing that this was the key to trapping her in his web. There was a sinister ecstasy in her impassioned pleas for more drugs and her struggling desperation was simply ecstatically seductive in his eyes.

As the long workday came to an end, Barbara sneaked into his office when no one else was around. Pleading eyes stared at him as she hoped he would give her something stronger for the pain that tore at her back and the anxiety that filled her mind. She started to speak but Jack held up his hand to quieten her.

"Barbara, I think we can develop a mutually beneficial relationship."

"I need help with this pain and I'm just desperate. Please help me and I will do whatever I can. What can I do for you to help me?" Barbara responded.

"You obviously need a number of things — medications and some money for your child. Barbara, I have some very definite needs too and we can help each other."

He moved closer to her and gently caressed the side of her neck. "Yes, I have some definite needs you can help me with, Barbara, and it will be well worth it for you."

Barbara knew with certainty where this was going, but saw no way out. Her mind reeled and she knew she had no options. He really could help her and her daughter and it just might be a small price to pay. She thought that after all, as a doctor he gets paid well and he has given her pain medications before. Jack could be someone who finally would bring her a stable and secure life. She thought that he might even learn to love her.

Taking her by the hand, Jack took her to the file room, locked the door and unbuttoned her blouse and bra. Jack was very pleased as he caressed her breasts and unzipped his pants. "I think you know what to do," he said with a sinister smile. Jack enjoyed seeing Barbara's quiet desperation as she did whatever he wanted. He wondered how far he could force her to go and over time enjoyed increasingly sadistic perversion to their sexual encounters. It became a cruel game with him just to see what she would do in her desperation. He loved to see her beg and the control he had over her was exhilarating and complete.

Chapter 17
The Need to Know

Zoë had convinced Patrick to come for a visit and help her get information about Asterman. He had hoped for a romantic weekend, but Zoë was on a mission and that would not happen. Patrick knew that she would never rest until she had the information she was seeking and she would undoubtedly assign him a good portion of the investigation. She wanted Patrick to meet Asterman and hoped that he would have some insight on the matter. The situation needed two heads rather than one.

Zoë found herself spending increasingly more time with Asterman. Because of her busy schedule, this was mostly in the evenings after hours. She told herself that she would not continue to sneak around to see him and added him to her list of patients that she saw on a regular basis. She began making notes in his chart and tried to develop a treatment plan for him. Almost everyone tried to dissuade her from doing anything with him, but the more she was in his presence, the more fascinating he became and she was absolutely convinced she could help him. After several thorough examinations of him, she drew some blood and did several other tests. The tests showed some minor electrolyte abnormalities and mild anemia, but certainly nothing that would give her a clue about his condition. He was malnourished without question and would often barely move and was rarely acknowledge her presence. Zoë realized that the only thing keeping him alive was his tube feedings and this certainly was doing an inadequate job. She had tried to feed him and would often take an hour to get a tiny amount of food into him. He seemed to dislike much of what was offered and would not swallow it. She remained determined to find out more about him.

Zoë and Patrick went to Asterman's room. This was the first time Patrick had seen him, although Zoë had described him in great detail and his response was typical of everyone's encounter with this strange man: amazement. Asterman lay there in his bed with his eyes closed as Patrick was both repelled and fascinated by his strange, thin body. His first thought was that Asterman had some kind of genetic abnormality or birth defect. He looked typically human but had a large head and skinny body, and somewhat resembled pictures he had seen in medical textbooks of patients with hydrocephalus and cerebral palsy. Patrick had a strong sense that Asterman was dying.

Zoë was emphatic. "You can't take any photos here, and it's strictly prohibited, so you have to draw him. Try to get several angles and some close-ups of his face as well."

She went over to Asterman and talked to him as she adjusted his head and pillow. Asterman seemed oblivious to what was happening. Zoë then called Patrick over to the bed and pulled back the sheet and lifted his gown to expose a somewhat barrel-shaped chest with almost undetectable widely set nipples, a sunken abdomen with no discernable navel, juvenile- looking male genitalia and scrawny legs. His skin had a pale mushroom kind of appearance and there was no hair on his body. Zoë then covered him but left his arms and upper chest exposed. Zoë continued to talk to Asterman and told him that Patrick was going to draw his portrait. With this comment, Asterman opened his large, dark eyes slightly and gazed at the both of them. Some fine movements of his face muscles could be seen and his thin hands moved slightly.

Zoë was delighted and began telling Asterman how they wanted to find out more about him and to see if they could help him get better. As Zoë talked, Patrick sensed some life coming back into the near corpse. She spoke to him in a logical, progressive manner as if he could understand her interest in him and her difficulty in figuring out anything about him. Zoë told him that he had not been well but she thought, with a little more information, she could help him to become better. There suddenly seemed to be a presence about Asterman that was familiar.

"Thank you."

Zoë said, "You're welcome." She was unaware that Asterman had said nothing as Patrick looked at her with a puzzled face.

"Zoë, you know he didn't say anything, don't you?"

"Patrick, he said 'thank you' and I know you could hear it."

"Nope, I know what I didn't hear."

"I know I heard him say 'thank you'. It was very loud and clear, and he was most sincere."

"This is all quite strange. My hearing is perfectly fine and I definitely did not hear anything."

Zoë was perplexed. She knew perfectly well that she had heard him without any distortion whatsoever. For a moment she contemplated the situation and deciding on a plan, walked over to Asterman's bed.

"Mr. Asterman, I am having a difficult time sorting out your problems. But I want you to know that I am really making every effort to figure out how to help you and I will do it. I am diligent and very persistent and will make it happen. You are very important to me."

"Thank you."

Again, Zoë heard the message very loudly and distinctly. She looked at Patrick, smiled and raised her eyebrows and then nodded affirmatively. Patrick responded by shaking his head from side to side, shrugged his shoulders with his hands outstretched and palms up.

"Zoë, you're either nuts or you are hearing his mind."

"So, I've become a mind reader? This is amazing! You know since I met him, I've had this feeling that we are somehow connecting at a non-verbal level. It's not just body language since he hardly moves, but it really does seem to be something much more profound." She looked over at Asterman, thinking that she might try something else with him to test this mind-reading idea, but he was soundly asleep. But there would be time later, she hoped.

Zoë pointed at Patrick's drawing pad and said: "We've got to get back to work. You had better hop to it. There is very little time and I've got a ton to do. The staff don't need to see you in here with him. Finish up as quickly as you can and meet me in the lobby at noon. The nurse will be back in here in about an hour. Don't forget to straighten his bed when you are done and talk to him if he wakes up."

Realizing she was late, Zoë quickly left the room and headed toward the nursing station to begin her rounds. She continued to think about Asterman and had to put him out of her mind while she attended to her other tasks.

Patrick prepared his drawing pad. Asterman still appeared to be sleeping. He decided not to try to awaken him but to proceed with his work. Patrick studied his face intently for several minutes. He had a small nose and a feeding tube was in his right nostril. The feeding tube really bothered Patrick and it seemed like such a cruel thing to do to someone. Asterman's mouth was small and his lips very thin. His ears were tiny and set low on his large, almost pear-shaped head. Patrick again wondered if his head size was due to increased fluid in his brain producing hydrocephalus. This seemed the most logical explanation. His skin was soft, almost like calf's leather and his hands and fingers small and spindly with small, pointed nails. There were no moles, freckles or spots and it looked like he had never been out in the sun with his ashy white skin.

Patrick began a charcoal sketch and decided right away to leave out the unsightly feeding tube. The first sketch was slightly off-center and included his arms and hands. The next sketch included his face, directly frontal, followed by a profile resembling a mug shot. As he completed closer sketches of his torso, hands and feet, Patrick saw that he was running out of time. He quickly sketched several other areas that he wanted to include, but was afraid to try to move Asterman since he did not want to disturb him. Several of the sketches would require additional work that could be done once he was back in his studio. As he finished, he noted that Asterman had begun to move slightly, but his eyes remained closed.

"It was good to meet you, Mr. Asterman. I'll try to come back and see you," Patrick said, feeling a bit odd about his comment to an unresponsive patient. Zoë had always insisted that everyone should talk appropriately to patients, even if they appeared incapable of understanding since one can never know for certain. Again, Asterman opened his eyes and Patrick had the sensation that Asterman was glad to see him also. They both smiled.

In the lobby, Patrick showed Zoë the drawings and she was quite pleased. He had been able to do six sketches, three of which were quite detailed.

"Would you be a sweetheart and make some copies for me? I want to get them to our group at our next meeting to see if they have any ideas about him that might help us. We are seeing them soon and can do it then. We definitely have to get more heads involved in this process."

"I will do some more touch-ups and take some large format photographs. Hopefully I can get them to you by the weekend."

"That's great. I really appreciate your help with this. So, what do you make of him?"

"He is even stranger than you led me to believe, and I can't even guess at this point, but he certainly is the most unusual and perplexing man I have ever seen. He may have some odd syndrome or possibly a genetic defect, but who knows? I've never seen anyone like him and he may give me nightmares. Did you get any other information about him?"

Zoë confided in Patrick: "I hunted through medical records last night and tried to find his chart when he was first admitted. There was nothing there and I think someone has taken his records. It is very suspicious to me. The only information we have is his present chart that only goes back several years, and the chart notes are incomplete and not helpful at all. However, I just found this one piece of paper down in the file room."

Zoë opened her notebook and pulled out the crinkled sheet of paper she had found. Patrick looked at it and read part of it aloud. "John Asterman, Medical Record Number 18-22-963, admitted September 23, 1983; date of birth: unknown; admitted by: Dr Roger Morris. Contact: Rachel Devane. We at least know when he was admitted and who admitted him. Who is this Rachel Devane person?"

"I was told Roger Morris is out of town, but I found an address for Rachel Devane. I am going to see her this weekend. Patrick, would you please check the local newspapers to see if anything happened about that time in 1983 that might give us a clue about him? He must have received those injuries in a crash or fire or something. Someone around here must know something more about him. I will talk to several of the older employees here and will definitely make a visit to Rachel Devane. I hope she will accommodate me and be willing to talk and maybe we can figure this strangeness out."

Patrick liked the idea of being a detective and accepted Zoë's offer. "I will start checking it out but remember, I have a day job and need to be back at work the day after tomorrow."

"Patrick, this is really important to me and I sincerely appreciate your help, but remember we have precious little time," Zoë said as she scurried off.

Chapter 18
Detective Patrick David

Patrick's goal for the weekend was to check out the local newspapers for any information that might give a clue about John Asterman showing up or being injured in 1983. After several non-productive stops, he went to the *Westchester County Gazette*, a weekly paper that had carried local news for over one hundred and fifty years. He entered the small office and was gleefully greeted by Marcus Newell, a sanguine, rotund and somewhat balding fellow with a generous mustache. He enthusiastically greeted Patrick and proceeded to tell him about the newspaper and how he had worked as an editor, reporter and even delivery boy at the *Gazette* for nearly sixty years. Marcus was supposedly retired but continued to show up for work and do whatever needed to be done. Today he was the only one in the office and was sitting mumbling at a crossword puzzle when Patrick arrived.

"Hi, I'm Patrick David. I would like to look at your archives for 1983 for some research I'm doing."

Marcus looked up and proudly boasted, "Well, we've got copies of every *Gazette* that has ever been published so you have come to the right place. Unfortunately, we ran out of storage space and had to put most of them on microfilm, but the information is all still right here in this office. Come around here with me and let's take a look."

Marcus led Patrick into an adjoining room and motioned for him to sit at the viewer. He pulled out a box from the files marked 1983 and gently, almost reverently, placed it on the table. He explained to Patrick how the viewer worked and how to make copies and then left him alone in the small room.

It would be nice if this were computerized, Patrick thought as he began with the January papers. He started the arduous process of reviewing every article published in 1983 and began taking notes. He had decided that, in addition to looking for the names of Asterman and Devane, he also would look for accidents and injuries since Asterman had been injured and of course, the gossip column might be useful. A small community newspaper's idea of 'all the news that's fit to print' is quite different from *The New York Times*. In the *Gazette*, there was no international news unless someone had taken a trip abroad and quite often very little national news. If it was not a local issue, it was not worth printing. Asterman and Devane were not mentioned as he carefully combed each edition. There were numerous recipes, family reunions, births, weddings, anniversaries and deaths listed in the *Gazette*. Jeb Johnson shot himself in the foot with his .22 pistol. Mae Langley had burned her hand and ruined her kitchen in a grease fire. The Collins had taken a trip to their roots in Ireland. There was a mysterious explosion in the middle of the night by the river near Croton Bay on May 4 for which there was no information. There were repeated reports of strange lights people had seen on several occasions.

Marcus came back into the room to find Patrick deep in thought staring at the notes he had made. It was looking like a dead end with nothing about Asterman or Devane.

"It's lunchtime. I'm sorry but I need to close up for an hour or so. Did you find what you were looking for?"

"I'm afraid I didn't," Patrick replied, still deep in thought.

"Well, what exactly are you looking for?" Marcus queried.

Patrick thought about how to be tactful in order to get the most information. He decided the simplest and most honest response was the best.

"John Asterman."

"Humm, Asterman. I haven't thought about him in years. Well, you won't find anything in the archives that I'm aware of. Why are you interested in Asterman?" Marcus's curiosity was suddenly piqued.

Patrick thought a moment about some non-revealing tales he might tell but decided to play it straight. At this point he surmised that Marcus would probably honestly answer any question that he asked him.

"My fiancée is a medical student who's working at Hampton Oaks and is taking care of Asterman. Most of his old medical records are missing and she asked me to help her get some information about him. He is not doing well and she was hoping to find out anything that might be of help for his care, particularly from the time he was admitted in 1983. She has no idea what is wrong with him, other than some previous injuries and no one at the facility knows anything about him." Patrick realized that he had never before referred to Zoë as his fiancée and it gave him a very good feeling.

"So, he is still alive? How about that? I thought he had died several years ago. Well, I can tell you what I know but I need lunch. You interested in buying?" Marcus's interest was high and he seemed ready to talk.

"Sure, lead the way. I appreciate your taking the time to talk with me," Patrick said smiling.

"And I appreciate your buying lunch. It seems like a good deal to me, food for information." Marcus closed the office, hung a 'back at two p.m.' sign and walked down the street with Patrick to Molly's Diner.

The restaurant was nearly filled with lunchtime patrons, but Patrick and Marcus found a booth in the back that afforded some privacy and avoided the clamor while they talked. They ordered lunch, sipped on their beverages and got to know each other. Marcus began talking and it became obvious that Patrick's best strategy would be to sit and listen. Marcus enjoyed hearing himself talk and had a way of weaving a story that conveyed much more information than was required. Occasionally he would get lost on his own circuitous path of his narrative and would have to be reminded what he was talking about to begin with. He seemed to be quite honest, but Patrick couldn't tell if he was stretching the truth for effect. There was no doubt that he liked to talk.

Marcus's story started with Rachel Devane's husband, Edgar, who was an industrialist deeply involved in shipping and commerce. Rachel was also from a wealthy family and had been a nurse in her younger years. She was well endowed financially with old family money and didn't need to work and was overly generous in helping almost anyone in need. They were married when she was probably in her early twenties and Edgar was mid-fifties. Edgar determined to impress his new wife, like she needed impressing, bought and refurbished a pristine old nineteenth-century mansion that became known as the Devane House, using state-of-the-art craftsmanship and artistry. He expected Rachel to entertain his business associates and be a pretty, congenial wife and hostess. This was not in Rachel's plans at all and this fact became a source of conflict between them. Rachel was much more concerned about supporting worthy causes and helping people who were down and out. Rachel was also much smarter than Edgar and studied everything. She traveled widely, studying non-traditional things like Buddhism, Taoism, the Vedas and meditation and was frequently gone to wilderness areas on what she called vision quests. She would be gone for months at a time but when she came back, would condescend to entertain Edgar's friends who she would then expect to contribute money to her charities.

Considering Edgar was occupied with his business ventures and not much of a homebody, the arrangement with Rachel was mutually beneficial. Edgar seemed the picture of health, but died rather quickly with pneumonia about three to four years into their marriage, leaving Rachel astonishingly wealthy and completely uninhibited in her pursuits. She quickly sold all her husband's holdings, banked and invested the money and began supporting numerous additional charities and humanitarian causes including Hampton Oaks.

Marcus had met and casually knew Rachel since her coming to Devane House, admiring her and making a point of formally meeting her soon after Edgar's death. In his words he took a 'real liking to her'. However, Rachel was not inclined to let Marcus woo her and promptly distanced herself from his amorous flirtations. Afterwards, they remained acquaintances rather than friends despite Marcus's persistence. She frequently had boarders in her home that would come and go as their fortunes changed. Most were much better off for having known Rachel. She had the ability to make dramatic changes in the direction of people's lives.

Apparently, John Asterman was one such person that Rachel helped. He suddenly appeared and no one knew he was there except the cook and housekeeper until he was taken to Hampton Oaks in September of 1983. Marcus, being the nosey person that he was, inquired to the housekeeper and learned that he was apparently injured when he arrived and that Rachel had cared for him and personally nursed him back to some degree of health for about four months. She would not allow anyone else to care for him and would often sleep on a cot in his room. If anyone knew where he came from or how he arrived at Devane house, it was Rachel and she never revealed this.

Asterman apparently improved dramatically for a short period of time and then began a rather rapid downhill course. Rachel was very concerned about Asterman and thought that he might die. Finally, near exhaustion, she arranged to have him admitted to Hampton Oaks for chronic care. Of course, this would be done since she was a primary donor to the Oaks. She had given very specific and somewhat unorthodox instructions for his care. Marcus had seen him once at Hampton Oaks on the pretense of seeing one of his friends there. His comment was, "He was the strangest dude I have ever seen. I don't know what was wrong with him, but he sure looked odd and very skinny." Rachel visited him frequently for at least a year but then one day suddenly stopped and had apparently not seen him since. Most people thought that she herself had become too frail to make the trips.

As for Rachel, she still lives at Devane house but does not socialize with the locals. However, there are numerous visitors who come, often five or six at a time, who meet with her for various periods of time. Many look like they are foreign and could be friends or business associates or have some common interest with her. She is not very active now, but Marcus believes she is still quite beautiful.

Marcus sat back, took a deep breath considering what he had said. If there was more to tell, he had forgotten or didn't know about it.

"There you have it. That's everything I know about that situation." Indeed, it was, because Patrick had a list of questions that Marcus shrugged off as not knowing.

Patrick persisted: "Do you think Asterman was related to Rachel Devane?"

"I wouldn't be surprised. She was really dedicated to him above and beyond the call of duty and seemed to have a particular affection for him, but who knows. She showed great affection for a lot of other people as well," Marcus observed. "I would think only a relative could love someone that ugly."

"Do you have any idea when he came to Rachel's home and was there any record of an accident that you know about? You did say that the housekeeper thought he had been injured." Patrick was really trying to get another clue.

"I would say, it had to be sometime in early May of 1983, considering she kept him about four months before admitting him to Hampton Oaks in September," Marcus mused as he stroked his mustache.

Patrick reviewed his notes. Since he had gotten some information with his prodding, he just decided to dig a bit deeper.

"I saw in the archives that on May 4 there was some kind of explosion in the middle of the night near the water at Croton Bay. All that was written was that there was a flash and a bang. What was that about?"

"People were seeing a lot of lights in the sky all during that year and someone called in and reported an explosion while they were looking for the lights. I can't remember who the caller was and would have forgotten even if I knew, but it was probably an anonymous caller anyway. I drove over there and asked around, but no one knew anything. I never heard any more about it, but most people said it was a sonic boom from those military jets. A lot of folks who reported sightings of the lights refused to give their names because they didn't want people thinking they were kooks. Most people won't even talk about stuff like that even if they know something."

Patrick was puzzled. "What about these lights? I have never heard of anything like that before."

The restaurant was clearing out and Marcus obviously wanted to talk more about the subject and was in no hurry to get back to work. He waved at the waitress and she came over to the booth.

"Jen, we need some coffee." Patrick was not particularly fond of coffee and asked for tea.

Jen smiled and chided, "Marcus, where did you get this strange guy that doesn't drink coffee?"

"He's just doing some research and came down to the office to look through the files. Oh, by the way, this is Patrick David. Patrick, this is Jennifer Wells."

"I'm pleased to meet you," Patrick said.

"Well, I'm always pleased to meet a good-looking fellow," Jen said as she smiled at Patrick.

Marcus interrupted. "Jen, would you have some time to sit and chat with us. Patrick wants to know about the lights and I don't know of anyone who has seen them more than you."

Jennifer was at first suspicious, but then had a liking for Patrick and the idea of talking to him was after all quite appealing. She was curiously drawn to the young man.

"The last of the customers should be out of here soon. I'll come over when they are gone. Your coffee and tea are coming right over."

"I will tell you what I know," Marcus began. "I have never seen them. I have been too late, too early or looking in the wrong place but there are many people in this area who have seen them and more than once. Some people think they have been around many years, even centuries, but most believe the sightings began New Year's Eve, 1982 up at Kent — that's east of Buffalo at Lake Ontario — when a retired police officer reported seeing them. It happened again in April near Brewster and Rochester where it frightened a mother and her daughter. Soon there were sightings all over the Hudson River Valley. Then they began occurring so often that people were outside looking for them all the time. It was the talk of this area and was even on the national news."

Jennifer checked out her last customers and cleaned their tables. She poured herself a cup of coffee and came over and scooted Marcus across the seat so that she sat opposite Patrick. They chatted a while until she developed a comfort level with him. Patrick seemed honest and he didn't appear to have some weird agenda. She decided that she liked him and liked him a lot. After all, he was very easy on the eyes and seemed kind and sincere. Patrick watched her closely, admiring her blue eyes, sandy blond hair and comely figure. He felt very drawn to her and not just at a physical level.

Jennifer sipped her coffee and didn't say anything at first. She obviously was thinking about what to say and how to say it. The story was unbelievable at best and she rarely talked about it. Many people simply would not believe her.

"So, you want to know about the lights? That makes you and a lot of other people around here. Most people simply won't talk about it. It all started about 1982, although I've talked to some that say there have been strange lights around here since the Indians lived here and maybe before. Who knows?"

She began by telling Patrick that literally thousands of local New York people had seen the lights on various occasions. Sightings were particularly frequent in 1983 and 1984 when many people actually photographed and videotaped them. A number of auto accidents had occurred as people were trying to watch the lights while driving.

"The first time I saw them was in the spring of 1983. It was in the late evening and I was parked with my boyfriend over by West Branch Reservoir at Carmel, NY when he called my attention to a cluster of bright lights off in the distance. We became intrigued as the lights kept coming closer to us. They were very bright and looked like airplane landing lights but there were too many of them. As this thing approached, we could see that the lights were all on a single dark metal-looking object. The lights were in a crescent or half-circle shape with one large light right in the middle. It was the weirdest thing I have ever seen. It was moving very slowly and made absolutely no noise. It came right over our heads, blocking out the stars and all we heard was the gentle rustling of the leaves on the trees. Not a single sound came from that thing! You could have heard a pin drop. I was really freaked out, hyperventilating and wanting to get the hell out of there but I couldn't take my eyes off it.

"The object stopped and then a bright white searchlight beam came out of it and moved back and forth like it was looking for something. Then the beam was right on my car and stayed there for at least a minute. I nearly had a heart attack. I wanted to run but couldn't. It was like we were in a trance. We just sat there frozen and my mind was just going crazy. Then all the lights went out and we saw this huge black shape that blocked out the stars where the lights had been. Then very slowly it began moving away and a bunch of dim red lights gradually came on and got brighter. It floated over the treetops and probably went half a mile when the bright white light came on again. Then it suddenly shot away like a bullet completely out of sight. I mean zoom. It didn't accelerate or anything and in a second it just was gone."

"Oh my God, that's incredible. That's overwhelming. What could it have been?" Patrick asked, shaking his head in disbelief but totally absorbed in the story.

"This thing, whatever it was, defied everything I know to be true about flying machines. It was gigantic, definitely solid, and absolutely quiet and was obviously moving very purposefully and under intelligent control. It was very disturbing that we saw something that was impossible by all known standards. Yet there it was. I thought about it for days afterward but couldn't make sense of it. My boyfriend got really freaky about it and wouldn't ever talk about it again and even began avoiding me like I had caused this to happen somehow. He was obviously very afraid and shaken to his core. This big, self-assured macho man was frightened like a child."

Patrick asked her a lot of other questions and was impressed with her sincerity. She had obviously had an incredible experience and could not begin to explain it. She mentioned how she had called the police and was told many others had seen the lights but then the FAA had assured them that it was only a prank by a bunch of guys flying in formation with ultralight airplanes.

"Did they think we are idiots or what?" Jennifer scoffed. "We know what we saw and what we saw was very big, very real and unlike anything of this world." She paused, obviously still quite peeved at the official explanation. She sipped her coffee in silence.

After several moments, Patrick asked, "Did you see them again after this?"

She had decided that Patrick was genuinely interested in what she had to say and became more comfortable in talking to him. The second event occurred several months later as Jennifer was driving home from a friend's house about ten p.m. on the Taconic Parkway that runs along the Hudson River.

"I nearly rear-ended a guy who was driving erratically in front of me and decided to suddenly stop. A number of cars had stopped, most pulled to the side of the road, and people were looking up and pointing at some lights in the sky. I thought, oh shit, here we go again and so I pulled over and got out. It was like whoever was controlling these things decided to give us a show. One swooped down really low over the Parkway with those bright lights and then the lights changed to all these intense really vivid colors: red, green, blue and yellow, and it just got closer. It covered the highway and I'm telling you, it was a lot bigger than a football field. It hovered and glided around maybe eight or ten minutes then slowly headed north out of sight. There were easily two hundred to three hundred people that I know of who saw it, including some cops." Jennifer spoke seriously but there was excitement in her voice.

Patrick learned from Jennifer and Marcus that there were thousands of reported sightings in Westchester, Putnam and Fairfield counties, with most occurring in the 1980s. Some investigators including the Project Blue Book guy, J. Allen Hynek came and interviewed multiple witnesses and there was a large public conference at Henry Wells Middle School to discuss the issue and get reports from people who had seen the lights.

Jennifer was irate at the local and federal officials who were condescending to everyone who reported anything. She felt that they were going out of their way to make the honest people who had made these reports sound like idiots. Even trained people like police officers, and those with military backgrounds and experienced pilots were ridiculed. The FAA stuck with its story that the lights were simply small planes flying in formation as a prank and the news agencies believed it and stopped carrying the stories. There were some pilots who actually flew in formation as a hoax and the witnesses who had seen both the airplanes and the lights could easily tell the difference.

Patrick was impressed that Jennifer had truly witnessed something remarkable that affected her view of the world. He was beginning to doubt his own rational views as the reality of the seemingly impossible unfolded. She was totally absorbed in thought as she continued her description.

"Whatever it was, was very real and not something we made on this planet. What it did was physically impossible, at least based on what little I learned from college physics. A lot of people who saw these amazing things won't talk about it because if you see something that simply can't be possible in the context of your daily life, what do you do?" She gestured with her fingers to enumerate her points. "First, you can say it didn't happen or I misperceived something or had a hallucination. Then, maybe I got it all wrong and just thought I saw something impossible. Maybe I smoked too much pot. Maybe I'm just nuts, but this would have to include a lot of other observant good citizens as well. There is another explanation that I believe is the true explanation. We think we know everything, but we don't know shit! Whatever this phenomenon may be, it is real and beyond our abilities and our comprehension." There was a long silence as everyone contemplated what Jen had said.

"There was another time too, wasn't there, Jen, when you were at home?" Marcus interjected.

"Yes, there was one more." Jennifer hesitated as if this were a very personal question.

"I know that it's difficult for you to talk about these things, but I sincerely would like to know. When did it happen?" Patrick asked.

Patrick felt that he was prying information out of her that she didn't want to share so he just waited in the hope that she would continue. The strangeness of these encounters was both fascinating and unnerving to him. He found himself thinking about the strangest person he had ever known, John Asterman. All of this information slowly but surely was chipping away at his worldview. There was something very important in all of this and he was beginning to feel that Asterman was somehow involved, but what could be the connection? He tried to put these ideas aside but the thought that Asterman might be some kind of ET fascinated him. However, he was not ready to discuss these thoughts with Jennifer or Marcus.

Jennifer sipped the last of her coffee and looked around the restaurant, then out the window at the trees. The sunlight sparkled on the golden fall leaves and for her, it was reassuring to see something so familiar and beautiful while talking about something so strange and unsettling.

"It has been six years ago this fall. I got home early and fixed some dinner. I was tired and decided to take a bath and do some reading. After reading for an hour or so lying on the couch, I fell asleep. Then I had a dream in which I was in a warm cocoon surrounded by soft white light and this humming sound began coming from everywhere. It was kind of like the sound the Buddhist monks make when they pray, although very soft. It was exquisitely serene and seemed quite real.

"I suddenly awoke and the house was filled with light. At first, I thought it was morning and that I had overslept when I realized that the walls were glowing. I had this incredible sense of peace seeing this glow and hearing this humming sound. As I talk about it now, it is frightening to me but at the time it was heavenly. Then the lights faded and the humming stopped so I got up and looked out the window. There it was, the strange craft above my house with its brightly colored lights silently floating. I went outside, waved to it and just watched it until it finally floated away."

Jennifer was again silent. Marcus was quiet and pensively rubbed his finger around the rim of his coffee cup. Her experience struck a chord with Patrick as he thought of a strange night in the Utah desert that wouldn't stay hidden in the recesses of his mind. No one said a word for what seemed like an hour, yet only a few minutes had passed.

Breaking the silence, Patrick said, "You've had remarkable experiences, not just once, but three times. Thank you so much for sharing this with me. All this information is mind boggling and my head is spinning, looking for answers. Why did this happen? There has to be some reason. What does it all mean and why are we being shown these incredible things?"

Jennifer continued, "That night I sat on the porch steps and cried. I have never been so emotional in my life. I was ecstatically happy and my mind was crystal clear. I knew what it meant to be alive for the first time. This little pot of begonias beside me seemed to be the most beautiful thing I had ever seen. I looked at the plants and held them in my hands and saw a billion years of life on our small, fragile planet. With the ecstasy there was sadness too. It was like I have a personal responsibility for life and this planet. I had the profound feeling that if we don't care for our planet and each other, we are in deep trouble."

"What are we supposed to do? Were you told something or is there a path we should take?" Patrick asked.

"I am not aware of a person or conversation or anything like that. I was simply given some kind of gift of awareness by someone or something. I don't know. It was like I was in the vast darkness and a light was turned on and I could see everything clearly. It was like knowledge, insight, a profound love of life and a sense that I am a part of something greater that is happening. We have to care for what we love. What we love will save us and what we hate will destroy us. This was one of the epiphanies of my life brought into sharp focus by them."

Jennifer had been talking for over an hour when Marcus, tired of sitting, suddenly became pressed for time. Also, Patrick was working the next day and had to get back to the university. As they prepared to leave, Jennifer walked them to the café door. Marcus said hurried goodbyes and bolted out onto the sidewalk and up the street. Marcus was a good source of information and he knew he would see him again.

"I've enjoyed talking to you. You seem to be a very special person," Jennifer said in a whisper. "I sense that you've had an experience with them, haven't you?"

Patrick was taken aback, hesitated a moment said, "I think I may have."

"You will find there are very few people you can talk to about these things who will take you seriously. We should talk again. I don't think it was an accident that you came here." Jennifer smiled.

"What do you mean?"

"You will find that people who have unusual experiences seem to have a spiritual connection that draws them together. If you don't understand it now, you will later. Keep a notebook of your strange occurrences and you will surprise yourself at the serendipitous connections you make. We need to keep in touch. Here's my number. Call me."

"I will do that. Thanks for your time." Patrick gave her his phone number as he left.

As Patrick drove back to his home, he sifted through the incredible incidents of the day and the wealth of information he had obtained. As Jen would say, it was serendipity. The events surrounding Asterman had become even stranger than before, and Patrick had the unsettling feeling that he personally might be involved in this strangeness.

"How does all this relate to me and Zoë? What about Jen? I don't know her and have never met her before and yet she seems to be involved in all of this as well? This is all so strange, so very strange. I've got to call Zoë and she's not going to believe this."

Chapter 19
Rachel Devane

Devane House was easy for Zoë to find, being about three miles from Hampton Oaks. Everyone living in the area knew its history and Zoë had actually passed by the aging but unblemished estate previously and wondered who lived there. The well-kept house and property emanated a serene and natural beauty with a magnificent view of the river from its hillside location.

Zoë had called earlier and spoken to a maidservant and yesterday received a message that Rachel Devane would meet with her today. She was somewhat intimidated to park her car in the driveway that curved up to the house and instead, decided to park in front on the street. As she ascended the long walkway, she saw ancient oak trees that were now almost devoid of leaves on this cold October day. The well-kept plants in the yard were already touched by frost. The view of the river and surrounding countryside was overwhelming in its beauty and she paused to take in the awesome scenery.

She rang the bell on the large wooden front door and shortly the maidservant who she had spoken with earlier answered the door and invited her in.

Zoë walked into a large foyer revealing intricately carved wood panels and a high vaulted ceiling that reminded her of a European castle. There were a variety of tapestries, sculptures, and immaculate old furniture that overwhelmed her eyes. She pictured this area being the focal point of many grand parties in the past and indeed it had been. Despite the expansive size of Devane House, it seemed both warm and welcoming.

"Ms. Devane will be down in a few moments. She asked that I make you comfortable in the library. May I take your coat?"

"Thank you. What a wonderful home this is! I've never seen anything so beautiful. It's a palace."

"This has been Ms. Devane's home for many years. It is her personal work of art and is indeed a wonderful place," the maid said as she took Zoë's overcoat.

The maid then escorted Zoë through several rooms and a hallway toward the back of the house to the library. The house was filled with artwork. It was almost like a museum with sensual sculptures, and what appeared to be old European Masters as well as modern art. There were many themes in the paintings, but Zoë noted that all of them seemed to express love and kindness and warmth that seemed to radiate into the house. There were also a number of more scientific-looking but yet quite beautiful photographs with some looking like the dramatic Hubble Space Telescope's pictures of planets, stars and galaxies. She saw some perplexing paintings or maybe they were photographic images of spiral geometric patterns that seemed to change and have a three-dimensional appearance almost like a hologram. These were particularly odd but somehow strangely pleasing and did not seem at all out of place.

"This is the library. It's one of my favorite rooms. Please make yourself comfortable and Ms. Devane should be with you shortly. Is there anything you need just now?"

"No, thank you. I am fine."

The library was sensational in every respect. There were more heavy carved oak panels with bookshelves extending to the ceiling. This room obviously was used frequently, or at least had been in the past. Eight worn but comfortable-looking leather chairs were scattered among four working tables, all of which were scuffed with signs of use. A large boardroom table was in the middle that could easily seat twenty people or more. She counted six laptop computers and noticed some audiovisual equipment. Zoë was quite surprised since she was not expecting anything so contemporarily technological. Although she was asked to sit at one of the small tables, she was compelled to look around at everything and check it all out.

As Zoë perused the bookshelves, she found a rich history of literature, science and art as well as a number of very modern and recent books. Toward the back of the library was a large cut-glass window from which there was a view of a beautiful garden. To the right were a group of shelves that appeared to be a favorite place where the furniture was a bit more worn and the shelves rounded and polished from use. Here was a mixture of old and contemporary books on a variety of subjects that had obviously been well studied. There was really no organization to the books on these particular shelves.

Zoë was surprised at the variety of topics which included philosophy, medicine, physics, astronomy, biology, evolution, religion, ghosts, the occult, UFOs, computer theory, and archeology to name a few. There were also a number of esoteric, scientific journals and a distinct lack of what she considered to be typical women's reading like *Vogue* or *Cosmopolitan*. On the contrary, this was all very serious stuff and heavy reading. Zoë felt somewhat relieved when she saw several gardening magazines, but the variety and depth of the reading material here held her fascination.

She pulled a book off the shelf on fractal geometry and thumbed through it, finding that it was a very scholarly, recent publication that had obviously been well studied. The pages had notes in the margins and several Post-its sticking out of the top. She turned to one of the marked pages and was taken aback by the complexity of the narrative. As she placed the book back on the shelf, she turned to see someone entering the room.

"Miss Abrams, I'm Rachel Devane. Welcome to Devane House. I'm pleased to make your acquaintance and glad you could come today. I see you are checking out my library," Rachel said with a soft smile.

"Oh, I hope you don't mind. I couldn't help myself. You have such an impressive collection and it's actually quite overwhelming. It is very good to meet you also. I hope this is not inconveniencing you."

They shook hands and exchanged pleasantries. Zoë was relieved to finally meet the mysterious woman she believed could help her. Rachel was tall and thin with straight, long, gray hair tied into a ponytail. Her countenance was soft and caring but her blue-gray eyes were delicately disquieting. She was poised but moved slowly and obviously with some pain, but it was only the wrinkled skin of her hands that suggested her advanced age. Zoë thought that she might be in her eighties, but her mind was certainly crystal clear and very sharp. From the looks of her library, her intellect must be astounding. Her quality clothes were new and she was dressed in a long gray skirt with a white blouse that was quite chic. She invited Zoë to sit with her at one of the small tables as the maid brought in tea.

"Miss Abrams, it is not an inconvenience at all to have you here. I currently have a lot of time on my hands and am happy to share it with you and I do enjoy company. As you can see, I read quite a bit and have a diverse taste in reading material. Well, actually, I am a prolific reader and have read every book in this library plus quite a few more. My mind stays very busy and I am always learning new things that I like to share with my friends. I think continuing to learn is the secret to long life. It has certainly made my life very interesting and happy."

"Ms. Devane, please call me Zoë. You're a lovely person and undoubtedly are very happy here. What an exquisitely beautiful home you have. I'm just completely overwhelmed by this incredible place and all the marvelous things you have here. This is just heavenly. It's like another world."

"Thank you for your kind words, Zoë. I've been blessed with so much good fortune and great friends, and have been very pleased to be able to share these with others. I'm glad you're here and enjoying the house but I think you're here for more than that. You have some questions for me, I believe?"

Zoë then explained how she had come to Hampton Oaks on a medical school rotation and had encountered John Asterman. She felt deeply moved to help him, but was thwarted by not being able to find his medical records or figure out anything about him. She described him and his declining condition and told her about his blood tests and all the searching that she had done for more information.

"Ms. Devane, everyone has given up on him, but I cannot. I firmly believed that something can be done to help him and restore his health. His medical chart has almost no information. His physician, Dr Morris, is nowhere to be found and probably off on a trip somewhere. The new facilities physician, Dr Adams, thinks he is terminal and doesn't want to do anything for him. He specifically told me not be involved with him but I'm doing it anyway. After a lot of searching, I found out that you brought him to Hampton Oaks some years ago."

"That's correct. I did take him to Hampton Oaks but haven't seen him for a long time. Now, tell me more about John."

"I have been both fascinated and troubled by him," Zoë offered. "I truly feel that he needs help and his health can be restored, but I don't know where to begin. Everyone at the facility thinks he is in a terminal condition and that all I would be doing is prolonging his suffering. They all say he will never be functional again and the most merciful thing to do is to let him die. Every time I am around him though, I feel that he is very much alive and that there is hope for his recovery. It's like he senses my intent and thoughts, and he speaks to me although he never says a word. There is just something there in his mind, some powerful communication that he needs me. I know that sounds crazy and I hope you understand."

"I do understand and appreciate what you are trying to do for him. He is very complex and I'm glad you can communicate with him. Only very unique and specially gifted people can do this. Please tell me more."

"Some think he has hydrocephalus, and that his brain is all thinned out with the pressure of his spinal fluid. I got out the ultrasound machine last week and put it on his head. He does not have hydrocephalus! He's got a big head, but he also has a large, otherwise normal-looking brain. I mentioned this to the staff and Dr Adams and they just dismissed it saying I didn't know what I was doing. No one understands him or seems to care and they have all given up on him and many are just freaked out by him. He has been getting worse in the weeks I've been here and I think he will die unless I do something to help. He is so scrawny now; he is pitiful."

"I am so sorry to hear that. I was hoping he might improve." Rachel shook her head slowly and a wave of great sadness spread over her face.

"Is there anything you can tell me that would help? I really need to know how he was before he went to Hampton Oaks. Was he injured? What are his medical problems? How did you come to take care of him in the first place?" Zoë talked rapidly having numerous questions.

Rachel pursed her lips considering the best approach to answering. It wasn't that Zoë's visit was unexpected, but there were many things she had to find out for herself about Zoë, things for which she needed to prepare that would ultimately define Zoë's life. The answers needed to be carefully considered and well stated.

"I am very sorry to hear that John is not doing well and I appreciate your concern for him. Maybe I can help you, but I don't know and I will tell you what I can. John came to me suddenly one night in the spring of 1983. He had been injured somehow and needed almost constant nursing care. I was taken with him, much as you are, and was determined to nurse him back to health. He was certainly larger in those days than what you describe for me now. His features were as you have stated but he was not wasted away. I was afraid to take him to the hospital because he was very different physically and spiritually and I wanted to protect him. People who are significantly different are not well liked or cared for by our society and are treated as less than human. I was a nurse for many years and knew it was my duty to care for this wonderful, battered man. I nursed, treated and cared for him by myself as long as I could, but it in the end it was overwhelming and drained all my strength. I was encouraged that he improved for a while, but he then began to worsen right before my very eyes. I realized that he was much, much more than I could deal with and that was when I took him to Hampton Oaks for care. They owed me a favor because I've supported them extremely well over the years. I continue to pay for his care, but I can't go to see him any longer. I have become greatly limited by this arthritic body."

"What about his injuries?" Zoë asked.

"His injuries were to his chest primarily; that is where he had the most pain and it appeared to be from blunt trauma. He had some burns on his face and arms and terrible bruises all over. He was fearful and did not want to go to the hospital and I did not force him. I had the feeling that if I called an ambulance, I would never see him again and it would be his undoing. He was so very different that I didn't know how people would react to him. Actually, I did know how people would react. They would treat him as bad as or even worse than physically different minorities are treated in most countries. He said very little, but he understood everything and we could communicate quite well even without words. He is the most loving person I think I have ever encountered. Being near him, I felt meditative and peaceful and almost as if I was in another world. It's strange to say this, but I feel as if many times he was teaching me something very important. Looking back now I cannot tell you specifically what he taught me, but I know for certain that I'm a much better person for having experienced him in my life. He knew that he had to be here at this place and at this time and it seemed that there would be an event he must be here for."

"I understand exactly what you are saying. There is something very special about him that really defies explanation, but why is he here and why is he so vulnerable? As you can see, I feel desperate to find out more so that I can help him. Did he tell you anything that would help? Is there any detail you can think of that might have some significance? Was he taking any medication or did he mention any health problem? Did he have a family history of any diseases? Did he have any allergies? What did he eat and drink?" Zoë almost pleaded for an answer.

"He never spoke of his family. He told me he had been well until he came here and was injured. He said that this place and his injury were a great shock to his body and he had to adjust. I had the feeling it was like someone living at sea level going to a high mountain and having the problems associated with the change of altitude. One time he said that everything was worse than he thought it would be. I don't know what he meant by that. I gave him some Dilaudid for pain but he wouldn't take it. He did take some aspirin but only for a short time then refused it. He had no evidence of infection so he didn't get any antibiotics. I tried giving him chicken soup and he spat it out with a repulsed expression on his face. He wouldn't eat anything with meat and finally seemed to prefer vegetable broth after we had offered a variety of foods. We made a large supply of vegetable broth and purée, and he did well with that. I knew he needed a lot of fluid and nutrition to heal his wounds, but it was still a challenge getting him to eat what I thought he needed. Gradually he began to perk up somewhat and his wounds appeared to be healing but he remained quite debilitated."

"Could he eat fish, cheese or eggs?" Zoë asked.

Rachel thought a moment and said: "He took mainly liquids and very soft food. I remember that he wouldn't eat eggs and certainly no meat."

"I think we may be onto something," Zoë confided. "The tube feedings he is getting now definitely have animal proteins and fats. I wonder if that may in fact be toxic to him. This is definitely something to work with. He may be a true vegetarian in terms of his biological make-up."

Rachel and Zoë continued to talk for several hours. They spoke of their common interests, personal and family histories and their passions in life. It was a very warm and friendly conversation, and both smiled amiably at each other while they sipped their tea. Zoë's questions were subtly probing and she had the intuitive feeling Rachel was withholding something from her despite the fact that she seemed sincere in her answer to every question. Zoë detected a powerful intellect hiding behind Rachel's weak, aging façade.

On the other hand, Rachel had been waiting to meet Zoë for a long time, a very long time, and studied her closely in preparation for what was to come. Zoë was a key player in the current web of confusion that hopefully would ultimately come together for a higher purpose. She liked Zoë a lot and right away felt a deep attachment to her. It was a great honor to meet this extraordinary, young woman. Their meeting was good and both parted with great optimism.

Chapter 20
The Halloween Party

"Oh my, three little ghosts attacking me all at once. I think you need plenty of candy so you will go away and not scare me!" Patrick poured a handful of goodies into each outstretched loot bag as the little ghosts squealed with delight and scurried off into the darkness.

"Those kids are so cute and I really love doing this for them. My being a father someday would be a dream for me," Patrick said to Zoë as he gave her a kiss. "It's great to see you again. I've missed you so much!"

"I've missed you too. It's been too long," Zoë whispered, hugging him tightly.

"Hey, what's going on out there? Let's have none of that. Get back in here so we can keep an eye on you two smoochers!" Scott hollered.

The B&B were back together again and Halloween was one of their favorite parties. There were a few costumes but most of the group had just driven straight away to get to Zoë's house and couldn't care less about dressing up. However, Deirdre had guessed this would happen and so brought face paint and a bag of theatrical wear that she had accumulated over the years from her little theater group She began busily making over anyone she could trap. The pizza had arrived and they all were crudely doing 'The Monster Mash' for the eighth time.

"I just love you guys and it seems that we have been friends forever. What would life be without you?" Erin called out as everyone was finally adorned and looking quite ridiculous rather than horrifying.

"Life would be dull and you know it, so here's to the Bold and Beautiful!" Scott held up his beer and everyone toasted and cheered. "We may be bold but tonight we ain't beautiful!"

"I think Deirdre didn't do well with my ghoul costume," Patrick said. "That last little kid laughed at me and then cried and ran for his mother! I thought I looked rather good."

"Patrick, how could you possibly think you look good as someone who has been dead for a century?" Jenna smirked.

The music played as they all laughed, danced, sang and relished being together again. The trick-or-treaters had all gone back to their homes and as midnight approached, Martine read several spooky stories from a book about New England ghosts. Her dramatic reading produced a lot of "ooohs" and wicked laughs.

"I know what we should do," Erin suggested. "Each of us needs to tell a true story about the most strange or eerie thing that has ever happened to you. This has to be no fiction but the real truth from your sordid previous lives. Grab something to drink and take a minute to think about it. I'm sure you are all full of deep, dark secrets you never wanted anyone to discover."

Everyone agreed that this seemed like a good Halloween idea and started contemplating what they would say. Zoë moved the jack-o-lantern and candles into the center of the room.

"Let's turn down the lights and sit in a circle and it will be just like going to camp and sitting around the fire," Zoë suggested and everyone concurred as they huddled in.

As the lights dimmed, the room took on a yellow eerie glow as their shadows flickered on the walls. "Oh, this is too good," Martine whispered and everyone cackled with delight. Their painted faces and costumes made them appear phantasmal.

"Now, let your minds go and think about some strange, dark event that happened to you in the past that you have repressed, tucked away in the dark recesses of your subconscious mind. Now, relax and take slow deep breaths and go deeply into your mind," Erin softly and deeply intoned.

"You sound like Elvira turned psychiatrist, Erin," Scott said, breaking the silence and giving everyone a good laugh.

"Okay, who will start? Who will tell the dark truth you have been hiding?" asked Zoë with feigned fear in her voice.

"Just let the spirits lead us. Somebody pass the spirits; my glass is empty," Scott chimed in with a Bela Lugosi laugh.

"I'll start," piped Deirdre. "Now, this is an honest, cross my heart and hope to die, true story and I don't want you to laugh at me. Listen up, Scott. When I was little, every day, this young boy and girl, who seemed to be brother and sister, would walk together to school and pass by our house wearing their backpacks. Every day, it was the same for at least a year. I could see them out the window as I sat and ate breakfast. Then one day they suddenly stopped walking by. They were just gone and I asked Mom about them, but she acted oddly and said that they probably had moved away. I kept watching for them, hoping they would return. I really missed seeing them, although I hardly knew them at all because they were very private and try as I might, they would never talk to me except to say hi. In fact, they wouldn't talk to anyone and always seemed to appear so very lonely.

"After a week or so, I saw them again, so I ran and told Mom and she saw them too. Mom appeared to be shocked and became pale and frightened and I thought she was going to faint. She wouldn't say anything for a long time, but I finally found out that the boy and girl had been killed several weeks earlier. I saw them only that one time and have never seen them again. They sure looked real to me, but they had been dead at least two weeks so they must have been ghosts. It's difficult for me to believe that but I have no other explanation. As I think about it, I have also experienced some other weird stuff too, but I can't beat this story."

"Oh, that gives me chills," Zoë said. "Don't you think you mistook someone else for them? Were there new children in the neighborhood?"

"There is no way. These two dressed the same, walked the same and had the same old backpacks. They would always look toward us with creepy expressions but never said anything. It was definitely them. That last day I saw them was like I was looking back into time at them before they died," Deirdre said legitimately mystified.

"Okay, I've got one. Let's move on," Erin broke in. "I've never told anyone but my brother about this and he thought I was nuts and to this day doesn't believe me. Please be friends and if you don't believe me, at least don't tell anyone else this story. When I was growing up, our house was next to an old growth forest. I think it has all been cut down and developed by now, but back then there were old Indian trails and huge trees hundreds of years old. We as kids hunted arrowheads and loved to hike around in the woods and every once in a while, would see a deer, a snake or a badger. Finding a banana slug was a real treat for us. I even heard a cougar growl once but never saw it.

"Anyway, one day my best friend and I were hiking. We were maybe thirteen or fourteen. We hiked to the top of a hill and were sitting on a log and talking about boys and what we would do when we grew up. We got up and turned to start back down the trail and there was a little man sitting nearby on another log watching us. He was about twenty feet away and looked like a midget dressed in brown and green and he had a strange, little grin. His hands were clasped together and he was twiddling his thumbs. When we saw him, we were scared to death and my friend screamed and jumped over a large log and ran home without me. I just stood there stunned, as much from the scream as the strange, little man, and was transfixed there watching him. He was really cute, like something out of a fairy tale book and I was totally absorbed watching him and he seemed fascinated with me. I wanted to say something but couldn't speak. He looked disappointed and actually seemed sad. Then he waved to me, jumped off his log and disappeared. I mean he disappeared; he didn't go behind a tree or anything. I went over to the place where he sat and there was nothing.

"This experience was unlike anything I had experienced before. It's interesting that my friend refused to talk to me about it and would never go for a walk with me again. She must have remembered at some level but to her it was as if it had never happened."

"Did you have your Lucky Charms for breakfast that morning, Miss Erin-go-baugh? Sounds like a leprechaun to me," Scott chimed, trying to make light of the story. "You obviously didn't find a pot of gold or are you hiding the fact that you are now independently wealthy and can keep us in beer the rest of our lives?"

"You know, no pot of gold but it does sound like a leprechaun. I've often wondered, could I have dreamed this or was it a hallucination? It was just too real and both of us saw it. Something really strange happened to us and I'm not sure what to make of it. There was nothing intrinsically bad about it but it was disturbing that we had encountered something so surreal and unnatural that just couldn't fit into our daily lives. My friend's reaction was strange too. Nothing really happened and it was just something that we saw and we weren't harmed in any way, but it really affected her and our friendship. I've had some other strange occurrences, but I will save them for next Halloween. You know, the more you think about this stuff, the more pops into your mind."

"It's your turn, Lucky Charm man," Erin said to Scott.

"I guess I have led a dull life but nothing unusual has happened to me."

"Scott, the fact that you were born was more than an unusual happening!" Erin sparred. "Come on and give us a story."

"Well, there is one thing. When my mother was pregnant with me, she dropped a phonograph record player, but it didn't affect me, it didn't affect me, it didn't affect me, it didn't affect me, it didn't affect me, it didn't affect me."

The group roared with laughter at Scott's broken record rendition that they subsequently heard repeatedly throughout the remaining evening. Scott apparently had no personal stories to tell but perhaps, he just did not want to share them.

"You know, it just didn't affect me," Scott had to say just one more time as he confidently sipped his beer.

"Well, I saw something once I couldn't explain," Patrick began. "About two years ago, some of my college buddies wanted to go deer hunting in Utah. I didn't particularly want to go but they were insistent and said I didn't have to hunt but they really wanted me to come along. I am not a hunter but figured I could do some nature photography and check out the scenery. We pitched camp and drove the Jeep out toward a box canyon where we thought there might be some deer. We found a lot of deer tracks, but they must have known we were coming because none were there.

"As we hiked back to the Jeep, we noticed a bright flash in the sky, like a ball of light that just suddenly appeared then disappeared. I thought it was a meteor or the sun reflecting off an airplane, but it was gone so quickly I couldn't tell what it was. We continued walking for a while and took a break in a small ravine that had some shade. As we sat there eating our snacks, we noticed this large silver ball-like thing silently floating in the air right down through the middle of the ravine. I got out my camera and took some photographs and noticed everyone just sitting there, looking at this thing like they were hypnotized or something. I was talking like crazy and everybody else was really quiet.

"I finally shut up and everyone just sat there for probably an hour or so. Then we began walking again, going back to the Jeep and the guys just complained that we didn't see any deer. I commented that even though we hadn't seen deer, we had witnessed some strange things. They all looked at me like they didn't know what I was talking about and kept on walking. I noticed that it was very late in the day, but it seemed like we had been gone only a few hours. It was dark when we got on the road again and no one seemed to remember what happened except me and even I was confused about how quickly the day ended. Everybody was very sleepy and I couldn't get a conversation going with anyone. In fact, I never got them to talk about it even though I tried several times. They honestly did not remember anything and I realized that they thought I was kidding. I was going to convince them with my photographs, but the pictures just looked like I tried to take shots of the sun."

"Sounds like you guys were burning peyote in your campfire and maybe breathing a little too deeply!" Scott pounced, responding to Patrick's story. "Definitely bad mushrooms. You should know better."

Patrick was emphatic. "We were not playing Carlos Castaneda and all we had were a few beers and peanut butter crackers. There were no drugs involved!"

"Yea, right! What is happening to the youth of America?" Scott lamented, unwilling to add any credence to Patrick's story.

"OK, that's enough for now — let's take a break, refresh our drinks and then we will return to 'Strange Stories I Have Known, Part 2'," Zoë announced.

Zoë and Patrick went out to the porch for a breath of the cold crisp night air. The moon was full and bright, casting eerie shadows across the yard. All the trick-or-treaters had retreated with their bags of goodies and gone to bed and left the night serene and quiet.

"You never told me about your Utah encounter. I thought I had heard all your secrets," Zoë whispered to Patrick as they held each other closely.

"You know, a man does not tell all of his secrets, but there is more to this story that I will share with you some time. I honestly had almost completely forgotten what happened until the first time I saw John Asterman," Patrick confided.

"Asterman? What about Asterman?" Zoë asked.

Patrick hesitated before continuing. "I don't know why but when I first saw him, the memory of that strange event flashed back in my mind. I don't know what it was except that there seemed to be something familiar about him that connected with the Utah experience. It's eerie but the more I think about it, the more bits and pieces of memory seem to be coming back. Right now, that's all I can tell you."

"Please let me know if you remember anything else. That's amazing and I'm very curious about what happened. I had no idea you had such an experience," Zoë mused.

"I'll keep you posted. You will be the first, well actually the second after me, to know if I remember anything else. I think all of us there experienced something quite remarkable that is hidden in our minds. You know it's interesting how many peculiar things happen in our lives that we just block out of our memory. Maybe these bizarre happenings are too strange for our brains to store along with our everyday experiences and so they're kicked out of memory. Maybe our minds trick us into thinking we are sane."

"I think you're right. When something happens that seemingly can't be true, I think our brains just forget it or hide it. It's like the very thing we see is a threat to our mental view of the world. It's interesting the way we think. Recently, I found that I was remembering things about my childhood that I had completely forgotten — odd lights in my bedroom at night, hearing etheric voices and that sort of thing. I always thought this was just my imagination. You know, the boogie man under the bed and the monsters in the closet, just childish fears. It shouldn't be difficult to know what's real and what is not. I've told you about that upsetting dream I keep having. What's with that? So, what's going on? Is this all not real and just in our minds? Do I need a head shrinker?"

"Zoë, what we are experiencing is very real. How this all relates to us, I do not know but I do think there is a relationship. Tonight, it's been good to hear what experiences others have had. I'm ready to hear some more."

"I agree. It's fascinating that we've all had some similar experiences at a paranormal level. What about your photographs you took on the trip? Do you have any of them?" Zoë asked.

"The photo shop didn't even print them. They were all fuzzy and overexposed. Just blobs of light. So much for the hard evidence I wanted," Patrick sighed.

Patrick and Zoë went back into the house and everyone was laughing, talking and having a good time. They loved being together and always had fun. It's a rare group of people that can be closer than family and get along so well together. Even when they disagreed with each other, they were never disagreeable and always showed respect for each other and each other's opinions. They could not have chosen better friends if they had tried.

"Sit, sit, everybody, sit!" Erin said with glee as she herded the group into a circle again. Grabbing their drinks, they rounded themselves into the circle as Erin turned down the lights again.

"We need another ghost story since it's Halloween, so I am forced to tell one," Jenna said as she suddenly began having second thoughts about telling such things to her friends. The carnival atmosphere of the evening and the alcohol had a great way of removing inhibitions.

"I swear, this is a true account, so, Scott, please don't make fun of me. I didn't believe it to be true for a long time and had to either admit that I was insane or that I had encountered a ghost. When I moved out of the dorm a few years ago, I rented a house with three other girls. The house was probably one hundred years old and the new owner renovated it to rent, and my friends and I were the first occupants afterward. It was a great place and had been modernized nicely. Life went on as usual for several weeks and then we began noticing what sounded like women singing in various places around the house particularly late at night. You couldn't really understand the words. It was more like they were chanting. We thought this was strange, but it really didn't seem to bother us very much.

"We checked the windows and the pipes and searched the house but couldn't find anything. We could still hear the singing and it always seemed to move around as we moved around trying to find a source. So, finally we just ignored it. As we became familiar with each other's routines of coming and going, other strange things began happening. As an example, my roommate Gail had an evening class each Wednesday and would come home about nine p.m. The rest of us usually studied together in the living room.

"One evening, shortly before Gail came home, we heard what sounded like her car pull into the drive and there were steps up the walk and onto the porch and the screen door opened. No one came in. So, we went to the door and opened it and looked out and there was nothing. No car, and nobody was there. Then about ten minutes later, we heard the same sounds, but this time Gail came in from her class. The sounds of someone arriving before they actually arrived happened with each of us in our house as well. The girls thought that I had come home early on two occasions while I was still at the hospital. It was like I had driven home and gone through my usual paces of parking the car, getting out, walking up the walk and opening the door in advance of my actually arriving at the house. It was like my spirit or double had preceded me home."

Erin thought a moment then continued her story. "Also, decorations of any type were not welcomed by someone or something in the house. Christmas was particularly deplored with decorated trees crashing to the floor, displays knocked over, and little things just simply disappearing. The TV would turn itself on and off and alarm clocks that no one had set to come on would ring in the middle of the night.

"One of our housemates couldn't take it any more and moved out, but the rest of us kind of adjusted to what we found to be an intriguing situation. It may seem strange, but we just acknowledged the events and weren't frightened by them. We decided to talk to the ghosts or whatever they were and tell them we didn't like what they were doing and invite them to move along if they couldn't be quiet and leave our things alone. Interestingly, making direct contact seemed to work and the strangeness gradually subsided. It has been at least six months since anything out of the ordinary has happened, so maybe they're gone. I can't explain what happened, other than to believe it was some sort of spirit or supernatural force causing these things to happen. So, if there is a moral to all of this I would say, don't be afraid of ghosts or whatever this was. You can talk to them and maybe they'll listen to you."

"My grandmother believed in ghosts," Martine responded. "She said, that she saw them all almost every day and could even tell if someone was going to die by the ghosts gathering around. She always said to never be afraid of them because they really can't hurt you and they are just hanging around because they don't know any better. I have not had any experiences with ghosts, but I have had a few strange encounters. In addition to her belief in ghosts, my grandmother always said that we all have guardian angels that hang around with us all of our lives. She thought they were there to help us more with spiritual growth than protecting us from harm, but I think I have seen mine and he has kept me out of harm's way several times."

"Him?" asked Scott. "I thought angels were supposed to be women with wings in white dresses." Scott had decided a long time ago that he had a problem with all this non-scientific belief in ghosts, angels and strange happenings. It was actually frightening for him to believe that there might be some supernatural aspect to life. He thought that it was only appropriate for him to make fun of such beliefs but on the other hand, he really didn't want to be too offensive to his friends.

"Didn't you listen in church or read *Paradise Lost* and learn that all the major hitter angels are masculine, like Gabriel, Michael and Ariel?" Deirdre shot back.

"You mean all the angels are men in drag? I'm crushed," Scott droned on.

"It doesn't matter what gender they are. The one that she thought she saw was male. Let her go on, please," Deirdre stated emphatically, getting increasingly miffed at Scott's critique of everyone's story.

Martine persisted, "Anyway, if you give me a chance, I will tell the story! The first time I remember seeing this man was when I was six or seven. I was in the hospital and very sick. I don't remember the details of the illness or much about what happened, but I do remember my father was crying and that frightened me a lot. Also, the priest was there and he put holy water on my head. There were a lot of people in the room when this handsome man in white came in, walked over to me and put his hand on my shoulder and looked into my eyes. He told me that I was going to be OK and not to worry and that he would always be here for me. He turned around and left and the next day I was much better. I asked my parents who he was and they looked at each other and said they thought that I had been dreaming. I insisted that he was real and that he was there but now I know that no one saw him except me. The last time I remember seeing him, I was eighteen and driving home when a tractor-trailer truck ran a red light and skidded and swerved right up to me. This same man was suddenly standing between me and the truck. I know that I would have died if the truck had hit me."

Deirdre was quiet for a moment and was choked with emotion. She waved her hand to the group signaling that she could not speak any more about this. Zoë hugged her and told her that it was a wonderful story and she believed what she had said. Deirdre had never told this to anyone and felt as if a large burden had been lifted from her. She was surprised at how emotional she had become and at the same time became filled with a sense of peace. There was much more but this was sufficient for now.

After a few minutes, Martine remembered another occurrence: "I've got to tell you about this one too. Just talking about this stuff has opened a bunch of memories. My parents and I were touring England, when I was fifteen years old. My father is quite a history buff and we had seen far too many castles and heard of too many kings and battles. All the stories were beginning to run together for me. We had driven to see Glastonbury Castle and motored through this neat, little village where everyone was dressed up in period costumes and it looked like a festival was going on. My sisters and I wanted to stop but Dad had to get on to the castle and said we would stop on the way back. So, we go to Glastonbury, do the tourist thing and head back about two hours later. When we returned to the little town, we couldn't believe our eyes. There was nothing there except a couple of old buildings and a pub and overgrown bushes.

"We stopped and walked around and there was no town, no people except for two old geezers in the pub, no animals, carts, horses, sheep or goats. Nothing! We asked in the pub about the festival and no one knew what we were talking about. Dad insisted that we just missed it and began driving around on the little back roads in the area. Then he claimed that it was on some other road. For once my sisters and I had actually been paying attention to the scenery and so we knew with certainty that the road we returned on was the same one where we saw the festival. Of course, my father wouldn't hear of it. My sisters and I talked about this for a long time and eventually decided that we had seen a glimpse of the town from an earlier time, probably several hundred years ago or more. We wanted to talk about this, but Mom and Dad just wouldn't consider it or say any more. The whole situation was obviously upsetting to them."

"Are you positive you just didn't get on the wrong road or there was a festival that moved away?" Erin asked.

"First of all, all of us saw it; it was on a main road, and we were impressed with all that was happening in the little village. It was like they had gone to a lot of trouble to make it all seem real and authentic to a bygone age. There were all these old-style buildings, people in animal-skin clothes and a bunch of sheep and goats, but there were no signs, no little tent with brochures or refreshments or anything like the Renaissance Faire we have here.

"We all looked at the map and there was no other way for us to go. It had to be on that road. Dad even stopped several other times, which was very unlike him, to ask directions and everyone was just puzzled by his questions. In thinking about this, I believe it was like some kind of time travel. It would have been interesting if we had stopped and interacted with the people there or if we would have discovered they were some kind of apparition. But I sincerely believe they were real, skin and bones real. It makes you wonder if you could really go back in time that you might possibly be able to change the course of history. Now that I think about it, I think that would be a very scary thing to do. I can't imagine the consequences."

"These have been some fascinating stories and I believe all of you were candid and truthful about these things you shared, except for Scott, of course, who has never been sincere about anything except wanting another beer. It fascinates me that all of us have had experiences like these that are so beyond the ordinary occurrences in our lives that defy rational explanation. I'm certain many others have had similar things happen to them. Is this not another common bond for us as shown by the strange and wonderful stories we have told this evening? There are more things in Heaven and Earth, Scott, than are dreamt of in your philosophy," Jenna chided.

"Women, pizza and beer; my philosophy, my life!" Scott proclaimed with a Shakespearean flair.

"We have heard from everyone except you know who. She's not going to get out of this that easily. Okay, Zoë, what is your story? You are the last one and you have to make this one the best," Martine prodded.

"Well, this is a great story that is true and it's something that's happening right now. I have a strange, fascinating mystery man that I need help from all of you guys to figure out. His name is John Asterman,"

Zoë responded. "Not so exciting thus far, is it? Trust me, it gets a lot better.

"When I started the rotation at Hampton Oaks, I encountered the strangest patient I have ever known. The staff said that I should not even bother to see him since he would die soon. It seemed that they were all trying to keep me away from him. Well, you know me. I had to check out the situation and became involved in a somewhat clandestine way, sneaking around the nurses and staff to see what this man was all about. The first time I saw him, it really shook me up. His appearance is so bizarre and unlike anything I have seen before that it actually shocked me. On top of that, he has these large, dark, penetrating eyes that stare right through you.

"After I got over the initial impact of seeing him, I began to feel that he was — how can I say this without sounding stupid — he was very alive, vibrantly so, and I sensed that he was loving, kind and wise. Also, I am certain he is telepathic. I know what you're thinking, but trust me, it's true, he really gets into your mind. Unfortunately, he is physically very weak and wasted and honestly looks like he was just saved from Dachau. Again, I keep having this overpowering feeling that I must help him, but don't know where to begin. He is calling out to me for help and that's why I need your help. Some of the staff are really spooked by him and will avoid going into his room at all costs while others share with me very positive feelings about him. He is unquestionably an enigma I must decipher.

"The story that Patrick and I have been able to put together is that he apparently showed up suddenly one night in 1983 at the home of a former nurse named Rachel Devane who became his benefactor. He had been injured somehow and needed almost constant nursing care that she provided for him. He apparently wouldn't go to the hospital but eventually had to be put into the nursing facility at Hampton Oaks. At Hampton Oaks he initially improved and seemed to be doing better but then began deteriorating. It's been a downhill course for him for several years now."

Zoë then related more details of what she had seen at Hampton Oaks, the story of her visit to Rachel Devane, and her suspicion that he might be vegetarian and having a toxic reaction to his animal product-based feedings. She said that she had started him on a vegetable puree, but it was too soon to tell if this would help. She also discussed her and Patrick's strange feelings when they were around Asterman and noted some of the staff's odd reactions to him.

"Patrick has really helped me a lot with this. As you can tell, this has turned into quite a detective case. Patrick, would you please show them the sketches?"

Patrick handed Zoë the sketchbook and she turned to the Asterman drawings. "Here he is," she said as she held up the first drawing for everyone to see.

"Wow, now that's impressive! I can see why he freaks people out. Look at the size of his head and those eyes," Scott said. "Looks like hydrocephalus to me."

"That's what I thought at first. So, I did an ultrasound and he doesn't have hydrocephalus. He just has a big head and a big brain. I think if he had a little more substance to his body, he might not look so out of proportion but he does look shocking in these drawings," Zoë related as she showed them the other sketches.

Martine observed, "His ears are tiny and low set and he has a diminutive mouth and nose and a broad chest. It looks like some type of genetic defect, almost like Turner's syndrome but he is male. I guess he's male. What's his history? What do you have on him?"

"That is the problem. His early records are missing. It is actually altogether mysterious, and Patrick and I have been on quite a hunt for information about him. The more we find, the stranger the story gets. By the way, he definitely appears to be male; however, he does not have much in terms of the usual accoutrements that go along with that. He appears infantile in that respect."

Zoë and Patrick then gave more details of their investigations, including Rachel Devane's history, discussions with the staff, Patrick meeting with Marcus and Jennifer and trying to find newspaper records about the purported accident that injured Asterman. She was barraged with numerous questions from the group that she answered to their satisfaction; at least she gave it her best effort.

"This may sound crazy but when I'm in his room and he is awake, I sense that he is very intelligent, aware of everything that is going on but is trapped in an injured body. Sometimes he speaks, or rather I think he speaks but he doesn't move his lips; very short phrases like hello, or thank you, yes or no. His eyes are large and creepy by our standards, and you get the feeling that he looks right through you. Some of the nurses and aides have told me that they will not even look at him if they go into his room. I have learned for a fact that he scares the crap out of Dr Adams."

"Zoë, I think you're reading too much into all this. When you have a guy as weird as this Asterman fellow, he just naturally gives you the creeps and that will make you feel and believe things that aren't really true. It's just your mind getting a little crazy with you. I agree that you should help this fellow, but I can't buy into thinking there's anything special about him like he has some eerie powers." Once again, Scott could not buy into a paranormal basis for this strangeness.

Patrick gave each of them a photographic copy of his drawings. They all carefully studied the pictures and remained completely enthralled with his appearance. The photos would provide them with a basis for further research on Asterman in each of their medical disciplines.

"Do you think he is human?" Erin asked rather bluntly.

"Whoa, you mean like an alien, an ET?" Zoë was startled, having never remotely considered this wild thought a possibility.

"That's exactly what I mean. I've seen drawings like that in UFO books and magazines. I don't know if any of that stuff is true or not, but I can't help but wonder especially when I see a picture like that of someone you tell me is real. Now, the opposite could be true. Maybe there is a group of people with some kind of syndrome that looks like Asterman that have been the basis for the idea of extraterrestrials," Erin replied thoughtfully.

"Erin, once again you are going off the deep end with your wild ideas. This guy is just some sort of genetic freak that tried to cope with the real world, got hurt and wound up in an extended care facility. That's it, pure and simple. He looks freaky and acts freaky and you want him to be someone unique and special and he's not. All of you are trying to make too much out of this. He is in terrible condition and will clearly die no matter what anyone does, even you, Zoë," Scott insisted.

Zoë shook her head and sighed in exasperation. "Scott, you just don't understand. There is a definite presence about him, something powerful, unique and noble. I can best describe this with an example of an experience I had in Hawaii. Summer before last, I was diving from a boat off Maui and this unbelievably large humpback whale swam around and came right up to me. Here was this magnificent, mysterious creature, unlike anything I had ever encountered breaking into my reality and right there in my face.

"I felt an unquestionable communication or connection beyond anything I've ever known. The whale could see me and I could see her but there was much more than that. It was like we were thinking with the same mind and were aware of each other on an essential level. My connection experiences with Asterman are strangely similar to what happened to me and that whale, but even more so because Asterman is so greatly intelligent and there is an undeniable communication with him. I sincerely sense that he needs help. Not just any help but my help."

"Zoë, you know I love you, but I just can't buy into that New Age nonsense. You're just letting your emotions get ahead of your intellect. Use your rational mind and you'll figure out what to do," Scott admonished her.

"I just can't let him die. There has to be information about him somewhere that can help determine who he really is, what happened to him, what his medical problems are, and how and if he can be treated. Dr Adams, the medical director, has ordered me off his case and will not authorize any additional tests. I think Adams wants him to die. He seems to have no respect and no patience with any of these people who are near death. Well, I'm not going to let this one rest. At least I got his feedings switched to a vegetable product. Maybe there is hope for him, but I fear for him when I leave," Zoë said with determination.

Martine responded, "There is a lot we can discover by checking his DNA, but I will need a blood sample or two."

"Consider it done," Zoë smiled.

Jenna added, "I know of several endocrinology databases I can search using the information that we've obtained that might be of help. At least maybe we can narrow down the possibilities. I agree that the DNA studies will probably be the most important thing to do."

"I think I will try to find some leads in the Clinical Genetics Database and will do an extensive literature search as well. In addition to the copies of the sketches, I will need notes on his physical examination and laboratory studies," Deirdre offered.

"This is great. You guys are wonderful. I knew you would not let me down. I can give you whatever you need." Zoë was delighted with all the support of her group.

Erin had been deep in thought since Zoë began speaking and then said: "Those sketches look familiar to me. I just know I have seen a drawing or photograph of someone very similar but I cannot place it. Maybe it was an old textbook or in a medical journal. I just know but I've seen a picture like that but for the life of me, I cannot remember where. I'll think about this some more, look in the library and I know of a few places I can check when I go home next week."

"I really appreciate everyone's help. Also, I don't think I need to say that we are running out of time. I think it is best that we keep all of this among ourselves and not discuss it with anyone else. There are patient confidentiality issues, of course, that I have broken by talking to you, and it is all just so strange that I don't think others would understand. I love you guys! Thanks for your help."

Scott interjected, "Don't forget that you were told to butt out and they could easily fire you from the rotation and create a stink with the dean of the medical school. You need to be very careful and I know you will. By the way, I think you're doing the right thing."

"Thanks, Scott. You are certainly right about the dangers, so let's all be careful. Keep me posted about anything you find out and I will do the same for you. You guys are great, and I really appreciate your help and friendship. This has been a great evening."

"This has been a great evening indeed! Here's to the B&B. It's like we have always been friends and we will be friends forever. All for one and one for all!" Patrick cheered, raising his glass.

"All for one and one for all! Friends forever!" everyone cheered as the glasses clinked together.

Chapter 21
Digging for Clues

Detective Patrick David of the Zoë's Investigation Squad continued his inquiries during his free weekends. He'd even taken a few days off from his work schedule to facilitate the effort. The task at hand was particularly difficult since many offices were closed when he was available. Patrick and Zoë had discussed their separate findings thus far and Zoë confided that she thought Rachel Devane was not giving her the complete story. Both of them thought that a good angle was to further check out the explosion story in the *Gazette* in 1983 since it was soon after this that John Asterman turned up with injuries described by Rachel that could have come from a blast.

Patrick checked several other regional newspapers but the *Gazette* had the only explosion story. He checked the weather reports and it had been generally clear with no thunderstorms. Also, there were no fireworks celebrations at that time either. If an explosion occurred, it would be likely that the fire department or paramedics were called. After checking several fire departments, he found that the fire and EMS system had changed and records were not available from 1983. He was finally able to get to the New Castle fire department one Friday afternoon while the firemen were having a meeting. Most of the firefighters were quite young and were certainly not there in 1983. This was disappointing to Patrick. At the end of the meeting, Patrick spoke to the captain and explained his research on the explosion report in the *Gazette*.

The captain responded: "I'm afraid I can't be much help to you. None of these men were around here in 1983 and I was in Connecticut."

Finding a person who might know about this was becoming a remote possibility.

After thinking about it for a moment, the captain then took Patrick to the back of the firehouse where there was a wall of about twenty plaques honoring men who had served the station for ten years or more.

"Let me see if I can figure who might have been here at that time. Fortunately, the dates of their service are recorded on their photographs."

The plaques were studied closely and narrowed down to five names. Several firemen came over to see what was going on and one offered that two of the men had died and one had moved to Canada somewhere and that left two names remaining: L.G. Bagnold and William Schmidt. Both men had retired and were presumed to be in the area. Patrick wrote down the information, thanked the men and set off to track down Bagnold and Schmidt.

Patrick discovered that William Schmidt had moved to Big Pine Key in Florida and he easily found his telephone number through directory assistance. Bill, as he insisted on being called, was quite a talker and was pleased to tell Patrick about his many years with the fire department. Patrick continued to try to get Bill to talk about May 4, 1983 and the report of an explosion, but could not pin him down to that date. "Bill, I really need to know if you remember anything about an explosion in 1983, either in May or any other month for that matter?" Patrick implored.

"I have trouble remembering things any more. But come to think of it, I believe it was L.G. that told me that one night when he was working, they called him to the scene of some odd accident down by the river. I remember he kept saying it was an odd situation, but he didn't say too much else. I really don't remember when it was. It could've been 1983." Bill continued to drone on about his life as a firefighter without giving Patrick any further information. Patrick thanked him several times and finally hung up the phone while Bill was continuing to talk.

L.G. Bagnold was difficult to find. His name was not in the phone book and the last address the captain had given him was a dead end. Patrick thought of Marcus and called him at the *Gazette*. After exchanging pleasantries, Patrick asked him about Bagnold.

"Oh, hell yes, I know Bagnold. He used to work for the fire department but is retired now. He's a rat. He didn't know how to be a friend, always cheating and weaseling out of paying for things. You had to watch your back with L.G. The last I heard from him was he was in Cold Springs up the river. I don't have an address. If you do find him somewhere, I would appreciate you not telling him where I am. I have no interest in seeing the scheming, little devil again."

Patrick thanked Marcus and headed for Cold Springs, hoping he would get there before dark. After asking at several stores and pubs, Patrick found someone who knew Bagnold and told him where he could be found. The house was a small unkempt single- floor wooden structure with peeling white paint with the grass overgrown in the yard and the bushes covering the windows. Patrick knocked on the door and was soon greeted by a suspicious, short, balding man with a sanguine face. Patrick explained who he was and the information he was looking for and after much encouragement was invited in.

"L.G. is the name, L.G. Bagnold. L.G. doesn't stand for anything. It's just L.G. It was my grandfather's name. I don't get many visitors but enjoy the ones that do come by. Can I get you a beer or something?" L.G. said, beginning to warm up to Patrick.

"I don't need anything, thanks. I am looking for some information you might be able to give me. Marcus Newell let me know where to find you. He sends his regards, by the way." That was not true, but Patrick thought it might help.

"Mr. Gazette. That's Marcus. He thinks that newspaper couldn't run without him and he may be right. I'm sure it would continue but it wouldn't be the same. He is something, isn't he? He's also tight with his money and won't spend a dime on anything."

"He is quite a fellow. He thinks that you're the only person that can help me out. I had talked to Marcus about an article in the *Gazette* concerning an explosion that occurred apparently near Croton Bay around May 4, 1983. There was only one story in the *Gazette* and nothing in any of the other papers. I think someone may have been injured but am not certain. I am trying to find out more about what happened. It was likely that the fire department and EMS were called to the scene and I am curious if you know anything about it. I know you worked with the New Castle fire department about that time since I saw your picture on the fire department wall that showed the dates you served there. I asked the captain at the station and he said that you and Bill Schmidt were probably on duty around that date."

Patrick hoped L.G. remembered something. If Bagnold did not have any information, he had reached a dead end. There was a long pause as L.G. put his finger to the side of his mouth as several conflicting expressions reflected his thoughts.

"Well, I do know something about it because I was there right after it happened."

"Please tell me what you can remember about it," Patrick urged.

"I probably shouldn't tell you anything. This is one of those things that I had put out of my mind and now that you have come here with your questions, I am having a flood of memories, things I haven't thought of since then. I was supposed to forget it, but I can't."

L.G. paused again and considered Patrick's question. His reluctance to say anything was quite apparent as he rubbed the stubble of his chin and grimaced.

"You were supposed to forget about it?" Patrick asked.

"Yea, and never talk about it to anyone." L.G. had now remembered it all and he knew he had to tell Patrick what had happened. The desire to unload the burden of his memories was overwhelming.

"You can't say I told you this because I will deny it and you will look like a fool."

"I understand. I will never associate your name with what you tell me or say anything that would lead people to believe that you'd told me," Patrick promised.

"Okay, now that we have that straight, I'll tell you what happened. On the day in question, and I believe it was May 4, we got a call from an unidentified man that there had been an explosion near the river edge and we needed to come right away. When we got there, military personnel were cordoning off the area. I don't know where these guys came from or how they got there that fast. I saw at least one jet plane fly over and a military helicopter. There was a small fire, grass and some bushes, and I pulled over and three of us rolled out the hoses and headed toward the flames.

"I noticed the soldiers covering some, what appeared to be, badly burned bodies and a large object that was partially in the water. At that point more soldiers with rifles pointed at us came between us and whatever was going on. They backed us well out of the way and the fire truck was commandeered until the fire was put out. We just stood there behind the barricade and did nothing since they wouldn't let us do anything. The truck was then driven back to us by one of the soldiers, accompanied by a civilian man in a black suit who told us in no uncertain terms that this incident didn't happen and would not be reported in any document or to anyone else and that our services were no longer needed. We were told to never discuss what we had seen again. I later found out that one of those bodies that they put under the canvas took off running while they were putting out the fire. The soldiers hunted for that fellow all night, but by morning everyone was all gone. They had even cleaned up the burnt bushes and grass. I was back there the next day and it looked like nothing had ever happened."

"Do you have any idea what actually happened? What was this all about?" Patrick quizzed.

"I've got a lot of ideas. Some may be right and some not. Those military guys frightened a lot of people and almost everyone wouldn't talk about it and so it became a non-event, if you know what I mean. It's interesting how when you've seen something strange and then somebody keeps telling you that it didn't happen and even threatens you, that it can be blocked out of your mind. But a few of us would talk in confidence in a hush-hush sort of way that we swore each other to secrecy.

"Most of us had seen the mysterious lights. Some of them were huge and some quite small. We heard reports of small, funny-looking people being seen near some of the lights. The military was obviously interested in the lights and had actually chased them on several occasions. So, my theory is the Air Force locked on to one of them, shot it down, and that's what we saw down by the river. As they say, that's my story and I'm sticking to it. But again, don't quote me!" L.G. said emphatically.

"Do you have any idea what happened to the one that ran off?" Patrick continued.

"There is no way to know. I was told all of the soldiers had left by dawn. They probably shot him. They were all over that place and they had some real heavy artillery with them. I don't think anybody could have gotten away but who knows. They did a big, thorough sweep of that whole area. Is that all you need to know?" L.G. yawned. "I go to bed early."

"One more thing, take a look at this drawing and tell me if you have seen anyone like this before." Patrick held up a small drawing of Asterman. "Could your missing man have looked like this?"

"Holy shit, that's him! Where did you get this?"

"He is my fiancée's patient and we are trying to help him. I must ask you not to say anything to anybody about this. We are still trying to sort things out and I don't want anyone in jeopardy. You have spoken to me in confidence and I am speaking to you in confidence. You have been a great help to me, more than you know. I am beginning to understand a lot more about the situation and it just keeps getting stranger. Thanks again for the information. I guess we are even. I gave you something and you gave me something and it will not go beyond this room. Well, I am out of here and I will let you get to bed."

Patrick left and started back to the city as he wondered if he had said too much, and as he thought about it, the more he worried that his showing Bagnold his sketch of Asterman was a big mistake. His concern was not so much for himself but for Zoë and even Asterman. He kept thinking about Marcus's comment that Bagnold was a rat.

Bagnold lay wide awake considering all that he had learned from Patrick. There would be no sleeping for him anytime soon as his mind raced over the implications of what he was told. His stock of beer in his refrigerator was gone by the time the sun came up. He was considering how to make some money on this information.

Chapter 22
Scott Larson

Scott had just finished his daily workout at the gym. He was very proud of his body and physical abilities and daily checked himself out by flexing his muscles in front of the mirror. With everyone in his family having been an accomplished athlete at some time or other, it was only natural for him to love sports. His mother, who was born in the Bahamas, had won several championships playing basketball, his two brothers were both doing very well in minor league baseball with hopes for the majors, and his dad had been safety for the Pittsburgh Steelers for eight years until multiple injuries forced him out of the game.

As an undergraduate at the university, Scott, who of course had a football scholarship, made the decision that he wanted to go into medicine, particularly orthopedics. His family was surprisingly disappointed in him, especially his father, in that his family had always assumed that he was going to stay with the ancestral tradition and ultimately be a star professional athlete as they themselves had been or aspired to be. His decision still troubled him because at family meetings, there was always undue tension and it was obvious that everyone, yes everyone, did not approve of his decision. Scott decided that he could remain athletic for the sheer joy of it, but would also pursue other areas of interest and the discipline of medicine, particularly sports medicine and orthopedics suited him very well.

In school, Scott enjoyed being the jock, the good athlete that everyone looked up to and admired for his physical prowess and for the simple reason that he was just a good guy. He received many accolades and was very popular with the ladies, not that he minded their fascination with him. Everyone wanted to be with Scott and there was no end to his female companions. His girlfriends were much more serious about their relationship with him than he was to them. His true interest remained with his sports, his friends, his growing interest in his studies and his determination to be a doctor. Medical school soon became a fait accompli.

Scott had become enamored of Erin since he met her on the first day of medical school. She was beautiful, intelligent, honest to a fault, sincere, and loved sports. But there was more than sexual attraction in their relationship. From the very first, they were like lifelong friends and there was, well, just something remarkably special between them. Erin loved the way he looked but also saw a beautiful, loving kindness in him that he continually tried to gloss over.

After showering and getting into his street clothes, Scott called Erin and asked if she could do dinner that evening. They would meet at their favorite restaurant, La Bella e Vita. This was a small family-owned place with delicious food and great ambience necessary for a romantic evening. Scott arrived early and sat at the table waiting for her.

"Hey there. Is this seat taken?" Erin smiled playfully and continued to stand until she was invited to sit. She was dressed seductively in a new outfit that more than adequately displayed her cleavage.

"This seat is just for you and no one else. It's the best in the house," Scott almost stuttered as she sat down. "You are gorgeous!"

"Well, thank you very much. I think you are right handsome yourself." Erin smiled knowing that she really had his attention.

Scott couldn't take his eyes off of Erin during the evening. She looked utterly delicious. It was obvious that she was preparing him for a very romantic evening. They had not been together for over a month due to their medical school rotations and they both relished their private time together. Scott had learned that he just couldn't jump into bed with Erin and expect to have a good time. There were no quickies with her and she demanded to be wooed, charmed, gently caressed and never rushed, and she was definitely a 'take charge' kind of girl.

The evening was wonderful. They caught up with the events of their lives that had transpired since they last saw each other and talked about when they could get together again.

"I have an idea. Why don't we go to your house and build a cozy, little fire in your nice fireplace? I just love being with you on that big couch." Erin smiled as she crafted her plans.

"That sounds great to me. I have the house to myself all weekend."

The November night was cold and a heavy rain had come in from the west. The room was cold and dark and the sound of the rain on the windowpanes sent a chill up Erin's spine. Almost in anticipation of the evening, Scott had prepared the wood for the fire. The small flame from the kindling soon engulfed the wood and the warmth and yellow light slowly filled the room. Then they curled up on the couch under a quilt. As they kissed each other gently and then more passionately, they threw aside the quilt and slowly began undressing each other as the room became warmer. Touching, caressing, kissing, exposing, gently teasing, delicately massaging, exploring soft moistness, then into each other more and more deeply, finally erupting into prolonged ecstasy.

The fire began dying with only a few glowing embers remaining. The dank chill of the outside began filling the room.

"I'll put some more wood on the fire," Scott offered.

"No, don't move," Erin said, pulling the warm fuzzy blanket up around them.

"Ahh, that feels good. I don't ever want to move again. You are so wonderful, Erin," Scott said, smiling broadly.

"You're not so bad yourself. I suppose I could do a lot worse. Don't let it go to your head, but you are a great lover. I've known very few great lovers, but you take the prize."

"You've known a few great lovers? Well, I'm glad I rank with the few. It makes me feel like a Marine."

"This was just a wonderful evening, the best. We need to have some private time like this every chance we can. I love spending time with you and having you all to myself. I'm so relaxed and feel so good. I can't think of a better evening in my entire life and my mind is just floating. So how do you feel and what are you thinking about?"

"I don't know. Why do women always have to talk?"

"What do you mean?"

"I mean, like now I feel all warm, cozy, kinda relaxed and sleepy and I really don't have anything to say. I feel a bit spent if you know what I mean."

"Well, it's different with me. I feel invigorated and alive, and my mind is working overtime. It's just a difference between men and women. Most men just do their thing and they're gone while women are just getting revved up. I think you understand that and I appreciate your doing the slow dance with me. But I am curious about what you're thinking."

"Erin, it was a wonderful evening and you are absolutely fabulous. I don't know what else to say."

"I think you keep a lot of things about your life hidden away. It's difficult to engage you in a conversation without you being frivolous. Do you really mean to trivialize every serious conversation? That's a sure sign that you have some hidden issues you should talk about."

"So now you're trying to psychoanalyze me? Well, I'm just an average guy who's had a fairly uneventful life and happen to love sports and want to be a medical doctor. Why are you doing this? Why can't we just enjoy each other and not talk about everything?"

"Scott, I love you more than anyone else and I want us to have a relationship that's based on trust, honesty and respect. I just feel that you're not being open and honest with me and with our friends when you make these funny cryptic gibes when people are saying something they consider serious. On Halloween, when we were talking about unusual experiences that we had, you were the only one who said that you have never had anything strange happen to you, and you're the only one who made fun of everyone else's experiences. I just don't understand that. Why do you do that?"

"It was all in fun. I just thought that I needed to be amusing and to keep things from getting so serious."

"You saw how Jenna was quite upset so that she was even crying and couldn't speak. I think you could've shown a little more positive and gentle support for her."

"That was just too heavy when we were just talking about ghosts and fairy tales. Ghost stories are supposed to be fun and happy and frivolous. Even if they're scary, it's still a fun kind of scary."

"These were not all tales. People were really being honest and actually experienced these things. You know them. They are not going to lie especially to our intimate group. Okay, so I'll give you some credit for trying to lighten the mood, but I was very surprised that you would not share any experience with the rest of the group. It was almost like you were aloof and somehow above the rest of us and way too ready to ridicule. You realize what a put-down that is to people?"

"That was not my intent at all and I am sorry that you're upset with me about it. I was just trying to keep things on the light side. It was a party."

"I'm not upset. I just want to know that you can and will share your feelings with me about whatever. Is it that you just can't talk about personal things?"

"No, I can talk about my feelings but it's very difficult for me. Some memories are actually frightening to me and I have tried to put them out of my mind. It's like if I don't talk about them, then it's not a problem. You understand what I'm saying?"

"Yes, I do understand, Scott. But I think we become better people when we confront our problems from the past and talk about them. It's certainly a way to develop trust with those you care about. I know you care about me and I hope you trust me."

"I do care about you very much and I trust you. Well, I suppose I do have some issues. I just like to keep them out of sight and out of mind. If there's anyone better than you to talk to about this, I do not know who it is, but I really don't want to spoil our good evening together." Scott was upset with himself for being perceived as a jerk and realized that his glib comments were more to protect his fragile ego than just being the comedian for the group.

"Okay, you asked for it. I want you to realize that this is actually very difficult for me to talk about. I am terrified of the water, especially the ocean. I have never been afraid of anything and I'm scared to death of water. I used to love to surf and some of the best surfing anywhere is along the California coast. In the summer after my freshman year in college, my friends and I decided to go on a surfing safari to as many great surfing spots as we could go to on our limited budget. We started in Northern California at Shelter Cove and worked our way down the coast. The weather and waves cooperated and we had a wonderful time.

"We were surfing at Huntington Beach and some large waves began coming in. We swam out and caught several spectacular waves that continued to increase in size. We had several excellent runs and as the waves continued to roll in, I went out again to a huge wave that was forming and I paddled like crazy to get beyond it before it broke. Well, it broke on top of me and I was slammed into the rocks. Then as a second wave broke on top of me, my whole body was battered and I knew that I'd broken my arm and maybe some ribs. I tried to swim but was tumbling and didn't even know which way was up. I gasped for breath and there was only water to breathe. My lungs burned and I struggled and knew it was all over. I became very relaxed and everything became quiet and I knew I was dead as I went down this dark passageway and came to a place that was filled with a golden light. I thought that it must be Heaven. There were three beings there and they looked like old men in robes but they were radiant, beaming and seemed to welcome me as if I was an old friend who had come home after a long journey.

"I don't know what was said but we talked, we talked for a long time and there were plans; there were things that I was supposed to do but also, I could choose not to do anything. It was my choice. I could stay there or I could go back. It was entirely up to me. I was under no pressure or encouragement to go either pathway. The place was absolutely indescribably wonderful and I really wanted to stay there, but I realized the overwhelming importance of my going back and doing whatever it was that I was supposed to do.

"The next thing I remember was coughing seawater and burning in my lungs, exquisite pain all over my body and a crowd of people around me. Five days later, I got out of the hospital with a bunch of stitches and a cast on my arm. I never went back to the ocean again and I still don't know what was said to me or what I was supposed to do. You know it's strange, but I think I'm doing what I'm supposed to be doing right now."

"Oh, my goodness, Scott. I had no idea and I'm so glad you're here with me now."

"I'm really glad I told you. Rather, I'm glad you've pried it out of me. I have not told this to anyone else and it actually gives me a sense of relief to let you in on my secret. So, now you know."

Erin just looked intently at Scott for a moment and gave him a big hug and kissed him passionately. His eyes were distant and serious. It was not the fun-loving Scott that she knew. As she held and caressed him, she could feel the tenseness leave his body. She held his face between her hands and could see the playful glimmer in his eyes returning. He then held her face, kissed her and gave her a wry smile.

"Thanks for telling me. I know that was very difficult for you to relive but I think you will be glad you did."

"And how's that for one hell of a story? I don't think any one of our friends can beat that one. Erin, I'm just not ready to share this with the rest of the group and would appreciate, you not saying anything about it. Maybe I can in time but not just now."

"I can certainly understand that and will not talk to anyone else about it. Scott, that's an incredible story. It makes me think that dying might not be so bad after all. What does all of this mean? Are we really here for a specific purpose and not by chance? This is more than my mind can take in right now."

"I just don't know but since I've told you this story, I feel that there is a memory that I have that is still hidden away that is starting to come back into my mind. This may seem strange, but I think you are part of this also, whatever it is. It's like all of our friends and we are somehow working together toward a common goal. It seems that I'm doing what I'm supposed to be doing and that things will happen as they should. I think we are all going to make history together.

Chapter 23
The Grim Reaper

Jack Adams took the patient list Meg Vandever gave him and headed off on his rounds. He couldn't dump this one on Zoë because she was off somewhere and couldn't be found. He detested old people and going into their smelly rooms and listening to all their complaints. Several people in assisted living had trouble getting to the clinic that day and it was his job to check on them. It was not unusual for them to eventually become unable to take care of themselves and require a move to the health care facility for constant care. This move took away their autonomy and much of their self-worth and was the last step before the exit.

First on the list was Sarah Bates, an eighty-two-year-old woman with all the complications of diabetes. She had renal insufficiency and was blind with diabetic retinopathy. Jack was seeing her because of a foot ulcer, another complication of her diabetes. She was lying in her bed and was terrified of him. She could sense his loathing of her in her decrepit state.

"Oh, Lord, oh, Jesus. The pain is killing me. Please don't hurt me! Please don't hurt me!"

"Sarah, you know we've got to do this and I don't like it any better than you!" Jack snapped at her.

"Please give me something for the pain. I just can't stand it," Sarah pleaded.

"Look, you don't need anything for pain. Hang onto your bedrail and I will get this done and get out of here." Jack was becoming more impatient as he closed her door.

Sarah began screaming with her feeble voice. "Help me! Help me! Help me! Lord Jesus, help me!"

"Shut up, you old bitch!" Jack shouted. "I'm getting this done and you are going to shut the fuck up."

She kept screaming and Jack grabbed her bath cloth and crammed it into her mouth. Then he jerked off her cover, ripped off the bandage to reveal a large, red, swollen ulcer that was much worse from the previous day. Infection had spread from her foot to the top of her thigh where blisters were forming. Jack quickly re-wrapped her leg as she groaned and writhed in pain.

As he pulled the bath cloth from her mouth, Jack smirked: "Sarah, I think this infection is the answer to all your problems. It's certainly an answer to one of mine. Everything will be okay. See you tomorrow or maybe not."

Jack wrote in Sarah's chart: Dressing changed without difficulty. Wound clean and dry with no evidence of infection. Plan: bed rest, dressing change on Thursday. No change in meds. Sarah's obituary stated that she died of complications of diabetes.

Jack's next stop was Ben Ellerman's room. Ben had Parkinson's disease and heart disease that were both fairly stable. At his last examination, he was found to have an aneurysm of the large artery in the abdomen called the aorta. Ben had been placed on some blood pressure-lowering medications, was having frequent examinations and he and his family had decided that he would have surgery on the enlarged artery in the next several weeks. Jack knocked on Ben's door and found him asleep in his recliner. Jack backed out the door and noted on the chart: exam unchanged. Plan: continuing monitoring aneurysm. An examination would have noted that the aneurysm had doubled in size and had become tender. The aneurysm ruptured at 5.20 a.m. the next morning and Ben died from exsanguination after briefly calling for help. Ben's obituary stated that he died of natural causes.

At the nurses' station, Meg stopped Jack who was in an obvious hurry to leave.

"What is it?" he snapped.

"Vera Menes has been having chest pain and indigestion. She has always had a lot of reflux, but her pain is really bad. I think we should get a cardiogram in case it is her heart," Meg said, very concerned.

"Give her some Tums! Anything else?" Jack was ready to leave and Meg was really irritating him.

"Dr Adams, I really think she should have a cardiogram. She has heart disease and…"

"No cardiogram. We are not getting cardiograms every time somebody has indigestion."

Meg saw that she was getting nowhere, but she was determined to get some orders out of him while he was there. "Very well, but I need to get some diet orders. David Zirella and Harriett Thuman need to be on soft diets."

"Whatever. Put them on any diet you want. Oh, is that freak Asterman still getting that vegetable mush?"

"Mr. Asterman is really doing great with the vegetable puree. I have been amazed at his improvement. That was a great idea Zoë had and it has made a major difference. It's a bit of effort to prepare but I think it has been worth it."

"You know, that is just a crock of shit. I should never have gone along with that idiot idea. We would probably be rid of him by now if it wasn't for her meddling."

"But Doctor…" Meg pleaded in desperation.

"Don't but me. Just stop that crap and put him on the cheapest tube feeding we have. On second thought, just give him water. It's time for him to move along."

Later that day, John Asterman was lying in his bed in the four-bed ward. His mind was much clearer and he could feel some strength returning to his small muscles. He held up his hand and flexed his fingers, something he had hardly been able to do for a long time. He bent his knees and lifted his head to look out the window at the passing clouds. Several nurses were gathered at the nursing station and he could just discern their conversation:

"I just can't believe Dr Adams wants to stop Mr. Asterman's tube feedings. He has improved so much. I don't know what Adams is thinking."

A shudder went through Asterman's body and he knew that there was no more time to spare and his years of planning had to be implemented now.

Chapter 24 The Squealer

"NSA, may I help you?"

"My name is George Dawkins and I am trying to reach Steven Pratt."

"One moment please."

"C4, may I help you?"

"Yes, my name is George Dawkins and I need to speak to Steven Pratt. It's important."

"May I ask what this is regarding?"

"He knows me and I have some information for him."

"I need to put you on hold for a moment."

Dawkins knew he had to make this call. Three minutes later there was a response.

"Hi, George, I haven't heard from you in a while. Things, okay?"

"Steve, I'm fine. Not too happy with retirement though. I could have worked longer. I was the most dedicated man on your team. You really shouldn't have let me go. You know I'm a good agent."

"George, you really were a fine agent; the best, but you know it was time for you to go. Perfection is not only a goal; it has to be an actuality. Mistakes just aren't tolerated. Anyway, I can't change what happened. The past is gone. Well, I know this isn't a social call, so what's up?"

"Is this a secure line?"

"You know it is."

"Do you remember the 1983 incident on the Hudson?"

"Christ, which incident, George? That whole area was hopping in 1983 and you know it."

"Do you remember the three EBEs as the ETs were called in those days and the one that ran away during the fire when nobody was looking? Did you ever find him?"

"Hell, no! We figured the thing hitched a ride back to wherever it came from. We covered the entire area with a fine-toothed comb and it was nowhere." Pratt's interest was suddenly piqued. "What do you know about it?"

"Well, I have reason to believe he is still around and alive but maybe not so well."

"Tell me more."

"I have this senile, old fart of a neighbor, L.G. Bagnold, who likes to hear himself talk. He was at the local diner the other night drinking too much as usual and rambling on to his friends when he mentioned that a young fellow had come by to see him, apparently asking a lot of questions about the 1983 incident. Bagnold was one of the firemen who showed up uninvited at the incident and was run off and told to keep his mouth shut. Apparently, he decided it was time to tell everything he knows to this fellow who came by for information."

"How unfortunate. How did you find this out?"

"I was sitting at a table right next to him and his cronies, eating dinner when he was spilling his guts out. He kept saying I'm really not supposed to be telling you this but the more he drank, the more he talked."

"Is this guy with all the questions writing a book or something?"

"No, but get this. Bagnold said this guy's girlfriend is apparently a doctor and has this strange-looking patient she can't figure out. Bagnold is certain it's the missing EBE because this guy showed him a picture and it is exactly what he remembers seeing."

"It sounds like a positive I.D. How did this guy make the connection with Bagnold?"

"I haven't figured that one out yet. There must be some connection between this patient and 1983 and this guy is just backtracking."

"Do you have a name?"

"No."

"Where does Bagnold live?"

"He's in Cold Harbor, 18 Pioneer Lane."

"How safe is the neighborhood?"

"We have had a few robberies on occasion but it is fairly safe overall. Why do you ask?"

"It may not be safe for long. Stay away from him and thanks for the information."

"Will I hear from you about this?"

"George, you know better."

Chapter 25
The Rat in the Trap

The knocking at his door finally got L.G. Bagnold out of his lounge chair. He was very tired and sleepy this evening and looked forward to retiring to bed early. Opening the door, he saw a man in a dark suit standing in the twilight. He noticed there was no car in front of his house.

"Mr. Bagnold?"

"Yes."

"I'm Steven Pratt. I am a special investigator for the government." Pratt flashed his I.D. at Bagnold who hardly had time to look at it. Pratt pushed past him into the small living room, closing the door behind him against the cold damp air as well as the view of the neighbors.

"Mr. Pratt, I was getting ready to go to bed and really need some sleep. I am a tired old man. Is this really necessary right now?"

"Trust me, Mr. Bagnold, this is quite important and cannot wait. I understand you had a visitor last week asking about something you saw in 1983? Would you please tell me about that?"

Bagnold was completely put out and protested that he didn't remember anything. Pratt became much more intense and Bagnold saw the futility of his protests. He remembered being told to never discuss the 1983 event and he suddenly had a foreboding that he might be sent to jail for finally breaking his silence. How did this man find out so quickly and who had snitched on him? Was the young man's visit a set-up?

"I'm in trouble, ain't I?"

"You are not in trouble now, but you will be if you don't tell me everything you know about this," Pratt said with an air of judgmental authority.

Bagnold took a deep breath and as was his habit, began at the beginning when he was at the firehouse and learned of the explosion. He told him everything that was said to his visitor including his belief that the Air Force had shot down a flying disk with extraterrestrial biological entities (EBEs) in it.

"That's really what happened, isn't it?" Bagnold asked.

"You are very astute, Mr. Bagnold, very astute. Now give me the details about your visitor last week."

Bagnold sat on the arm of his chair as Pratt darkly hovered over him. He began talking again in his circuitous storytelling mode as Pratt listened and recorded the conversation with his hidden pocket recorder.

"He was a very friendly guy. He started off by saying he was interested in an article in the *Gazette* concerning an explosion that occurred apparently near Croton Bay around May 4, 1983. He thought someone might have been injured but was not certain. He was trying to find out more about what happened. He thought it was likely that the fire department was called to the scene. He found out from the fire station personnel that I had worked with the New Castle fire department about that time and he tracked me down, hoping that I had remembered something. I told him that I was there at the scene right after it happened."

He then related the story that he had told Patrick about seeing the fire, the object at the edge of the water and the bodies.

"What else did he say?"

"I told him that I later found out that one of those bodies that they put under the canvas took off running while they were putting out the fire and the soldiers hunted for him but apparently never found him."

"What did this fellow say to you?"

"He showed me a picture and asked me if it looked like the beings I saw. It certainly did. This thing in the picture looked exactly like those bodies!"

"Where did he get the picture?"

"Well, it was not really a photograph but a drawing, a very good one at that. He said that he drew it. He said it was one of his fiancée's patients. She is a doctor, I guess."

"What else? Think. I need every detail."

Bagnold went over everything that he could remember. He knew that Patrick lived within driving distance, but he could not think of his name or where he came from. Pratt was becoming increasingly perturbed with him as his voice became louder.

"Think, old man. I need a name!"

"I'm so tired. I just need to sleep. Can we do this tomorrow?"

"Now! You have to think of the name now. Think! Is there anything about the name that you can remember?"

Bagnold struggled trying to recall anything. "It sounded Irish, maybe and like there were two first names."

"Time is getting short. There will be no rest for you until you cough it up." Pratt was now pacing the room and breathing heavily.

Beads of sweat formed on Bagnold's wrinkled forehead as he searched his brain for the name. Mentally he searched every letter of the alphabet and thought of every name he could think of under every letter. He was gripped with foreboding and a cold fear was seeping into his body, knowing that this was not going to end well for him. He knew with no uncertainty that he must remember the name or this obstinate man would beat him to a pulp. His mind was reeling with names and it finally came to him.

"Patrick, Patrick David. That's his name. Patrick David."

"Are you sure? You're not making up something, are you?"

"That's his name. I know it." Bagnold was emphatic, proud of himself that he finally remembered and relieved that he would now be left in peace.

"Do you remember the doctor's name or where she could be found?"

"No, he never mentioned it. I promise you. I do not know and I would tell you if I knew."

Pratt was much more relaxed now. He asked several more questions until he was convinced that Bagnold had told him everything he knew. The trouble was he knew too much.

"Can I go to sleep now?"

"You sure can. Take a nice, long nap."

Pratt then walked behind Bagnold and shot him in the back of the head. The silencer assured that there was no sound heard outside the house. Pratt took the money out of Bagnold's wallet and opening all the drawers in his dresser found a small tin box of cash and change that he emptied, taking the money. The staged robbery was complete and Pratt faded into the darkness undetected.

Chapter 26
Perversion

Zoë's rotation at Hampton Oaks had come to an end in mid-November. Earlier, on her last day, she met with Jack Adams and reviewed with him all of her assigned index cases. Jack was aggravated because she had taken on more patients than he asked her to, had not limited herself to the patients he wanted her to, and it was obvious that she had continued to see John Asterman, despite his removing her from the case.

Zoë presented all of the cases to him efficiently and in detail and made many excellent recommendations for care. She would have outshined most advanced medical residents despite her being a medical student and soon-to-be physician. Jack was glad to see her go. She had created too much new work and he resented how well the staff liked her. He looked at her evaluation letter and at the choices of: honors, high pass, pass, and fail. He checked 'pass' and noted: average student with little potential. This was the lowest grade he could give her that she could get in order to pass the rotation.

Jack wanted no more interfering students. He knew Zoë would not be positive about him and he hoped that might be sufficient motivation for the dean of the medical school not to send anyone else. In any case, he knew that he would not agree to have any other students there.

It was time for Jack to go home, so he headed to the unit to check with the nurses before leaving. He loathed being called as soon as he walked out the building. It was fortunate that he had stopped there because the nurses needed several additional orders for medications and would have soon called him. He quickly signed the orders and again headed toward the door. He went up toward the side entrance in order to get to his car more quickly. This was through a residential area of the building and staff had been asked not to use this as a thoroughfare. As he hurried out of the building, he heard weak screams coming from the back hallway. Normally he would have cared less but he also heard a voice he recognized repeatedly saying: "Fuck you, bitch!"

"That little son of a bitch! I just knew he was going to be trouble!" Jack said under his breath as he ran toward the sounds. The door had a chair pushed against it to keep it closed. Jack rammed the door with his shoulder and the chair splintered down the back. Draco Reen lay naked on top of old Ms. Parker as she pleaded: "Please don't rape me! Please don't rape me!" Jack grabbed Reen and threw him to the floor and kicked him in the butt as hard as he could.

"You God damned little pervert. Get the hell out of here! You're fired! You son of a bitch, I never want to see your degenerate face again." Jack picked up the splintered chair and threw it at Reen as he ran naked down the hallway with his pants trailing behind.

"Shit!" Jack said as he took several deep breaths. Miss Parker was crying and kept repeating: "Please don't rape me."

Jack covered her and said: "Oh shut up, it was just a fuck."

Jack aborted his plans to leave, called for a nurse and then went directly to Frieda Harrison to relate what had happened and that he had fired Reen. Jack hated everything about his job. This was just one more thing for him to deal with that pissed him off.

Chapter 27
Erin's Family Secrets

Erin went home for a long weekend three weeks before Christmas, the first since June. Life had suddenly become very busy with school, her summer job and all of her projects but she knew it was time to go home and check on her mother. She had written to her mom regularly but that was not the same as seeing her. It was good to be home. It was a place where the things of her childhood remained as if time had stood still and her comfortable old bed was always waiting for her.

She looked around her neighborhood and had the distinct feeling that the big street in front of her home had somehow gotten smaller. It seemed much larger when she played in the yard with her friends throughout the summer. She had fond memories of jumping rope, playing hopscotch and watching the people in their cars as they went by. Her front porch was a great observation deck for all the activities and she could remember her friends and neighbors parading by and those spectacular August thunderstorms. She remembered the smell of fresh, crisp air and her mother baking bread and those wonderful smells from the kitchen as her mother fixed dinner.

"Hi, Mom. I'm home," she called as her mother came down the stairs and hugged her tightly.

The smells of the yard, the house and especially the kitchen, opened floodgates of memories of good times long past: summer fun, Christmas, holidays, wonderful meals with family and friends and laughter. Constant laughter at ridiculous jokes, gag gifts, constant picking and making light of tough times, made life in this house wonderful. The family was now dispersed and Mom lived alone in the big, old house after her dad had died three years ago. Her brother and sister had married and moved to the west, had families and were just too busy to visit. It was sad, but a good kind of sad, to be filled with great memories.

"Erin, it is so good to see you. I've missed you so much. It has been too long since you were here. I thought you had forgotten about me."

"Mom, you know I always think about you. I love you and miss you. My life has just gotten way too complicated. I don't have time for anything any more, but I will never forget about you."

They continued chatting in the kitchen as her mother made dinner. Erin looked about the house that had been so familiar for all these years and was surprised to feel that she no longer belonged there. The figurines on the cabinet and the paintings on the walls that she had so dearly loved as a child were still wonderful and intriguing, but she did not feel the ownership for them that she once had. They now seemed separate from her.

"Jim Allison died last week. You know, he was married to Ophelia. They were good friends with the James's. You remember them, don't you? Well, his cancer finally got him."

Her mother droned on as Erin tried to recall names and faces of people she barely knew, and times and events she didn't remember. Some of the stories Erin's mother told about her childhood, were really about her older sister. Erin started to correct her but didn't. She loved and respected her mother but knew that their paths were separating.

After dinner, they bundled up and sat on the porch and enjoyed some Chardonnay. Wine was a special treat they both enjoyed and an evening glass of wine while watching the sunset had become one of their favorite traditions. Despite the cold air, the sun was warm on their faces.

"So, do you have a young man in your life?"

"Yes, Mom, I do. He's a real special guy."

"Thinking about marrying him?"

"Marriage is not so important to me right now, but I do want to be with him as much as I can. I think you would like him a lot."

"I would love to meet him. Bring him by to see me some time. Don't forget about your old mother. You know I want you to be happy and I want to be a part of your life."

"Mom, you know I will. You will always be an important part of my life."

"Erin, I'm very proud of you for all that you have accomplished and for the very special person that you are. You are going to have a wonderful life and I want you to do whatever your heart leads you to do. I am doing fine and really don't want you to worry about me. I need to tell you that in the spring I'm going to move over to an apartment at the Willows retirement community. This house is just too big and too much for me. You, Holly and Jeff aren't coming back. If you want anything out of this house, I want you to take it because I am getting rid of almost everything. There is little of any value here. I've already talked to Holly and Jeff and they're not interested, so I want you to look around this weekend and let me know if there is anything you want."

"Mom, are you sure you want to get rid of everything?"

"It is all baggage. Where would I keep it and what would I do with it? My life is not in my possessions but in my experiences. You know, the only things you can take with you are what you eat and drink. So have another glass of wine!" She smiled as she refilled Erin's glass. "I will be very happy at the Willows. I've got some friends there now and they have something going on every day. I'm getting tired of cooking and I won't have to unless I want to."

"Is there anything I can do or help you with?"

"No. I have it all together. I want to make these decisions now while I can and not wait for somebody to have to do it for me. I've never been a burden on anyone and I'm not starting now."

"As much as I hate to say it, I think you have made a good decision," Erin said, reaffirming her mother's choice.

"I know I have and I'm comfortable with my decision. I'm glad you understand. Tomorrow in the morning we will go on a treasure hunt but don't expect to find much treasure. Most of it is trash and junk."

They continued to talk throughout the evening around a wood fire that they built in the living room fireplace. It was quite cold once the sun had gone down, enough so that they settled on the couch together under a warm blanket. It was a great evening, talking and reminiscing. After an hour or so, she noticed her mother had fallen asleep. She gently woke her and took her to bed. Erin then went to sleep in her own bed, enjoying the flood of memories that had come to her.

The following morning, Erin and her mother began going through each room of the old house, looking at everything. There were many memories in the house and it was painful to think that all of it would soon be gone. Erin found a music box, some small paintings, a chair, a desk lamp and a teapot she wanted to keep. The furniture was good, but much worn and Erin did not have a place for it.

"Mom, what did you do with Dad's old books and magazines?"

"I threw out a lot of his stuff. He was such a pack rat. I had no idea he had as much as he did. There is still quite a lot in the attic. We'll take a look when we finish down here."

"He was really interested in strange stuff, UFOs and the like, wasn't he?"

"I think he read everything ever published about all kinds of weird stuff. He was actually obsessed with it. One of the biggest arguments we ever had was about the money he spent buying those crazy books and magazines. I know he hid a lot of his spending from me and I just couldn't convince him to save that money."

"Why do you think he was so enthralled by all that?"

"He never wanted me to tell this to anyone because he didn't want people to think he was crazy. He had several extraordinary experiences during his lifetime and was convinced that we are not the only intelligent beings on this planet. I think I am the only person he ever talked to about it. He wouldn't say anything to anybody about what he believed and even denied believing it if it came up in conversation. I happened to mention his interest to a close friend once and was quickly reprimanded by him. He said that it was all so bizarre that the person of average intelligence was completely incapable of understanding or rationally comprehending it. He said that the mind could not accept it and therefore everyone believed it couldn't be true. It would be like believing in fairies or witches. He always said that he would like to have one person in the world that he could talk to seriously about his experiences."

"Well, what happened to him to make him think that?"

First of all, your brother and sister don't know this and out of respect for him, please don't tell them or anyone else. They couldn't care less anyway. I have always been able to trust you with anything."

"My lips are sealed."

"Erin, I feel like I can talk to you about anything in the world. That is a wonderful relationship to have with someone. Thank you for that."

"My curiosity is killing me. Please go on."

"In World War II and the Korean War, your father flew frequent reconnaissance missions over enemy territory and was often followed by glowing balls of light. They had a nickname for them: Foo Fighters."

"Is that it? Glowing balls of light? Is that why he was caught up in all this?"

"Hardly. He was under direct attack by the enemy on several occasions and he claims that the lights ran the enemy planes off. He was convinced they were protecting him."

"Protecting him? That is way too strange."

"Indeed! After he got out of the service but before we got married, he said he was lying in bed one night and one of these balls came right through the roof and into his bedroom. He saw three small, childlike creatures and they talked to him and gave him instructions to do something, but he could never remember what it was. Several years later, after we were married, they showed up again. It was night and in our bedroom. All I remember was waking up and finding him standing by the window and being very excited. He said that they had come back, told him that he had done a good job and gave him another task to do. Again, he couldn't remember what it was."

"Was Dad, okay? Did he have some mental problems or hallucinations? Did you ever see anything? Could you confirm anything that he said that he saw?"

"Erin, your father was a rock-solid person in every aspect of his life, but he became obsessed with reading everything he could about the occult, ghosts, UFOs, psychic stuff, physics and astronomy. It began affecting our lives and I had to insist that he give me some undivided attention every weekend. Finally, he agreed to that and stuck by his word our entire married life. But sometimes, he would get that faraway look in his eyes and I knew what he was thinking and it wasn't about me. He was obsessive but I don't think he was mentally ill.

"One time, I suggested that he might want to talk to his doctor about some of these things and he told me in no uncertain terms that the doctor would say he was crazy and he was not going to do that. I think these events were real. One of his army buddies told me one time that he thought your dad was the luckiest person alive because those Foo Fighters would seem to come out of nowhere and protect him from an enemy attack. Sometimes after he had some of these experiences at home, I would wake up and there would be buzzing electrical energy in the room and maybe even a glowing mist that would quickly disappear. Something was definitely going on."

"Did anything else strange happen?"

"I want to say no but now that I think about it, we did have some weird things occur around here. Think about it yourself and you may remember some of the things. You know, I have just put this stuff out of my mind because it's so crazy."

"What do you remember?"

"Well, the first thing was some knocking in our old apartment in the middle of the night and footsteps. We wrote that off as being the neighbors or the building settling but didn't really believe that. Then things would mysteriously go missing and weird stuff like that."

Erin recalled her story from the Halloween party. "Do you remember when we lived by the woods and my friend and I saw the funny little man sitting on the log?"

"I sure do. Your very good friend, what was her name? Jennie. Jennie Wells, I believe. That poor kid would never come back to our house. That encounter really scared the wits out of her."

"I was really mad at Jennie. She would never even talk to me after that. I don't know why she became so upset. I guess she just couldn't handle it."

"Erin, I think we have all had some of these strange experiences. It was not just limited to your father. The more I think about it, the more I remember little, quirky things that I have just put out of my mind. One more thing, on the day your father died, he saw one of the lights again. I was there and remembered seeing a flash out of the corner of my eye but nothing else. He said that he was told that his family would carry on his mission. He smiled and seemed very happy and then passed away."

There was a long pause as they both remembered Erin's father and their lives with him.

"Thanks for telling me about Dad."

"Let's go up to the attic," her mom said with a smile. There's a lot of your dad up there. They climbed to the top of the stairs and the musty smell caused Erin to sneeze three times in rapid succession.

"Bless you. It's a bit dusty to say the least," her mom said with a laugh.

"Thanks. It's really a mess up here. Where are his books?"

"Over there in those boxes. There is a light just above them you can use to see better."

Erin turned on the light and found four large cardboard boxes filled with books, magazines and various articles. Some were quite old and others were bought just prior to her father's death. She wiped off the surface of a small table nearby so she could have a closer look at some of them.

"Erin, this is all that is left of his things. I've gotten rid of his clothes and shoes and he really didn't have anything else of value. You can have any or all of these. Whatever you don't want will go into recycling when I move out. I don't know what else to do with all this mess. Who would want it?"

"Good grief, it would take me forever to go through all this stuff. Frankly, I don't want to spend all of my time with you this weekend going through boxes and besides, the dust is really getting to me."

"Well, before you give up, take a look at that box with the yellow tape. Those are the ones he treasured the most and kept in a special bookcase. He probably read them a dozen times or more."

Erin opened the box and put several stacks of books on the table. There were also at least thirty journals and stacks of articles. Although she did not know it at the time, all of these were classic books and articles that every parapsychology and UFO researcher in the field knew well. She felt an eerie connection with her father and this strange subject matter as she decided to definitely keep the contents of this box. As she looked through his papers and publications, she saw something that caused her to gasp. On the cover of one of the journals was a drawing of an alien that looked exactly like the drawing Patrick had made of John Asterman. The caption read: 'The Night Visitors Where Do They Come From and What Do They Want?'

Chapter 28
Who Is John Asterman?

As Christmas approached, Zoë once again found her mind turning to thoughts of John Asterman no matter what she was doing. He was increasingly haunting her every thought. When she tried to relax or sleep, his intense eyes were there in her mind and the energy of her thoughts worked constantly, trying to understand this strange and enigmatic man. It was not that thinking of him was stressful or unpleasant but instead, it was quite peaceful and gratifying, having a curious soothing effect on her. She was now trying to focus on the facts of all she knew about him.

Within the last twenty-four hours she had spoken to every one of the B&B friends, all of whom had made it their personal crusade to help her discern the truth about who or what Asterman really was. Genetic anomaly, endocrine anomaly, birth defect, combinations of many factors and everything had been considered but nothing fit into a logical concept. Her discussion with Erin was most disquieting. After Erin returned from visiting her mother, she called Zoë and told her that within the UFO literature, multiple drawings and descriptions that she had seen would indicate that John Asterman was an alien, a non-human intelligent being from another world who somehow became trapped here in New York. Could this be a scenario of an extraterrestrial being stopping on Earth for maybe a snack and to get some gas then unexpectedly getting injured, lost and being left behind? He then somehow winds up with Florence Nightingale, aka Rachel Devane, who tries to nurse him back to health but finds out he's more than she can manage. So, she puts him into Hampton Oaks where he has languished for twenty-seven years. As outlandish as the idea sounded, it was the only reconstruction that made any sense. After all, John Asterman not only didn't look human, he also didn't act human. Again, she couldn't get over the uncanny feeling that many times he could sense her presence, read her thoughts and communicate with her without saying a word.

There was also the fact that many people she interviewed had said that they had a strange, creepy feeling whenever they were around him, even if they didn't look at him. Zoë had observed that the staff seemed ill at ease and several were disquieted enough to refuse to work near him altogether. As Zoë sat contemplating all of this, sipping a cup of tea, her concentration was broken as her phone rang.

"Hello, this is Zoë."

"Hi, Zoë, this is Martine. I've got some interesting information for you about Asterman."

"He's an alien from Mars. I just knew it. I think I figured this one out," Zoë blurted out.

"Well, I hate to burst your bubble, but I'm afraid not. All the tests show that he is very much human with a full complement of twenty-three paired chromosomes and he is definitely a he, with both an X and a Y chromosome."

"I'll be damned! I had just very logically figured out that he is an alien from space. Well, there goes that idea. Ha! Back to the drawing board! I had hoped for something much more exciting and I'm actually kind of disappointed. How sure are you about this? Could there be a mistake?"

"Sorry, but we double checked both blood samples and there is no doubt about it. I must say that the thought crossed my mind that we might find something extremely unusual, maybe alien but he's just another *Homo sapiens*."

"I guess I was getting crazy in my thinking. There are no aliens. How could I have let myself believe that he is from another world? I've seen too many science fiction movies."

"As long as you stick to science, you won't go astray. Just stay with the facts. We are going to do a few more tests to see if we can account for some of his physical anomalies but that will take a while. I'll give you a call when we have more information. Take care. Gotta go."

"Thanks, Martine. Talk to you later. Let's try to get together during the holidays."

Martine had already hung up. Zoë contemplated the results and said aloud: "John Asterman, you may be human, but you are by no means like anyone I have ever seen. Who are you?"

Chapter 29
Free at Last

Macey Grabel sat in her room at Hampton Oaks gazing out the window at the forest. Most of the leaves had fallen and the sky was clear. A light frost covered the foliage in the shadows. She covered herself with her blanket as the winter air seeped into her room through the closed but not so tight window. Nodding off into a numbing sleep, she dreamed of earlier times, times long before Hampton Oaks. She ran along the trails by the river, sprinting full of energy in the warm sun. Even now, she often dreamed of running because that had always been her favorite sport, but much more than that. Running was freedom and life for her. The trophies had long ago been boxed up by her children and taken away.

"We need to get rid of all this clutter," they said. "She doesn't need all this stuff now." Little did they know the joy that her mementos brought to her limited world. They could have put them away after she died.

Old age for Macey had been a progressive loss of health and personal possessions. Her pride and dignity had long ago slipped away. She greatly missed visiting her dear, wonderful and mysterious friend late at night when no one was around. Now, she could no longer walk. The irony of her situation was that her mind was clear and sharp, but she was a prisoner in a body that would no longer function. Her voice was weak, halting and breaking and no one took time to try to listen to her. She kept her mind busy with the details of life around her to avoid thinking about her sad state of existence. An irrational fear kept creeping into her mind that she would soon be alive in a body that was dead, and she would be buried alive with no one knowing that she still existed. Then she remembered that her friend had told her that everything would soon be much better and her fear passed.

She awoke with the familiar licking on her leg. Webster was a little white Westie given to Macey by a friend eight years ago. She nodded and Webster jumped onto her lap. His soft fur, warm snuggles and enthusiastic licks were a wonderful comfort to her. Although pets often visited Hampton Oaks, few lived there and many on the board of directors wanted them banned because they invariably became a problem. Macey had been fortunate thus far to keep her beloved pet, but she feared the time when he would be taken away.

Macey watched as the little dog proceeded on his routine: sniffing the chairs, playing with his squeaky green frog, chewing his bone, loudly slurping water, eating a bite of food, using the litter box and then sitting and looking out the window. He would then lie on his pillow and look up at Macey as if trying to fathom who she was and what she was thinking. He was in awe of her and could sense her deep thoughts that were beyond his ability to understand. For Macey, Webster became an extension of herself. She watched his every move and imagined that she was the little dog. Her reality faded away as her mind focused its entirety on Webster, envisioning herself with tiny paws, thick white hair, and a wiggling tail. She imagined lapping the cool water and sniffing the floor for traces of a scent. Her world completely disappeared as she became the happy little curious Westie who was alive, healthy and unshackled by disease. Her mind was free in the little dog. She could run, jump and experience the world as she had not in many years.

"If only I could leave this old body behind," she whispered. After several minutes, she circled around the base of the chair, looking at the familiar, old woman who was no longer breathing and had slumped in her chair. Walking over to the window, she stood on her hind legs and looked over her paws at the ducks in the garden pond and longed to run and chase them.

Chapter 30 God Only Knows

Deirdre Lindquist had come up for the weekend to see Zoë. Both had some time off and greatly enjoyed their mutual company and catching up with the latest news and gossip. They had been sightseeing, doing some Christmas shopping, and arrived back at Zoë's house in the early evening.

Zoë updated her about her recent experiences with the Hampton Oaks staff and patients and noted: "The nicest little old lady died over at Hampton Oaks this week. She would have been ninety next month. I always enjoyed seeing her and will really miss her kind words and beautiful smile. She had this cute, little dog that brought a lot of joy to her. Her family lives in the city and never came around and they don't want any of her possessions or the little dog, so the staffers are trying to take care of things for her. It's really sad to see someone deteriorate and die even after a long, good life. I guess that's just the way things are, and I guess it's God's will that we shouldn't live forever."

Deirdre scowled. "I'm sorry, but I have a real problem with that thinking. What do you mean, God's will? I just don't get it. Hundreds of thousands of people are killed by disease and in hurricanes, tsunamis and earthquakes every year. Terrorists are blowing up children and innocent people in God's name. Africa is literally dying of AIDS and famine and the Church is against birth control and condoms. Is that God's will? If it is, then God is not the loving entity the Church people have tried to lead me to believe. If anything, he is capricious, arbitrary and callous, and certainly not loving. He lets one hundred thousand people die in Pakistan in an earthquake and here in America lets me have a comfortable, protected life, money, a college education and a graduate degree in medicine. I didn't do anything but get born in the right place at the right time. No, Zoë we are here by chance and what happens to us is by chance.

There's no providence involved, and some people are lucky and some people are not."

Zoë was silent as Deirdre's questions and comments passed through her mind. These were questions she had struggled with all her life. It really was more than a struggle for her; it was torment for her to try to believe in the God her parents had told her about and what she had experienced in the world.

Deirdre continued: "You know if God really exists, and I have serious doubts, then he must have said, 'Hey, let's do a big bang and find out what will happen'. Then boom, energy, matter, galaxies, stars, planets and people, all evolving from God's big idea. Is he bopping around making people live or die? No! If he is there, he is just watching where all this is going to go. He is not controlling anything."

"Deism," Zoë murmured.

"Excuse me?" Deirdre replied.

"Deism. That's the basic belief system of a lot of the founding fathers of the U.S. You know, Washington, Jefferson, Franklin and those guys. Basically, God is seen as a clock maker. He makes the clock, winds it up and leaves it alone to run however it will and for as long as it will."

"Well, if I believed anything about God that would be it. I don't see God going around doing good things for good people and dispensing evil to bad people. Zoë, just withhold your beliefs for a moment and look at the world. It is just not that way," Deirdre said thoughtfully as the tone of her voice returned to normal.

Zoë had thought about these things many times before and had tried to reconcile the facts with the religious beliefs of her youth. She wanted to believe that her experiences in life would make her better and stronger but somehow, she found it difficult to believe that suffering is good for the soul.

"I understand what you are saying and intellectually, it makes sense to me. I'm not sure how to say this, but I see the bad things and the good things that happen in the world and it doesn't all make sense, but yet I feel a spiritual connectedness to God or something that is a lot greater than I am."

"Connectedness? Like you talk to God or something?" Deirdre wondered.

Zoë again thought a moment and began: "It is not easy to explain, but sometimes I have a strange sense of direction and a purpose that is somehow beyond me, beyond my control. Occasionally I realize that I have made a major difference in the life of someone I don't even know, or I am somehow in the right place at the right time for someone. I feel drawn to some people I've never seen before and then realize that I have something special to offer them or they have something special to offer me. As an example, I had a strange urge to pull into a McDonald's, a place I never go to and then found a lost, sick child behind a dumpster. Once, I missed a ride because of a bad storm. The car I was supposed to be in crashed and I would have been killed had I sat in the passenger seat."

"Coincidence. That happens to everybody," Deirdre retorted.

Zoë realized Deirdre was a deep skeptic and wondered how she might convince her, or even if it was possible to convince her, that there might be some greater force affecting their lives. Some people are just unmovable in what they believe and will not change their minds under any circumstances, even if there is hard evidence that refutes the belief.

"Deirdre, of course there are coincidences in life, but there are too many times things happen that I rationally cannot account for. I must tell you that I had the same feelings that you have expressed after my mother's death, and a long time passed before I began to change my feelings. Sometimes I sincerely sense direction in my life and equate that to God, spirit or whatever you want to call it that relates to me on a personal basis. But you know, I'm beginning to think that God is more concerned about our spiritual growth than our physical comfort."

"How so?"

"Maybe the physical world does run by chance and the whims of people with power and control. Bad things happen to good people and good things happen to bad people. I think the importance lies in how we live our lives with the cards we are dealt. We are too hung up on being right or wrong, black or white and almost every religious or ethnic group has the attitude that I'm right and you're wrong. There is no hope for us unless we live our lives as caring, compassionate people, and we are given opportunity every day to live compassionate lives. Everybody is a winner in a world of compassionate people and when the world is not compassionate, everyone loses. If God is in our lives, his or her presence takes form in our compassion and our love. Our view of God as an old, judgmental man, sitting on a throne is all wrong. God or whatever we want to call him is not a vindictive, old man. He is a spirit of being," Zoë mused.

"I do think there is more to us than the sum of our parts. How much more? I don't know. I used to think that science had all the answers, but the more I've studied the new findings in physics, the stranger things have become. I really want to believe that everything is neat, orderly, and measurable and can be broken down into knowable parts. It is not that way at all. In quantum physics, it is like the observer actually affects reality in some mysterious way. It is like your consciousness actually creates reality and that reality doesn't exist without consciousness. Kind of sounds like science fiction, doesn't it? Particles, atoms and molecules can become entangled with each other in strange ways so that even when great distances separate them, a change in one will produce an immediate change in its partner. Nobody understands how or why this happens. Einstein couldn't believe it but finally had to admit it was true.

"The more we learn, the stranger things become and it just defies logic. I used to think the idea of having a spirit was ridiculous. Now, it wouldn't surprise me at all. Okay, so I'm open to some of these ideas, but I still need my facts and I will not change my mind just because someone says I should. I have to know and understand. Right now, I know I definitely need a glass of wine. How about you?" Deirdre said with a smile.

"I believe I most definitely need wine," Zoë said. "Heavy conversations require good wine. I don't know if we've resolved anything, but it does feel better to talk about it."

"Cheers! May the Force, God or whatever be with you."

Chapter 31
Face from the Past

As the New Year began, Patrick David had not seen Zoë for several weeks and had been putting in many hours working at his new job. The work was difficult, but he was continuing to learn new things every day and enjoy the process immensely. In so many ways the archaeological work was like a great treasure hunt that continued to produce fascinating finds. In the short time that Patrick had been working, a wealth of new information and artifacts had been discovered that could easily take several years to fully evaluate. The interesting part of the discovery process was that each new bit of information prompted the need to find more information to add to the details of what sometimes seemed to be a large jigsaw puzzle.

A huge pile of wrapped artifacts was stacked in the corner of the laboratory. Patrick meticulously opened each pack, recorded the identifying information in the logbook and photographed each surface. A metric ruler was visible in each photograph to facilitate accurate measurement. Most of the current batch was soft limestone that unfortunately weathered very easily, rounding out normally sharp edges resulting in a loss of detail. Many of these do not photograph well and Patrick often needed to draw the barely discernable details and then photograph his drawing into the database. Some of the regular specimens were artistic beauties that Patrick drew just for the sheer joy of it. At this point, he had been working non-stop for nearly four hours and had to take a break. There was so much to do and Professor Horowitz was really pressing him to complete the current cataloging before his next trip that would be coming up within the month.

Patrick made a quick pit stop, grabbed some crackers and a Pepsi from the vending machine and hurried back to the laboratory. There at the photo table was Horowitz looking over his entries. Patrick became very uneasy feeling that Horowitz didn't trust him and was checking up on his work. This was not the case. Horowitz trusted Patrick immensely or he would never have hired him for the job. He only wanted to check the progress of Patrick's work to this point.

"Great progress," Horowitz said without looking up as Patrick came into the lab. "Try to get more contrast on J583 and R801."

Patrick wondered how he could have possibly had enough time to look at all the entries. Maybe he just randomly picked a few.

"All the others look good," he said as he picked up Patrick's drawing pads.

"I haven't photographed all of those drawings yet, sir, but will do it before I go today."

He flipped through a stack of drawings of small sculptures, steles, and vessels. At the bottom of the stack was one of Patrick's drawings of John Asterman that had mistakenly wound up in the pile. Horowitz was deeply focused on the drawings and commented on each one as he studied them in detail.

"Good. Good. Too bad we don't have more detail on this snake. This one is excellent, just look at the pattern of feathers in the headdress." He then held up the drawing of Asterman and grunted: "Way too much detail here that doesn't accurately depict the original. Try to restrain your artistic creativity and make it look more like the original. Good job overall. Try to keep up the good work. Let me know if you need anything."

Horowitz put down the drawings and left as quickly as he had arrived.

"What the hell is he talking about? What has he seen?" Patrick said aloud. "I've got to find out more about this."

Chapter 31
Anguish and Revenge

Draco Reen sat on the bed in his meager apartment holding his mother's picture. He was completely morose at having been fired from Hampton Oaks. Icy winter raindrops hit the windowpane as night fell. Tears streamed down his face and splashed on the image of the stern woman whose fiercely bitter eyes looked back at him. Those eyes were always piercing to the heart, always angry, always letting him know of her disappointment in him.

He clutched the picture tightly to his chest and rocked from side to side fearing his mother's anger for yet another failure. She was always angry and he was the cause of her anger. He was the reason for all the unhappiness in her life. He was the reason she could have no more children. He was the reason for her headaches and the pains in her stomach and back. He had failed her once again. If she were there with him, she would slap him, and would cry in anguish. He hated to see her cry. It was always his fault. There was nothing he could do and she would punish him again for his miserable failure.

He thought of Jack Adams, who had brought his secure world to an end as the dark clouds of his mind swirled. He felt sick and dizzy as he decided what he must do. There must be revenge so that his mother would no longer hate him. He opened the dresser drawer and under his socks found his old pistol. Taking it out, he checked to make sure it was loaded, placed the gun under his belt, put on his coat and went out into the cold, rainy night.

Chapter 32
Trading Places

Jack had been called to see an elderly woman who was in heart failure and was just admitted to the hospital unit. After examining her and initiating appropriate treatment measures with the nurses, he headed toward his office, longing to get out after a seemingly never-ending day. Since the onset of winter, the early darkness poured like thick, inky fog through the windows turning the dimly lighted hallways into darkened tunnels.

As he approached the ward, he sensed a powerful urge to go in. Jack shrugged off the feeling and walked past the door when he stopped as if someone had physically turned him around facing the door. As he reached for the door handle, he felt both an urgency to enter and a dread of what was inside. The gun aimed at him in the darkness missed its first opportunity to hit its mark as he quickly went in.

Inside he noted that everything was strangely quiet. Where were the nurses? The nursing station was brightly lit and empty. The rest of the unit was dim and the patients appeared to be asleep, except for one. John Asterman's bed was in the corner by the window. His unblinking stare shined like giant cat's eyes in the darkness. Jack had never seen anything like this and was both startled and fascinated. He remembered his previous encounters with Asterman and fear crept into his being, but now he couldn't take his eyes off him and was drawn ever closer. As he moved in further, he did not hear the door open nor see the dark figure enter the room behind him.

Jack sensed Asterman calling to him, but no words were spoken. Tonight, Asterman was completely different and his body appeared animated for the first time in Jack's memory. He was no longer limp and pallid but was vibrant and actually glowing in the darkness. Jack realized he was in the presence of a magnificent creature regaining life after being nearly dead for many years.

Behind him, there was a sudden click of a pistol being cocked and ready to fire. He turned to see Draco Reen standing there, trembling with anger and aiming the gun at his head. Knowing he was about to die, Jack gasped and broke into a cold sweat as his heart pounded like a hammer in his chest. Suddenly, Reen's desperately angry face instantly changed to a look of pure horror. His eyes dropped from Jack and looked at Asterman. Reen's breathing became labored and he clutched his chest as crushing pain overcame him. The pistol dropped to the floor and spun like a pinwheel. Reen gasped and slumped to the floor and rolled back to display his ghastly dead face.

Jack trembled and his twitching mouth was agape at what had just happened. He stared at Reen's dead body and slowly turned to Asterman who was now sitting on the edge of his bed. Jack was completely transfixed by the visage of the magnificent man-creature that was before him. Asterman smiled ever so faintly and silently motioned for Jack to come nearer to him. Jack was terrified, not knowing what to expect but there was no doubt that Asterman had somehow saved his life. But to what end?

Jack hated his life and the people around him and he hated the world. He was empty. Any goodness that might have ever been within him was long gone. He was a shell of a man and he now wished that Reen had shot him and put an end to it all. As he moved closer, Jack felt soothed and mesmerized and yet totally overwhelmed by the presence of this incredibly intelligent and charismatic being.

"Who are you? What are you?" Jack asked, almost pleading.

"I am you and you are me," Asterman whispered as he grasped Jack's arm.

Chapter 33
Old Enemies and New Friends

"Adams, what the hell is going on?" Frieda Harrison demanded, seeing Draco Reen's body on the floor.

Jack was quite composed as he explained to her that he had come in to check the unit, found no nurse and was about to call her when Reen came in.

"He apparently was going to get even with me for firing him — using that thing," Jack said, nodding at the pistol. "It looks as if he had a heart attack during all the excitement. I tell you it was a close call for me. I was seconds away from being history."

Frieda contemplated the situation and said: "Heart attack. That's exactly what you will put on the death certificate, myocardial infarction secondary to anxiety attack. I don't want the staff, police or news media involved with any of this. I'll be damned. What a thing to happen. I've wanted to get rid of him but certainly not this way!"

Frieda looked at Jack for a response. She was amazed at how calm and collected he was since he normally would have overreacted and created a problem.

"Of course, I think that is the best way to handle this," Jack answered, nodding in affirmation. "I am just glad the charge nurse wasn't here when all this happened. She might've been killed or injured.

"It's all rather strange. Grace, who was the nurse here tonight, very suddenly became quite ill, called me and had to leave. That is most unlike her and she was quite concerned about having to leave her post. I sent her home and hope she is feeling better," Frieda said reaching down and picking up the revolver.

"The trigger is still cocked. Be careful, don't shoot yourself," Jack said, pointing at the weapon.

"Dr Adams," Frieda began, peering over her wire-rimmed glasses at him.

"Would you please call me Jack?" Jack answered, trying to be as gratuitous as possible.

"Well, that's a turnabout. I would be happy to call you Jack," Frieda responded. "I think I am finally beginning to like you. Anyway, Jack, after years in the army, I can handle a gun."

With that comment, she popped open the cylinder, unloaded six shells, snapped it closed and pulled the trigger with a snap. "Empty. Now I need to get rid of this thing," she said while wrapping it in a towel. "I'll talk to the staff in the morning and take care of the phone calls if you will help me get him down to the morgue and write the death certificate. We need a quick cremation."

"Consider it done," Jack retorted as he retrieved a gurney. He grabbed Reen's arms and Frieda his feet and they heaved him up on the stretcher.

Jack and Frieda closed Reen's eyes and covered him with a sheet. The horrified look frozen on his face was disquieting.

"Does he have any family?"

Frieda thought a moment then said: "I think he lived with his mother most of his life but has lived alone since she died five or six years ago. His father is dead and I'm sure he has no other relatives. He never listed any contacts. He was a loner and never got it on with any of the staff or locals. Pathetic little pervert."

"He was a sad fellow. I had no idea he was so screwed up," Jack said as they wheeled him to the morgue.

Jack and Frieda returned to her office and after making a pot of coffee, she and Jack talked for several hours. She couldn't get over how much Jack's personality had improved after he was nearly killed. For the first time he seemed like a genuine, warm human being. Frieda actually liked him a lot and wondered how she could have misjudged him so badly. A bond had developed between this unlikely pair.

John Asterman, or so it seemed, lay in his bed with his eyes closed and a grimace on his face. His body, once glowing and vibrant, was now flaccid and weak and the mind within him filled with rage, a rage that would soon destroy him.

Chapter 34
Guatemalan Discovery

Patrick's new employer was a highly respected archeologist. Jacob Horowitz's life was archeology. As a child he found a flint axe head and his obsession for everything old and hidden began. He loved and was inspired by the story of German archeologist Heinrich Schliemann who believed in the truth behind what the world thought was a myth and eventually found the ancient city of Troy. Horowitz's passion was discovering the hidden past and connecting the stories of ancient peoples to the present time. For him, history was not dead but very much alive and full of surprises.

He literally knew about every significant archeological find. The rich heritage and archeology of Central America was his Troy and armed with legends, subtle clues and satellite images, he had found his purpose in life in the search for early Mayan and pre-Columbian history. He often said that many ancient people had more wisdom, insight, and creativity than modern people do with all their computers and technology because they knew how to use their brains. Horowitz's family was his students and colleagues. The significant others in his life were victims of his passion for his work. He sat transfixed to the data on his laptop computer, oblivious that he was flying over the Caribbean.

Patrick was taking a nap in the window seat after reviewing his notes for their expedition to Guatemala. This was his third trip and each time they found a trove of fascinating data and artifacts. Patrick's primary job was to catalog, photograph and draw the findings. He was doing considerable drawing since a lot of the weather-worn details were difficult to record on a photograph. With an agreement with the Guatemalan government, selected objects were taken back to Horowitz's lab and studied in detail and later returned or otherwise shared with interested researchers and institutions. For Patrick's efforts he got a decent stipend and was a co-author on several publications that Horowitz was writing.

The flight attendant came by with refreshments and Patrick awoke and Horowitz put up his computer. Both of them were ready to be at their destination. Horowitz was anxious to move to the dig site as soon as possible and they both agreed to grab some provisions and eat on the way. They reviewed their plans and Horowitz went into his lecture mode. He was always lecturing and always teaching. On their first trip he briefly digressed from his plans and took Patrick to Tikal. Patrick was overwhelmed by the panorama of impressive Mayan ruins of over four thousand structures in the humid tropical forest. He was told that over two hundred thousand people had lived in the area in classical Mayan times and they had a wonderfully rich culture by anyone's standards. He was amazed that there were scores of sites in the surrounding Petén area, some partially excavated and others not at all. It was a newly discovered site that held the interest of his mentor.

"The world of the Maya extended over Guatemala as well as Belize, Mexico, Honduras and El Salvador. The Mayans believed their society to be as stable and permanent as we believe ours is today. Egocentrism is not based in truth or fact. All societies are impermanent. Everything changes and societies must undergo change and evolve or they are all doomed to extinction. Consider the great empires of the world, the Assyrians, the ancient Chinese, and the Romans, to name only a few; they are all gone. We think we are unique and will endure forever. Not so. It is not all about power and might. Exploding populations and diminishing resources is a disaster waiting to happen and certainly one facing us today. Climate can and will change, new diseases appear, volcanoes and earthquakes wreak havoc, and who knows when a big chunk of rock may fall out of the sky." Patrick was totally engrossed in what Horowitz was telling him. His mentor had developed a wonderful and very logical perspective on human history.

"There is another aspect that I find particularly interesting. That is when an indigenous culture that has been stable for many years encounters a technologically superior race. Think about the Spanish destruction of the Aztecs; the Native Americans that were wiped out by the European white men moving west, and our ancestors, the more mobile and skillful Cro-Magnon peoples who out-competed the Neanderthals for resources.

"In almost every situation in which native peoples encounter advanced races, the old culture is wiped out or assimilated and drastically changed. These once noble peoples become a remnant of the past. Their stories and what ultimately happened to them are in the ruins and the artifacts we are looking for. It is like being a time traveler going back into history and finding the truth of what happened. The truth is often not what we think it should be."

Horowitz continued to talk without interruption about his excavations at the current site, K3, which was proving to be very rich in high quality limestone panels with intricate carvings. This was particularly good since most of the Mayan limestone structures were soft, porous and crumbled relatively easily. The site was remote and well hidden, and had not been looted. Unfortunately, there is a considerably lucrative black market for high quality Mayan artifacts. He once again related to Patrick, perhaps for the third time, his involvement with the hunt for the mysterious Mayan location called Site Q that was first known through pilfered artifacts. After forty-five years he believed this famous 'snake head' site had finally been established to be at La Corona. Horowitz was obviously quite proud of this finding. As usual, Patrick said very little, but took copious notes like a good student.

The plane finally touched down, they cleared customs and soon saw their driver and guide, Rafael Rodriguez, happily waving to them. The Jeep, already filled with ample supplies, was ready and they headed off on their journey. They were on the main road for nearly two hours then turned onto a poorly paved secondary road for what seemed to Patrick to be an eternity.

Horowitz had put a great deal of trust in Rafael after working with him for many years on various projects. Rafael had been working at clearing vines and brush from the site and had taken a series of photographs that they were trying to study as the Jeep heaved and swerved down the road. After making several more turns, Patrick was completely lost and could not see any road at all. Rafael, smiling as always, quickly forged ahead on a pathway that was only in his mind. Suddenly there was a clearing and Rafael announced that they would now walk. They packed up their gear and supplies and hiked along a barely discernable trail for about three hundred yards when they came upon a looming pyramid with a small temple sitting atop. There was a paved courtyard, some terraced structures, and a large platform. Most of it was covered by foliage and the platform was cracked and a number of blocks of limestone had fallen away, possibly from earthquakes. However, the site was remarkably intact and the stonework was exquisite.

Nightfall was rapidly approaching, so they hiked back to the clearing and set up camp. Patrick and Rafael did most of the work while Horowitz studied the photos and planned the next day's activities. The morning would be spent reconnoitering the area. Rafael had several things to show them that he had uncovered recently. Horowitz wanted to dig a trench but couldn't decide where to dig. Patrick hadn't planned on digging in the jungle heat and he hoped they would stay occupied with other things.

On the following morning they awoke to the sounds and smells of Rafael cooking breakfast. "I cooked a lot. It will be very hard work today and you will need it." Rafael smiled as he held up a pile of sausage, eggs, chilis and tortillas.

Horowitz was still agonizing over where to dig his trench. "Maybe we should dig two trenches, one at the platform and another at the pyramid."

Patrick moaned under his breath at the prospect of all that digging since they had no other help at that point. The temperature continued to rise as the sun peeked through the canopy of trees and the humidity was stifling.

"Why don't we wait until we have finished our survey before we decide on digging? There is plenty to see and document without digging for it," Patrick almost pleaded.

"We will take it a step at a time. There is a lot to do," Horowitz relented.

The forest was alive with the sounds of birds and monkeys as they returned to the site. They climbed to the top of the pyramid that extended just beyond the tops of the trees. Dense jungle was present in all directions. Several other brush-covered mounds could be seen, suggesting that structures were hidden beneath. A vine-covered mound was about half a mile to the west and it was not unreasonable to think that another pyramid was hidden there. The area was obviously a bustling city with thousands of people in the past. Multiple photographs were taken, and Patrick drew a rough topography map as Rafael and Horowitz looked into the small temple at the top.

As they descended from the dizzying top of the steep pyramid, Rafael became excited.

"I must show you something I found last week! The sunlight is in a good place now. There, beside the pyramid is a wall and courtyard with remarkable carvings. Hurry, we must see it now."

Rafael was right. The sun was at just the right angle to the wall to shadow the intricate carvings and put them into relief. As they approached, it was difficult to get a good view at first then they were right upon it. The intricate detail was unlike anything they had ever seen at any Mayan site. The craftsmanship was superb. Horowitz knew that the discovery of this place would make him famous. They backed up slowly to take in the entire scene that stretched out before them. It appeared to be a religious ceremony. Gifts had been placed and hundreds of people were reverently bowing to the figure in the center. Above the figure were depictions of the sun, moon and stars. Patrick stared in disbelief. The figure, whose left hand was extended as if in a blessing and whose right hand was lifted to the sky, looked for the entire world like John Asterman.

Chapter 35
What's Missing?

The ten days in Guatemala had been agonizing in many ways, but for Patrick it was very rewarding work. Thousands of photographs and measurements were taken and an incredible array of artifacts was discovered with very little digging. Horowitz finally got his trench dug after changing his mind more than several times. He said that it all came down to a hunch and a great hunch it was because in the end, about four feet underground, was a decorated slab that everyone believed was the top of a tomb.

With time running out and no help, the decision was made to cover and camouflage the trench to protect the discovery until Horowitz could return with more help. Patrick had catalogued several boxes of unique specimens to be carried back to the laboratory in New York. Everyone knew that their activity in the area would raise some suspicion and the site would have to be secured. Horowitz hoped he could get help from the university and the Guatemalan government to help secure the area before looters found out about the site. This apparently undisturbed area was a great find that couldn't be hidden forever and Patrick realized the importance of moving ahead quickly before anything was lost.

Patrick had hoped to sleep on the plane returning home, but Horowitz would give him no rest. They reviewed hundreds of photographs and planned in detail what they would do on the next trip, a trip that had to occur very soon.

Once Patrick was back in New York, he called Zoë but only got her answering machine. He was longing to see her and being away for nearly two weeks had been more difficult than he could have imagined. The university had sent a large van and Patrick loaded all the equipment and the precious artifacts, notes and journals and took them to Horowitz's laboratory and began the unloading process. The photography laboratory technicians nearly died when he was flooded with all the film and digital images they had taken. Horowitz was already starting to look at the specimens. Patrick, who was totally exhausted, could not understand how the man could work so relentlessly day after day.

"Professor Horowitz, I desperately need to go home and get some rest. I am just wiped out. I'm not thinking clearly and don't want to screw up anything."

"Go! Go! Get out of here. I need you tomorrow. Get here by eight," Horowitz said without looking up. He was totally engrossed in a small, carved statue. "Look at the detail. This is just amazing. Incredible!"

"Thanks! I'll get here as soon as I can."

Horowitz waved him out of the room and continued his work. Patrick's head was pounding and his body exhausted. He was hungry but too tired to eat. The only thing he wanted to do was sleep.

"Oh shit, I hope it will start," Patrick said as he saw his old dust-covered Volkswagen in the parking lot.

Reluctantly, his car finally started and he made his way home while struggling to keep awake. It seemed as if he had been gone for months and his house was a welcome sight because he knew he would soon be in his own comfortable bed.

As he touched his key to the lock, he noticed that the door was ever so slightly open. The heavy door was always stuck a bit, but he remembered securing it before he left. Maybe his old roommate had come by, but it would have been strange for him to leave the door standing open. Patrick pushed the door open, entered the house and stopped in his tracks, looking aghast at the scene. Everything was ransacked and in shambles. The cabinets were emptied onto the floor and his books and pictures strewn down the hallway. Every drawer was emptied and most of the furniture overturned. Even the mattresses were off the bed.

"Damn, I've been robbed," Patrick said aloud, now very much awake. "I've got to call the police."

Two police officers came very quickly and Patrick showed them the scene. One of the officers took Patrick outside while the other looked around the house. Patrick explained that he had been out of town for several weeks and had just returned to find that he had been robbed. The officer questioned him at length as he took notes.

"Have you had any problems with robberies or vandalism in the past?" the oldest officer asked him.

"No. It is a very quiet neighborhood for the most part."

"Do you have any idea who might have done this?"

"No. I would assume it is someone from outside the neighborhood."

"What did you find missing?"

"Well, I haven't really looked around to see. Everything is torn up. I guess they were looking for money or something."

"Anything valuable in the house?"

"Not really. I'm just a student and don't have very much. My books, CDs, stereo, and camera are probably the most valuable things I have."

"Any money?"

"I usually keep thirty or forty dollars tucked away in my desk in case I run out."

"Drugs?"

"Drugs?"

"Yea, drugs. Do you have drugs in the house? Marijuana, meth, coke, or that sort of thing."

"Oh, no. No drugs."

"Is there anyone with any issues with you? You know, like a score to settle. Maybe some gambling debts? That sort of thing."

"No. I can't think of anyone who might be upset with me, and I don't owe anybody anything except for my student loans."

After a few minutes the second officer came out and began questioning Patrick.

"Have you touched anything since you got here?"

"No. I haven't touched a thing. I just came in and looked around and phoned you guys."

"So, you touched the doorknob and the telephone? Anything else?"

"Uh, no."

"Who knew you were away?"

"My friends and the neighbors next door. That's all."

"Do your friends play practical jokes?"

"No. Why do you ask?"

"Let's go inside a minute and look around."

Patrick and the two policemen went back into the house and walked through each room looking at the mess. His bedroom was hardly recognizable with his mattresses askew and his desk overturned with the drawers dumped on the floor. Patrick's eyes searched the room and there on the floor were his calculator, pens and pencils, two twenty-dollar bills and his father's gold retirement watch.

"Does this seem unusual to you?" the officer asked him.

"I'll say! The only thing of any value that I have is lying right there on the floor. They didn't take anything, so they must either have been vandals or were looking for something."

"Looking for something? What might they have been looking for?"

"I have no idea."

"Are you sure nothing is missing?"

"I don't think so but look at this mess. I am so tired right now my brain won't work. I've been awake for nearly two days and feel like I'm dreaming."

"Well, check things again as you clean up and let us know if you find anything missing. Here is my card. By the way, it looks like the front door lock was picked. You should probably change your locks. A dead bolt is a good investment."

"Thanks. I'll do that."

The officers went out to the squad car and sat there filling out the report.

"What do you think?" the younger officer asked his partner.

"He seems to be straight but somebody sure as hell was looking for something that they thought he had. I wonder if they found it."

"I am very curious what they were after but we may never know."

Inside, Patrick put the mattress back on the bed, pulled the covers up and fell into a deep dreamless sleep. The following day as he cleaned up the rummaged house, he found his personal diary was the only thing missing.

Chapter 36
Memories of Who I Am

Zoë had planned to go to into the city, meet some old friends from college and maybe take in a play, or at least that was her initial intention. As it came time to make a decision to call her friends, she found her mind thinking about Asterman and once again, she was drawn to take the road up the Hudson River Valley. As always, she enjoyed the drive and the beautiful scenery. The journey up the valley was always spectacular and it was difficult to believe that such a serene beauty lies just north of the constant hum of New York City. Zoë could feel the tensions of the day slip away as she drove farther into the countryside.

Today the bright sun was warm and the air was cold and crisp, and there were early signs of spring coming. Dots of pale yellow-green on the barren trees and the sprouting green leaves on the forest floor heralded the end of winter. She had been overwhelmed by her clinical rotations and studies and desperately needed a break. Patrick was off on another trip to South America and the rest of the B&B was on call. The group had not gotten together in ages, but that would have to wait. She had to see John Asterman again.

Her sleep had again been troubled for nearly a week. Her recurring nightmare vision had stopped, but now, almost nightly, she would awaken with Asterman's enigmatic face and piercing eyes emblazoned on her mind. It was as if Asterman was trying to tell her something, but she could not understand his message. Also, what did the results of the genetic testing mean? Is he just some poor soul riddled with genetic defects, or could he somehow be something else, very special and utterly different from us? It just didn't make sense.

Zoë was proud of her life's journey and that she had been able to fulfill most of her goals, maintaining her health, and enjoying great satisfaction with her work. She knew that this had been accomplished by her hand and not providence. She wanted to believe, to have faith, to know that God was guiding her path and would take care of her. She wanted to believe that things worked out for the best because of some grand plan, but she could not force herself to accept this.

The ultimate reason, of course, was the anguishing death of her mother. Zoë remembered her mother as her best friend and confidante who died much too soon. She was a beautiful flower that quickly withered and died. Cancer, that horrible disease, sapped her life away. Zoë had prayed night and day for a miracle of healing, for a cure of body and spirit. She had known with all her heart that if she totally believed and trusted in God, her mother would be made whole and live. Not only did her mother not live, but her death was slow and agonizing. She fought to stay alive, refusing medicines that would cloud her mind until her last breath. Zoë was there. She cried tortured sobs into the depths of her soul, knowing that God had not only denied her prayer, but had abandoned her. Doubts crept into her mind and she blamed herself for failing to be good enough to merit God's favor. What had she done wrong? How could she fail her mother?

The counseling went on for over a year and it helped her deal with the pain, but the pain would not go away. She still remembered her mother's priest repeatedly saying that it was God's will. God's will! Damn! How could God, who is supposed to be loving, be so cruel? Zoë began to think of God much like her father: aloof, insensitive, and uncaring. She believed that God, like her father was lost in his work, which was his only purpose. If there was anything good that was going to happen in her life, Zoë would have to make it happen. She found herself driven to set high goals and standards for herself and not trust anyone to do something for her. She believed that good things would come to her only because she would work hard and make it happen. To her, God was out there somewhere doing his creating thing and deciding who would live and who would die, but Zoë would take care of herself. Maybe Deirdre was right. These things that happen are just coincidence.

"I'm not going to be hurt like that again," she whispered.

184

She saw a rest stop and decided to pull over. She got out, drank some bottled water and gazed out over the valley.

"This is great! I just love this place," she said aloud as she smiled. Watching the slowly flowing river seemed to wash away some of the pain of her memories. She took another sip of water, stretched her legs and got back into the car.

Back on the road her mind was about the future, her upcoming residency and Patrick. Patrick! Now he was always in the back of her mind. Why was she infatuated with this medical school dropout, jack of all trades guy who never finishes anything? He was a perpetual student: lazy, goofy, immature, intelligent, fun, adorable, and yes, good in bed. She thought how her life would be with him and shook her head. He was just not the lifetime love she had dreamed of. She thought she needed someone more stable and committed, someone with a purpose, someone who fits her idea of a good husband.

"I'll find the right person," she whispered.

The exit to Hampton Oaks came into view. She didn't know how but she was determined to get some answers and maybe there would be something, even the smallest detail, that would help her to understand. Now that Asterman was improved, he would surely be able to communicate better with her and allow her some closure. She would simply tell him what she knew and just ask him the hard questions. She had to know.

As many times as she had come through the large front door and proceeded down the hallway, it was always deserted and like a surreal visit to a previous time. As she entered the new section, she was again back in the present. There is where the people were, walking and talking and ignoring the past. As she rounded the corner she bumped into Annie Bellington.

"Zoë, it is so great to see you! How have you been?"

"Hi, Annie. It is good to see you too. I got the weekend off and thought I would stop by. Is Dr Adams or Frieda Harrison around? I never got to meet Dr Morris. I would like to see him if he's available," Zoë asked, hoping she could talk to them.

"I am sorry, but they are all off today since it is the weekend. I know they will be sorry they missed you. Usually someone is here on Saturday morning but not today."

"That's too bad. I hate to have missed them. I never really considered that they might not be here, but I should have called ahead. So anyway, I will be moving to Boston for residency soon and it may be a long time before I get back again. Annie, I feel so much attached to this place and just had to come back. I really do miss it and all the great people here too."

"Well, congratulations on your residency, Zoë. We are very proud of you! I just knew you'd get a great residency. You know, you will always be a member of our family. Boston is where you wanted to go, wasn't it?"

"Yes, it was my first choice. Dr Adams said that I would never get into the program and I did want to tell him face-to-face that I made it. You know, kind of rub it in. Not that he would really care but it would've been nice to see him smirk."

"Zoë, I've got to tell you this, but I think Dr Adams really would care and wouldn't smirk. You would not believe Dr Adams if you saw him today. I mean he certainly looks the same, but he has changed from being the biggest asshole I've ever known to a wonderful, warm and decent human being. I thought it was just an act at first, but he really has had a change of heart. I guess he saw the light and decided it was a lot easier to be a good person rather than a jerk. I can't believe I'm telling you this. None of us have really recovered from the shock. Frieda Harrison has gone ape over him and you know, she is as tough as nails. But everything is a lot better around here. He is a completely different person and patients, that I never thought would make it, are thriving."

"Well, I find that very hard to believe. Did he get religion or have a stroke or something?" Zoë asked with a scowl, being completely unimpressed.

"Zoë, be kind. I don't know what has happened to him, but we love the person he has become. I think there is hope for everybody," Annie said with a big smile.

"Well, I don't know what to say, but thanks for the great news. I certainly wish him well. I really had a great rotation here despite that dreadful man. He must be on medication. I will definitely come back again to see all of you, but it may be a while. By the way, mind if I check in on Mr. Asterman? I think about him a lot. How is he doing?" Zoë asked, anxious to see him.

"Oh, honey, didn't you know? John Asterman died."

Chapter 37
Not the Person I Knew

Zoë drove down the winding road from Hampton Oaks and turned toward the village. Despite the bright sky and the sun's warm rays, she felt sad and deflated since her chance to unravel Asterman's mystery was now gone. If only she could have gotten more information from him when he was alive, she thought. Annie's account was straightforward, but she knew little about the medical details. Zoë had never turned up anything from his medical records when he was first admitted, except for the scrap of paper that confirmed an admission day. It was as if Asterman had never existed. Who was he? His genetic testing confirmed that he was human. He didn't appear to have any known genetic or endocrine disorder. Deirdre, Jenna and Erin had spent many days researching diseases or conditions he might possibly have and turned up nothing. They all agreed that an injury would not have caused him to have his unique, strange appearance.

After Zoë changed Asterman's feedings to the vegetable-based diet, he began showing dramatic improvement. It appeared that his meat-based nutritional supplement was poisoning him as she and Rachel Devane had surmised. With the vegetarian diet he improved daily and by the time Zoë had finished her term at Hampton Oaks, he was turning his head, moving his extremities, and becoming more responsive. She had made Jack Adams promise to continue the vegetarian feedings on the day she left for the city. She wondered what he had really done and even thought that Jack may have deliberately killed him. Maybe that was what Jack was so happy about.

Asterman's condition continued to improve for about another month and he was even beginning to make some raspy whispering sounds as if trying to talk. Annie said that the nurses told her they had never seen such a miraculous improvement in someone who looked so near to death only several months before. When everyone thought that he might make a full recovery, he suddenly became agitated and within a day, had worsened and became drawn up into the fetal position. Within a few hours he stopped breathing. The nurses attempted resuscitation but to no avail and then he was gone.

No one seemed to know what had caused his demise and Zoë's hopes for an autopsy were dashed when she learned that he had been cremated shortly after his death. Rachel Devane would not permit a funeral, but she sent a small vase of flowers and a note to the staff thanking them for their care of him. Zoë knew that there had to be more answers and there was one more place she must go before returning home.

Annie also mentioned that shortly after Asterman's death, a strange man in a dark suit came by specifically to see Asterman and was quite interested and almost pleased in knowing that he had died. He wanted a copy of the death certificate and she wouldn't give it to him until he flashed some kind of badge at her. His name was Pratt, I think, and he was from some government agency I never heard of. He looked at Asterman's records and said, "Well, how about that." He then thanked her and left.

Annie then said something to Zoë that was very disquieting to her. This suspicious man was trying to find out Zoë's name and address, but Annie didn't trust him and denied any information about her. She told him that her job did not have anything to do with the medical student rotations and did not personally know any of them who came through Hampton Oaks. Zoë asked Annie if she knew anything else about the man or why he wanted her information and said she noted that he was just checking some leads.

As Zoë meandered her way through the village then up the hill to Rachel Devane's beautiful, old Victorian house, she contemplated all of her experiences here and considered what she would say to Rachel. Surely, she knew of his death and probably a lot more about him that she had not revealed to her. She remained fixed to her car seat for a moment as her mind teemed with so many unanswered questions. Who was John Asterman and what was the real connection with Rachel? What actually happened thirty years ago and why wouldn't Rachel give her more information? Zoë wanted the truth and she intended to be steadfast and blunt with her to get some true and honest answers.

"I will not leave until I find out what this is all about," she asserted loudly as if she were talking to someone.

Taking a deep breath and rallying her determination, she got out of the car and strode toward the front porch. As she approached, she began to hear people talking beyond the garden gate toward the right side of the house. Pausing at the front door, she decided not to ring the bell but go where she heard the voices. Walking around the corner she came to a vine-covered iron gate. She distinctly heard someone say: "I think our visitor is here." Unable to see beyond the vines and bushes, Zoë slowly opened the creaking gate and proceeded into a lovely, well-manicured garden that was in early spring bloom. The air had warmed considerably since the morning. There were numerous plants, shrubs, a small pool with a fountain, and a rock garden. The scene was breathtakingly beautiful and Rachel Devane was standing near some hanging baskets in an arbor in the back. To Zoë's overwhelming surprise, Jack Adams greeted her with a warm smile, a gentle hug and a kiss on the cheek. Zoë was completely caught off guard and unable to speak or react. She simply stood there and looked at him in amazement.

"I am so glad you came. We have been expecting you," Jack said with a warm and friendly voice.

Yes, this was the same man who only months ago reviled everything and everyone and seemed to have total disdain for her. She could not believe what she was seeing and her mind reeled in disbelief. Was this some kind of fake, engendering façade, and who on earth knew that she was coming?

"Dr Adams, you were expecting me?" Zoë asked skeptically.

"Sure, Rachel and I were just talking about you. We knew how much you like it here and suspected you might come by sometime. It is so good to see you," Jack replied with a broad ingratiating smile that Zoë had never seen before. She could not imagine such a smile on Jack Adams's face.

Zoë just nodded, not knowing what to say but was unable to return his smile. Her negative thoughts and memories of him filled her mind.

"Yes, welcome, child. I am so glad to see you again," Rachel Devane said, taking Zoë's hands in hers and then kissing her on the cheek. "You look so lovely today. You are a beautiful person and today your true beauty really shines through. Look at her, Jack."

"Yes, she is truly beautiful in every way," Jack concurred.

"Thank you," Zoë hesitantly replied, not knowing how to deal with such compliments.

Rachel smiled and said: "I know you are hungry. I will go get us some tea and a bite to eat. Please enjoy the garden. We must talk when I return. It shouldn't be long."

"Zoë, come take a walk with me," Jack said as he gently took her by the hand.

Zoë now was completely confused and her mind conflicted, knowing what she knew about Jack Adams from last fall and the Jack Adams she was seeing today. She even wondered if he was the same person. His hand was soft and warm and there was a remarkable sense of caring about him in both his manner and speech. His previously scowling face showed almost no lines and had softened to the point that his countenance was almost angelic. He had bright, clear eyes and a captivating little smile on his face as he talked to her.

"I know you have a lot of questions but don't think about them now and just listen with your heart. Your heart will never betray you. This is very important so please give us some of your time. Here, let me show you the garden. It is beyond beautiful here and will only become more wonderful as the season progresses."

The garden was coming alive with early spring flowers and new pastel light green leaves and shoots. Jack was completely enraptured with the enchanting, tranquil scene. Everything he pointed out to Zoë, was as if it was the first time ever he had seen anything like that. Within Zoë's thoughts, she remembered her childhood and the beauty of a spring day that seemed so new. Jack was playful and seemed filled with sheer delight, almost like a young child.

"Come over here and look at these crocuses and daffodils peeking up through the soil. I have not seen anything so wonderful as the new life and beauty of this precious planet."

"What an incredibly beautiful garden this is," Zoë replied, getting caught up in his enthusiasm. "Blue sky, fresh air, beautiful trees and flowers. It is great to be alive."

Jack stopped and looked into Zoë's eyes. "Yes, it is. It certainly is good to be alive," he said slowly and emphatically.

Zoë had been with Jack many times and always sensed bitterness and anger. In her mind she had decided that he was an evil person. She looked at him now and wondered how he could have possibly changed into such a pleasant person. She sensed profound joy and gratitude in him. It was as if everything he saw or touched was being experienced at a profoundly basic and deep level. She saw him smile and laugh and expected that he might squeal with delight when he spied two birds building a nest. Zoë knew this transformation was nothing short of miraculous as she tried to cope with this new paradigm of Jack Adams. She found herself thinking of John Asterman as they walked because she remembered the caring, delight, and wonder of being in his presence. Earlier she had mourned his passage and now she was thankful that she had been a part of his life. Strangely, he still seemed very close to her.

Jack and Zoë walked through a large archway and she noticed an unusual mobile-like structure hanging from above. It looked like it might be made of acrylic or polished crystal and had a most unusual shape. As the sunlight shined on the slowly turning structure it emitted a rainbow of dazzling colors that produced a changing pattern of light on the walkway below. The light patterns reminded Zoë of the geometric fractal-like paintings that she had seen in the house when she first visited Rachel. Jack and Zoë stopped and gazed at the scene of changing images. There was something almost hypnotic about the alluring patterns.

"It is a *Manus Deorum*," Jack said, anticipating Zoë's question. "It explains the universe. Watch it for a few more moments and you will understand."

As Zoë watched the single simple image repeated in unending complex changing patterns that merged to form an object then returned to the original image, she understood the meaning. The entire universe and everything that exists is a manifestation of only one thing.

"When everything is broken down into its smallest possible parts, there is only one thing; there is the face of God. We are all made of this aspect of God. God is within us and we are within God. God is the structure of the universe," Jack said.

Zoë was taken aback by this wonderfully spiritual and philosophic description that seemed to come from the creator himself. She was at a loss for words and struggled with her emotions.

"Everyone, please come," Rachel called as she brought out the tea and a platter of sandwiches and fruit.

"Cucumber sandwiches. I hope you like."

"Yes, I do," Zoë replied.

"Me too," Jack said with a wink.

They sat at a small table in a corner of the garden by the house and enjoyed the refreshments. The serenity of the garden and Rachel's warmth erased many of Zoë's concerns. They sat in a comfortable silence enjoying their meal, perfectly aware of the others' thoughts much like a couple married for many years who know each other so well they only have to nod and smile.

"We are so glad you came," Jack and Rachel said almost in unison and then both laughed.

After tea, Jack got up and walked across the garden to observe a pair of birds he had just spied. Again, he looked like a child, seeing something wonderful for the first time. A small white dog joined him and they both delighted in playing by throwing and retrieving a stick. The little dog was very happy running about the garden and chasing the birds. He ran over to Jack as he sat on a bench, put his little paws up on Jack's lap and licked his hands. Zoë thought that she heard him call the dog's name. Yes, she did. It was Webster, Macey's dog.

Rachel began, "Zoë, this is very important for you to understand. Everyone and everything throughout the universe is a part of the same Great Spirit, the same universal mind, the same oneness. We are all connected and are a part of the same spirit no matter where we are in space or time. We are rather interesting beings because we are entirely spiritual but are having a physical existence. This is the way we grow and evolve in that our complex and difficult physical lives are necessary for our spiritual growth. Always remember that your true nature is spirit."

"Okay," Zoë said with uncertainty as she wondered where the conversation was going.

"Years ago, most people considered themselves a part of the natural world and were also aware of their spiritual nature. This understanding has all but vanished in the modern world. We live only in the physical aspect of things and believe that the world and its resources and creatures are only for our use. We no longer see ourselves as part of nature. We have become greedy and greed has nearly devastated our world. Everything is about money and the accumulation of wealth. We do not see beyond our own lives and have made our physical existence completely separate from everything else. This is a delusion. Anything that we cannot see, touch or measure does not exist for us. I want you to know that we are not separate from each other. We are not separate from the earth and its beings or the universe and its beings. We are not separate from the creator, the source of all things. Do you understand what I'm saying?"

"I think so. My mother said something very similar to me when I was young."

Rachel stopped a moment, looked intently at Zoë and slowly said: "You are spirit temporarily living in a physical body. You have a beautiful physical body, but it will age like mine and will surely die and eventually become dust. However, your spirit is incredibly more beautiful than your body and you don't even know it. Your spirit has been around a long time and has made many journeys and has grown stronger and more beautiful. Your spirit will last forever. Look deeply into yourself when your mind is calm and you will begin to see your true nature. There is purpose and meaning to your being. We must allow the spirit to guide us."

Zoë thought a moment and replied: "I do have a difficult time thinking of myself as a spiritual being. I went to church with my mother and I was quite confused about things. All I remember was that I was going to Hell if I wasn't good. The people running my church were against everything and everybody that didn't think as they did."

"That is a problem with many religions. Somewhere they lost sight of the importance of being one with the Creator and our fellow beings and instead have focused on ideological differences that separate us from who we truly are. Differences are not tolerated and this becomes the basis for fear, hatred, bigotry, xenophobia, genocide and the misery that stems from this estrangement from goodness."

"Sometimes I just don't know what is right or wrong. It just seems like it depends upon which religious dogma you ascribe to or which culture you are born into or how society feels at any given time," Zoë said.

"Well, Zoë, good and evil are very real and I think it is fairly easy to make a judgment about any religion or philosophy that espouses hate over love, war over peace, injustice over justice, tyranny over freedom, greed over altruism, and bigotry over tolerance. It is important for you to know that you need to protect your soul, for evil can destroy it. It is the love in your heart that protects it. Without love, your soul is lost."

"I thought souls were supposed to live on forever," Zoë said, considering what Rachel had just said about lost souls.

"Yes, they are supposed to, but some do not. If enough hatred and malice fills a person, their soul will leave their body an empty shell."

"Will it die?" Zoë asked.

"Effectively, yes. It is taken back by the Source and never seen again."

"Are there soul-less people walking around?" Zoë was fascinated.

"Not for long."

"Now this is crazy. How does someone get a new soul?"

"Remember that you are a spiritual person with a temporary physical body. The person that you are is your soul. So, yes, a new spirit can reside in a body that has lost its soul. Souls are remarkable and they go where they need to go. This is the way we grow spiritually."

Rachel then turned and looked at Jack who was continuing to play with Webster and enjoying her garden. She nodded and smiled broadly at how happy he and the small dog were together.

Chapter 38
Transcending Fear

Zoë was resting peacefully after her long and eventful day, when suddenly, like a thief breaking into her house, the horrid dream began once again. I cannot let this happen, she told herself as her mind became fully awake, but yet her body was asleep. I will fight whatever it is and it will not overcome me again. The phantom dream proceeded and she was unable to stop it as fear streamed into her heart and mind, but she was determined not to be overcome this time. The darkness surrounded her and she became increasingly colder. It was as if her very life was being drawn from her helpless body. Not again! I won't let it happen! I will not die!

Then, a tiny, feeble light appeared in the distance and slowly grew brighter and she began feeling some warmth from its pale ember glow. Slowly, ever so slowly, the golden light approached as if she were far in space and the light became increasingly brighter. Quickly the darkness flew away like the rapid coming of a beautiful dawn as life returned to her and warmth and energy filled her body and enveloped her in brilliant light and energy and an unbounded sense of peace. A familiar, radiant, young man with eyes of love and understanding came to her, brandishing a delightful smile. He was familiar, like an old, treasured friend. As he bowed politely at the waist, he took Zoë's hand and kissed it, then embraced her and kissed her cheek. Zoë's eyes were moist with joyful tears and her heart filled with gratitude for his presence that ended her fear forever.

"Zoë, you can stand against the darkness. You can be the light in the darkness as you have seen my light come to you. You can fill the void and be a source of hope for everyone. Never doubt that you can change the world and the course of history for the benefit of all."

"I don't understand all of this. I'm just struggling to believe that I might have some purpose, some real goal in my life and that life is not meaningless. I am just a young, helpless girl and I'm afraid of the dark and being alone."

"You are not alone and you have never been alone. You think that you are meek and helpless, but you are strong and powerful. Just trust that the future will unfold for you as it should and follow your heart. Your heart will not lead you astray."

Having given her his message of hope, the magnificent glowing man smiled again, touched her gently and handed her a single red rose. Zoë desperately wanted him to remain with her. She wanted to ask him more questions but that time was not now. As he slowly disappeared from her view, she remained surrounded by the wonderful empowering light that he had brought to her. Now it was time for her to wake up. She willed herself to be awake and immediately opened her eyes to her bedroom that was dark and quiet. Her mind reeled from the experience as the room filled with a heavy smell of unseen roses. She was ecstatic and elated and her body tingled as she lay there smiling in the darkness of her room while her soul was filled with the brightest of lights. She began to know that a wonderfully good future was ahead for her.

Chapter 39
Patrick's Notebook

Steven Pratt's meager office did not reflect his years of service for the government. This was one of many offices he had had over twenty-eight years. All were windowless, austere and nondescript. On his desk was a photograph of his wife and two children. The photo was a window to the past and was over twenty years old. It had been a very long time since he had seen any of them. They used to wonder if he was still alive, but after not hearing from him for years, even if they were curious, they no longer cared. He was now consumed by his work, maybe obsessed is a better term, and nothing else mattered. He had no hobbies or outside interests and his only regular contacts were within his division and that was strictly business matters. He firmly believed that the security of the world was on his shoulders and there was nothing that would stand in his way of doing his job.

There were others within the secret hierarchy as well as in civilian groups that were in direct conflict with him, trying to achieve inroads into what he was trying to destroy. In the compartmentalized, secret world in which he lived, the right hand often did not know nor care what the left hand was doing. For him, his detractors were misguided and didn't understand the awful truth of the great menace threatening mankind that must be destroyed.

Pratt had worked his way up through the ranks of military intelligence. He sincerely believed that what was good for America was good for the world and he hated anything and anybody who was even remotely anti-American, including what an unbiased person would consider discontented, patriotic, American citizens. There was no gray zone for Pratt who saw everything in black or white. Orders were to be obeyed and no questions asked. The prime directive governed everything: Destroy the Menace. He did not understand feelings or compassion and for him, morality was a flexible concept of the mind. The government and the military did what was right for the country and this was an undisputed fact for him. His attitude did not go unnoticed by his superiors who considered him the perfect agent.

Pratt was tested early in his career by being informed that his best friend, with whom he had been working closely for two years, was giving military secrets to Soviet agents. Pratt was to follow the man, without being seen, to a restaurant where he would observe a package drop-off in the men's restroom. He was told that someone would then pick up the parcel. If the pick-up was observed by him, then he would have the proof of his treachery and Pratt must eliminate his friend. Pratt witnessed the exchange and happily, for God and country, killed the agent and eliminated the body without a trace. There are remarkable ways to make someone mysteriously disappear, to never be seen again. He had been trained well. No one, except his superiors, ever knew what had happened and their only concern was that the problem had been fixed. There was no remorse, only a sense of pride and dedication in doing what was right for his country.

Late one night early in his career, Pratt was awakened from sleep and escorted to the local military base where he was flown to a remote site. It was there that he saw something that shocked him to the core. There were three bodies lying on tables as if on display. Two were dead and the third badly wounded but moving. He was instructed to say nothing by a man in a black suit. He moved closer and saw that the bodies resembled human beings but were definitely not human.

"Look at them closely and remember them. They are our mortal enemies. The human race is in jeopardy because of their presence here. Some people want them here, even some in our government, but their presence must be eliminated at all costs. They must be destroyed as well as those traitors who work with them. This is your job, above all else."

The lecture was long and stern and filled with disdain for the small beings and what was viewed as their evil agenda. Their evil agenda was never specifically known to Pratt. In his job, no explanations were required or given and he was just to get the work done cleanly with no witnesses.

"They will take over our world unless we stop them now. You will track down every lead, find them, kill them, and leave no evidence behind. I think you know what to do here."

With that, Pratt pulled out his 9-millimeter pistol and shot the struggling creature in the head. This was his first, but not his last encounter with the beings.

Pratt's current assignment appeared to be straight- forward. He had obtained intelligence on the presumed EBE, alias John Asterman, and found out that he had died and had been cremated. But there was still more that Pratt wanted to learn about the situation. Too many people had contact with Asterman and it appeared that some knew the truth about him. The person who leaked the initial information had been taken care of. Now was the time to find out who else had knowledge of him and to what extent were they involved in his escape and protection. He had a lengthening list of people who needed to be eliminated.

Pratt placed a book on his desk and took out his notepad. The book had a flexible black cover and was filled with handwritten pages. On the inside cover was written: Patrick David, My Journal. Pratt slowly began reading every word and occasionally making notes about specific entries.

"Great day with Zoë. I never laughed so hard or had as much fun. I feel as if I've known her forever. She's so beautiful. I think I'm in love!"

"Medical school is such a drag. I'm so tired of memorizing things I will never use. I feel stifled. Everything is so dry. Do I really want to do this? I'm losing interest."

"Zoë hates me. She thinks I'm a complete looser for dropping out. Wouldn't even talk to me today and looked the other way. I am a *persona non grata* to all my friends."

"Got some delivery jobs and making a little money. Went to a game with Scott last night. At least he didn't give me any grief. He says everybody wants me to stay with the group. Right now, they are pissed but they will get over it."

"She wants to be friends. What the hell does that mean? I know she thinks I'm not good enough for her. I think it may be over for us."

"It was like old times today with Zoë. I have missed her so much. I still feel her disappointment in me."

"B&B meeting last night after the movie. Got trashed. Love those guys. Zoë spent the night — on the couch."

"Horowitz called with great offer to do research with him. It looks very good. I think I'll do it. Zoë might think I'm doing something useful for a change. I'll tell her this weekend."

"Great party with the B&B last night. I'm so glad I have them as friends. I told them about the Horowitz job. Zoë seemed pleased. I think she is warming up to me again. Maybe there is hope."

"Zoë has found a strange patient she is trying to figure out. Funny-looking sick guy. No one knows what's going on with him. She wants me to help find info about him. Another chance to get on her good side."

"I saw Zoë's mystery patient today. Wow, he is really weird. Did some drawings for her. I enjoyed doing it. I miss my art. She hasn't been able to find out very much about this guy. Wants me to look for news articles for 1983 about a fire or explosion he may have been injured in. That shouldn't be too difficult. Anything for Zoë."

"Things are getting interesting with Zoë's patient Asterman. This weekend she told the B&B about him and they are all getting in on the action to see what might be going on with this guy. Everyone seems to think he might have some kind of birth or genetic defect. Who knows? He might be an alien or something."

"I need some sleep. Between working for Horowitz and helping Zoë on her weird patient, I'm getting no rest. I found from the local paper that there was an explosion down by the river about the time Zoë's patient showed up at Hampton Oaks. I also found out that there were a lot of mysterious lights in the sky during that time. I wonder if there is a connection. I met an intriguing, young lady, Jen, who has seen the lights on several occasions."

"Got some leads at the fire station about who might have been around at the time of the '83 explosion. I'll make some calls tomorrow. This detective work is fun. I wish I had more time to dedicate to it."

"Horowitz has made a big finding in Guatemala. I began cataloging some of the artifacts today. They are unusually intricate and unique. This is turning into a great project. I'll have to put Zoë's work on hold for a while."

"I got a great lead on Zoë's alien. This guy Bagnold was a fireman who saw a downed saucer-like object and some bodies. He claims one ran away. Could this be Zoë's Martian?"

"Zoë talked to a woman who apparently took care of the weird patient and later put him in Hampton Oaks for care. She thinks they might have made him sick by putting meat in his diet. Zoë is a vegetarian after all. She is going to try him on a veggie diet. No one has come up with an explanation of whom or what this guy is. It is all very strange."

"It's odd but after talking to Jen at the café, I had some forgotten memories of my strange experience in Utah several years ago. I have the strangest feeling that I was somehow destined to meet Jen and that she would help me make sense of my experience. Also, she thinks the ETs will come back. She thinks that we are all somehow connected with each other in these experiences. I think she is right. Who knows when they will show up again?"

All the remaining entries were about Patrick pining to see Zoë and about his evolving project with Horowitz. In the back of the book, Pratt found a pencil drawing of John Asterman that was labeled: Zoë's Alien.

Steven Pratt flipped the journal closed and contemplated all he had read. There was no doubt in his mind that John Asterman was the extraterrestrial that had escaped from him in 1983. Also, Patrick, Zoë and many others were deeply involved with this EBE and knew too much. This Jen person appeared to be a contactee and was perhaps orchestrating something between these people and the EBEs. Something was going to happen there. More surveillance was necessary. All of this would have to be watched very carefully before he acted, but he would act and decisively too.

Chapter 40
Metamorphosis

Jack went to his office and found a stack of papers Frieda had left for him to sign. He sat quietly at his desk. Closing his eyes, he went into a meditative state for a few minutes. There was little for him to do today so he then reviewed all of the orientation information that was given to him on his first day there. Everything seemed both familiar and yet new. He leafed through all the books on his bookshelf and closely studied a book on health and spirituality that had been placed on his desk by a well-wisher the day before. He opened the curtain to allow the light to pierce into the darkened room. Jack smiled as he spied two of the residents sitting in rocking chairs on the garden patio and waving their hands and walking canes in a most animated conversation. Brilliant white cotton ball clouds dotted the azure sky and Jack believed that it was one of the most beautiful scenes he had ever beheld. He thought that the earth was truly a magnificent planet.

After a brief rap at the door, Barbara rushed into the room. She was apprehensive and filled with angst and desperation glared from her eyes. All the staff knew that Barbara was on the skids. She had gone from being a pleasant, hardworking, yet somewhat burdensome nurse to one who was depressed to the point of being morose and increasingly unreliable. At one time stylish, cute and petite, she now had the persona of a callous hooker desperate for money. Frieda had warned her to clean up her act and tried to get her into counseling and was planning to fire her.

"Jack, you've got to help me. You know I'll do anything for you," she said as she unbuttoned her blouse. "I've got to have a fix. I'm out of everything. I'll do anything, Jack. You've got to help me! I need it bad!"

She quickly came over to him, buried her face in his neck and put her hand between his legs.

Jack slowly took her hand away and put his arms around her, kissing her face, her eyes and her lips. Holding her away from him, he looked deeply into her eyes. His face was filled with kindness and compassion. She was shocked having never seen Jack this way and did not know what to say.

"Look at me, Barbara. I want you to relax and look at me. You have lost your way and it is time for you to get back on your path. The stress and anxiety you feel will go away. I want you to know that you are a good person and a beautiful person. The pain you have felt in your back is going away. You do not need to take drugs any more. Your need to take drugs is going away. You are going to find joy in your life every day from now on and you will find ways to cope with whatever life gives you because life is good and, Barbara, you too are good. You do not have to do anything that you do not want to do. You only need to make yourself happy. It is not anyone's responsibility but your own to make you happy."

Jack continued to talk with a soft, melodious, hypnotic voice that flowed into Barbara like the warmth of the sun. Her tense body relaxed. The taut lines of her face faded. The desperation in her eyes slowly disappeared. She felt tremendous love for Jack as she had felt for no other person. She felt that she had not only been forgiven for a life of pettiness and self- indulgence, but that she had been given another chance to live a meaningful life.

"When things are difficult, Barbara, I want you to remember what I have told you today and recreate the feeling you have in your mind right now and you will be all right. You can do it." Jack put his hands on the sides of her head, looked again into her eyes and kissed her softly. Buttoning her blouse, he touched her face and told her how pretty she was and that she should go.

"What has happened?" she asked in disbelief.

"Good things, very good things. Now you should go," Jack smiled.

Chapter 41
The Night Caller

Patrick lay in bed thinking about everything going on in his life. His detective work had kind of unnerved him. He had always taken life at face value and had not really considered the mysterious side. However, his life was becoming increasingly mysterious as if he were following a path not completely under his control. This feeling bothered him for he had always considered himself in charge of his life and responsible for the decisions he made. Was he not the captain of his ship and the master of his fate? Yet there seemed to be a flow of the current pushing him in a direction that he didn't understand and that he was resisting.

The phone rang and Patrick, thinking it was Zoë, answered saying: "Hey, Love."

On the other end of the line a familiar but unexpected voice said: "Hey, Love, yourself."

"I'm sorry; I thought you were someone else," Patrick said being completely embarrassed.

"So, you don't love me. I've heard that one before. Patrick, I'm sorry to be calling you so late. This is Jennifer Wells. I met you and Marcus Newell at Molly's Diner some time ago."

"Oh yes, I remember you. Thanks for the time you spent with me and for answering my crazy questions. Sorry, I wasn't expecting any calls tonight. You caught me off guard," Patrick said.

"I'm sorry. I usually don't call people at this hour, but I think this is very important so could you please bear with me?" Jennifer urged.

"Sure, I couldn't sleep anyway. What's up?"

"Remember when I told you about my last experience at my house with the lights?" Jennifer asked.

"Yes, that was when the room was glowing and you later saw that triangular thing outside," Patrick recalled.

"That's the time. Well, it happened again tonight and I just needed to talk to you — you above anyone else. It's about you," Jennifer said.

"Okay, what happened this time?" Patrick asked, somewhat concerned.

"Like before, I had fallen asleep on the couch and then the room filled with this glowing light and I heard the chant-like sound. It was just like it was before. My mind was clear. I was sensing incredible things and became aware of you. Not like you were there but rather like you were being discussed in very reverent tones. You are held in high regard and so is this person you love. Her name as Zoë, isn't it?"

"This is way too creepy. This really scares me. How could this possibly have anything to do with me or Zoë? What's this all about?" Patrick was dumbfounded.

"I am supposed to help you in any way I can. It is wonderful and exhilarating and there is so much love and hope. I know this doesn't make sense to you. It doesn't to me either. Patrick, they know about you and have plans for you and I think it is very good. Please don't worry about this. I think it is wonderful. Something remarkable is going to happen and I think we are going to see them again."

"Jennifer, you are shaking me up. I don't know what to say. Why would I be involved in this? Actually, I have been lying here in bed thinking about all these weird things tonight. You know, it's odd but ever since I met you, I keep remembering a strange encounter I had in the Utah desert several years ago. Everything you said somehow activated my memory of that event. I encountered someone or something and I don't know what it was. I think it was very important and I hope I will eventually remember it all."

"I think you will remember. These events are so unreal to us that we have to change our worldview for us to even recall what we have experienced and make sense of it. I just have a very good feeling about this and don't want you to worry. It's like everything is working out as it should. There's something else I need to tell you. Something else very unusual and actually kind of funny happened tonight." Jennifer hesitated.

"What's that?"

"I came away with the distinct impression that I need to buy a house. Well, it was really more than an impression; it was like I was expected to do it. Isn't that odd? Maybe they are into real estate. What do you think?" This gave them both a good laugh. "I'll let you go to sleep now. Keep in touch. Oh, is your girl's name really Zoë?"

"Uh, yeah. Damn, this is weird."

They said their goodbyes and Patrick hung up the phone, thinking that everything was getting stranger and stranger. Outside the house, a tiny black box, that was not there the previous day, was connected to the phone line and was so small and subtle that it would never be noticed.

Chapter 42
It's All in the Genes

Martine was due to arrive soon for a short visit. She had called two days previously and insisted on coming to see Zoë and Patrick this weekend at Zoë's house. Patrick was really overwhelmed with his work and it was only with Martine's persistent prodding that he finally agreed to the meeting. Martine was quite mysterious about why they must meet, but absolutely maintained they must talk in private. To add further mystery, she wanted to be certain that they would be alone and undisturbed for several hours. Patrick and Zoë both thought she wanted to talk to them about her research or a direction change in her career plans. Could she be engaged? Would they hear about wedding plans? Patrick said that she was too busy to have a love life and Zoë agreed.

Patrick knocked at the door and let himself in. He had brought his bag of notebooks in case he could get some work finished. He always enjoyed being with Zoë, but he hated being there distracted with a large backlog of work hanging over his head. He knew that Professor Horowitz would expect a report Monday morning and he must get that finished. Also, he let Zoë know about his stolen diary and was quite confused and concerned that someone would go to all that trouble just to come after his personal notes. It did not make any sense and it worried him immensely that he was targeted for the information in his diary.

"I just knew Martine wouldn't be here. She's always late," Patrick grumbled.

"It's good to see you too," Zoë said with a smile.

"I'm sorry, but this is just a bad weekend for me. I've become a slave to that damned job. I shouldn't have agreed to take it. Where is she?"

Zoë hugged him and gave him a big kiss.

"Just relax. Everything will work out for you. You are doing a great job and it will help you so much in the future. Just be patient. You don't have much longer. Martine will be here soon and we will get this meeting over. Let me massage your back. You're just too tense."

As Zoë worked the tightness out of his neck and shoulder muscles, she could feel him beginning to relax. She reassured him of the value of his work and that he shouldn't let it get to him.

"You normally have such a cool and calm demeanor; how did you get yourself into such a snit?"

"I feel fine as long as I just go with the flow. Anytime I have to do an important job, it actually frightens me and I get very uptight about it. I just know I'm going to blow it and I know that this is just my crazy perception, but it has always been a problem for me. I think that is why I backed out of medical school and probably a lot of other things. The sense of responsibility frightens me and I am just overwhelmed with it."

"Well, you know that you can do anything you set your mind to do. It really is an issue of mind over matter. You can learn to relax and take pleasant, safe and secure feelings with you no matter what you do. On my first pediatrics rotation, I saw four screaming children and hysterical mothers one after another for about three hours and I nearly freaked out. I had to actually leave the building to calm myself down. Later, one of my friends who was a dental student taught me a number of relaxation techniques that have helped me a lot. He used relaxation tapes that were a form of self-hypnosis so that I could program my mind to relax even when the situation was tense. It really does work and can take the stress out of most bad situations. I've got some of the tapes around here and I will get them for you to try. It will make a big difference if you just give it a chance."

"I think I would prefer getting a daily massage from you. That felt great and thanks so much. You are very good for me."

"A little massage can be arranged on occasions," Zoë said, giving him another hug.

A knock on the door announced Martine's arrival. She came in, hugged them both and put down a large stack of papers and notebooks.

Zoë got them some tea and they moved to the kitchen table where there was room to spread out Martine's bundle.

"Okay, I'm sorry for being so weird about this but I have a lot of important things to tell you and this is the only way I could do it. I certainly couldn't talk to you on the phone."

"You're getting married, aren't you?" Patrick interrupted.

"Hardly. Men are the last things I need in my life right now, although a good wife might be of some help! I would go for a good woman right now," Martine said in her best dramatic tone. "There is so much I need to say and I don't know where to begin, so I'll just start and please bear with me. As you know, we did a preliminary check on the DNA of this Asterman guy and found that he is without a doubt human. I nearly stopped at that point but did a few additional tests and found something phenomenal."

"Just get to the point; we don't need all the drama," Zoë said as she became more impatient.

"Well, this is dramatic and it has taken me a long time to figure out this puzzle and it will take me a while to explain it, so just cool your engines."

"What puzzle?" Patrick asked impatiently.

"Okay, just hear me out. Remember that I got blood samples from you guys and a bunch of other students to use as controls for the Alzheimer's studies? When I first looked at Asterman's DNA, I found some mutations in several genes that were unusual. Then I decided to analyze his DNA compared to a bunch of controls including DNA from you both. To make a very long story short, you are both related to this Asterman guy."

"What are you talking about? How could that possibly be true?" they both protested in unison.

"I don't know how that could be, but it is unequivocally true. I have rechecked the data multiple times. In fact, I ran the data against our whole registry and you are the only people he is related to."

Patrick and Zoë were stunned as they wracked their brains, trying to remember any strange relatives or family secrets that might account for a missing ancestor. Also, how could they both be related to Asterman and not be related themselves?

"So, are Zoë and I cousins or something? How could we both be related to Asterman? There is just no connection with our families," Patrick queried looking quite puzzled.

Martine assured them that their genetics were sufficiently different that they were not related to each other at least for the past half-million years. Martine could see that she had a lot of explaining to do and still didn't know if it would make any sense to them.

"I know that neither of you know much about genetics, so I need to give you a short course so we can all be on the same page."

"Fire away," Zoë entreated. "I've got to hear this."

"There are several ways of tracing a person's ancestry by looking at their DNA. All genes undergo mutations over long periods of time and multiple generations. These mutations usually make little or no difference in how the gene works but they are passed along from generation to generation and the only way they are detected is by genetic testing like I did in the lab. These mutations can be considered almost like fingerprints. For instance, if a woman claims a man is or is not the father of her child, a simple genetic test can compare the child's DNA with that of the candidate father and determine if he is truly the father. One half of the child's DNA is from his mother and half from his father, and each have unique and identifiable mutations that prove the relationship. This kind of testing is used all the time in paternity cases and DNA identity has become crucial in forensic medicine, enough so that people convicted of murder and rape have been freed when old evidence has been reevaluated with DNA analysis."

Patrick looked at Zoë and said: "She thinks we are really stupid. We've seen CSI on TV."

"Did I say I'm finished? There is a lot more. Certain genes mutate at a relatively predictable rate, as an example, say once every twenty thousand years. By knowing this, the number of genetic mutations can be used to date the actual age of some frozen animal in a glacier, or an ancient mummy, or to trace how far back in history two species have a common ancestor. This technique is used a lot in evolutionary biology. As an example, chimps, gorillas, orangutans, and human beings have a common ancestor and by using this technique, it is highly probable that our mutual ancestor lived two million years ago. Also, we have a common ancestor with Neanderthals that lived about half a million years ago. Another point I need to make, and this will be apparent to you in a minute, is that some genes can be specifically traced back to a male and some genes back to a female ancestor. In the case of the male, we look at genes in the Y-chromosome."

"That makes sense because only men have Y-chromosomes that are passed along to their sons. Well, they also have an X and a Y, but females have only two Xs. So, if you look at the Ys you know it's a male lineage, right?" Patrick interjected, being obviously proud of his logic.

"Definitely right. So, again for an example, using this technique, scientists have been able to establish that in central China, eight percent of men share the same Y chromosome that seems to be linked to Genghis Khan. Y is always from the male. There was also a study in Ireland that linked about twenty percent of the male population to a fifth-century warlord named Niall. Are you still with me?"

Zoë and Patrick nodded like two elementary school children.

"We can never know for certain if a gene from an X chromosome is from a male or female ancestor because both men and women have X chromosomes. But there is a special DNA in a cell that is always from the female and testing this DNA is the way to determine female genealogy. This test uses DNA from mitochondria extracted from cells. Mitochondria, the little energy powerhouses in our cells, are related to ancient bacteria that were acquired by primitive cells millions of years ago. This DNA is unique and it always comes from mom. The reason for this is obvious when you think about it. An egg has a nucleus that contains the DNA from the mother. It also has a lot of cytoplasm that contains mitochondria. A sperm is tiny compared to the egg. The head of the sperm contains the DNA from the father and no mitochondria or any other genetic material. It is basically all DNA with an oscillating tail that provides motility. If the sperm cells were larger, it would be very difficult for them to maneuver to the egg to fertilize it, so Mother Nature has streamlined the little swimmers."

"So, all the DNA in the mitochondria in my body came from my mother and none from my father?" Patrick asked.

"Right again. Therefore, if we want to look at the female lineage in your family, we analyze your mitochondrial DNA.

"Now you both need to look at this," Martine said, spreading out multiple sheets of raw DNA data. "I was going to scan all of these but I decided to bring the originals so you would see for yourself and there wouldn't be any questions about my veracity. First, this is a series of DNA analysis patterns from you two as well as some other control patients. The column on the left has some known gene markers that everyone has. As you can see, everyone has essentially the same genes but there are scattered mutations that make everyone's pattern unique."

"Is this mitochondrial DNA?" Zoë asked.

"No, this is just regular cellular DNA. Martine explained. "If we compare this to Asterman's DNA, there are a lot of similarities, but a number of his genes identically match both yours and Patrick's DNA." Martine then showed them multiple matching bands between their DNA profiles and Asterman's that clearly showed that they shared genetic material. "Now look at this one here that looks at Y chromosomes. Here is the Y chromosome analysis comparing Asterman and Patrick. Everyone stared at the image clearly marked with JA for John Asterman and PD for Patrick David. The chromosomes were identical at every major comparison point. There was a long silence as everyone considered the implications.

"I don't understand how this could be," Patrick almost stuttered.

"Let me finish. There is more to consider," Martine said seriously. "Here is the mitochondrial DNA analysis that looks at female lineage. The image was again marked with initials. Zoë saw JA for John Asterman and ZA for Zoë Abrams and the bands of gene patterns in question were again identical."

"Oh, my God. This doesn't make sense. Are you sure you did the tests correctly and used the right samples? There must be some mistake." Zoë was obviously shaken by the unequivocal evidence.

"Zoë, I have checked and double checked. Remember, you gave me two tubes of blood from Asterman and I got several blood samples from each of you last year? There is no question about the findings."

"I know the blood came from Asterman because I drew the samples and labeled them myself," Zoë said as she remembered drawing Asterman's blood as he watched her every move.

"There is something else I need to tell you and this is probably the strangest thing yet. You remember when I said that Asterman had some other unusual mutations when I first looked at the samples? Well, these are truly unique mutations and I have searched a number of databases around the world that are accessible online. These mutations have not been reported before." Martine then went off on a technical account of the genes, mutation frequencies and quickly lost both of them.

"Hey, hey. Come back to Earth. You have totally lost us. You will have to simplify things a lot for us to understand this technical talk," Patrick demanded.

"I'm sorry but I'm still trying to make sense of it myself. One of my mentors, Professor Johnson is my advisor and a real confidant. He is the neatest person, a Jesuit and geneticist. I sincerely believe he can be trusted and have talked to him about all kinds of personal and other issues. His integrity is impeccable and I am very comfortable with my relationship with him. I felt so overwhelmed by all of this and actually couldn't make myself believe it. He is someone I can trust to talk to about this data, someone who knows a lot more genetics than I will ever know. I know that we promised each other that we would not say anything to anyone, but I desperately needed help with this one so I swore him to secrecy and his promise is good as gold. I told him the whole story and all our theories about Asterman and was convinced that the DNA analysis would show that he had a genetic defect and that would be the end of it. I was frankly blown away and could not make sense of this because I didn't believe or want to believe what I was seeing."

"So, what did he say about it?" Patrick and Zoë demanded in unison.

"He has looked at the data and as crazy as this all sounds, he thinks that Asterman is a descendent of both of you. Not an ancestor, but a descendent. He is like your great, great, great, great, great… grandson."

Patrick and Zoë were speechless as they both realized at the same moment that John Asterman had to be an earthling from the future who had traveled back in time to see them, his ancestors. John Asterman, a descendent, a strange and unusual man, who evolved from them over many future generations. They looked at each other as they sat in silence with their minds swirling with questions and disbelief.

Martine had one last observation before she had to leave: "If we look at these new mutations, considering what we know about these particular genes and their mutation frequency, it is our best guess that Asterman is from eighty thousand years in the future."

Chapter 43
Patrick's Night Visitor

Martine's findings had rendered both Patrick and Zoë shaken to the core, to say the least. The implication of this finding was beyond mind-boggling and they each struggled to even discuss their vacillating feelings about the whole affair. Now that Asterman had died, they could not get their questions answered. They wondered if anyone else knew about this and for a while they couldn't decide if they should tell their friends in the B&B but eventually, they did tell them all the details with Martine's help. Their reactions were similar, with confusion and wondering to what purpose these things had happened. Why would Asterman come back to this time to meet them? Surely, he wasn't just on a travel adventure from another time period to see who his ancestors were. However, if they could believe Rachel Devane, there was a purpose in all of this yet to be determined.

The week had been exceptionally long for Patrick and once again he was near exhaustion as he readied himself for bed. The night was chillier than usual for April and the wind whistled outside his window heralding the approaching rain. He thought about Zoë and wished she were back with him. He would call her but knew that she was very busy taking medical calls on one of her final clinical rotations and probably didn't have time for him. He found himself yearning for their weekend together in two weeks. He thought about what Martine had reported about the DNA studies and realized that he and Zoë would one day have children, but he couldn't think about it now. All he wanted to do was sleep.

Patrick set his clock for six a.m., pulled up the covers and quickly fell into a deep, renewing sleep. He slept soundlessly for several hours, then began to dream. He and Zoë were walking in the woods and came to a clearing that was filled with warmth and light. They were ecstatically happy and like happy young children, danced around in the soft green grass. She was beautiful with her flowing hair and gleamingly playful eyes. Patrick took her in his arms and kissed her deeply and wanted her with all his heart more than ever before. It was a wonderful, magical place with just the two of them when a persistent knocking, at first softly, then increasingly louder awoke him from his beautiful dream. Patrick was then wide awake with the pounding at his front door.

"Who the hell is that at this hour?" he muttered irritably as he glanced at the clock. It was three a.m. The continuous pounding became even louder and vexingly more persistent. He turned on his bedside light, got up and walked out into the hallway and down to the front door. Through the peephole, all he could see was the outline of a man with white hair. Thinking someone might be having a problem, Patrick unlatched the door, opened it and saw an elderly man dressed in a black raincoat standing there. His windblown white hair, wrinkled face and white mustache gave him a mad scientist appearance. He was smiling broadly as he abruptly pushed by Patrick, coming directly into the warm house. Patrick stood there with his mouth agape, not knowing what to say to the persistent stranger.

"Patrick David, I am delighted to meet you. You don't know me and let's just say I am a friend and leave it at that. I'm sorry to be so blunt and to barge in on you at this late hour, but it is crucially important that I talk to you now. Patrick, time is of the greatest importance and I must communicate to you some extremely important essential information right now," the old man said with an intense sense of urgency.

"Who are you and what do you want? I don't appreciate your barging in here in the middle of the night!" Patrick snapped in complete exasperation, pointing to the still open door demanding that he leave.

The man's eyes pleaded with Patrick and he sincerely begged him to stay. Patrick shivered as he became aware of the cold damp air pouring into his warm house through the open front door. He closed the door, grabbed a jacket off the coat hook and put it around his shoulders. The man walked past him and proceeded into the den and just stood there as Patrick followed him and clicked on the desk lamp. The man's face was kind and sincere and he gazed at Patrick with a look of genuine admiration. He wore a stylish older dark sweater, and trousers and a long black coat and muffler. He held his gloves and dripping black hat in his hand.

"What do you want?" Patrick implored him.

This was not a lost stranger or beggar and it didn't appear he needed shelter for the night. The man was most determined to talk to Patrick whatever it took to do so. He just stood there looking at him with a gleam in his eyes and his persistent smile. He remained absolutely silent as if savoring their encounter.

"Okay, you win. I'll talk to you if I have to. Sit. Please sit down," Patrick said as he pointed to a chair. "What do you want from me?"

The grandfatherly figure said nothing and motioned to the couch for Patrick to sit down as well. When Patrick finally acquiesced to his request, the visitor then sat in a chair opposite him and looked intently into his eyes. He spoke with profound authority and Patrick felt obligated to hear him. Despite his grandfatherly appearance, the man had a compelling demeanor and Patrick surmised that he usually had his way.

"You would not believe how many people have wanted to meet you and it is a great honor for me to talk to you now."

"I don't understand."

The old gentleman pursed his lips contemplating what he would say, looked up at the ceiling and took a deep breath. He began speaking as a father would speak to his son.

"I have to speak to you about your future and the future of mankind. It is very important that I talk to you and that you clearly understand what I tell you."

"Excuse me? The future of mankind?" Patrick was confused at this surreal, clandestine conversation.

"You hold the future of mankind."

Patrick now definitely felt dizzy and his mind was in a fog, as if he were still dreaming as he told him about aspects of his life no one should know. What is he talking about? Am I still dreaming? He keeps talking to me and telling me all about myself, everything I have done from where

219

I grew up and went to school, and my grades and all of my friends and even the details of what's important to me. He keeps talking and talking and everything he says is true. This elf of a man seems so familiar, yet I don't think I have ever seen him before. Is he one of the visiting professors I met at school or one of the patrons of the Anthropology Department? How can this strange night visitor know about me? It's like this character intimately knows me even more than my parents knew me as a child.

"There is not much time and I need for you to understand that you are a very special and uniquely important human being. You may think that you are just an average person, but you are truly remarkable in every respect. There is a mission that we are asking you to undertake, a unique mission for the entire future history of mankind."

"A unique mission?" Patrick asked, utterly confused.

"Indeed. I know that this is extremely difficult for you to understand because of your limited perspective living here at this place and time. It is all about perspective. Think about your neighborhood and your view of it from your house. If you were to stand on the spire of the church, you would have an altogether different view. Think about the view from the orbiting space satellites, the moon or Mars. What if you could see the past, the present and the future all at once?"

"That's impossible."

"Is it now? You have very parochial ideas. You are part of the stream of time and the stream exists without beginning or end. It twists and turns, is divided and rejoins, is impeded by things like rocks and dams but it is always a moving stream. It is your task to allow the stream to carry you where it will. It is the intent of billions of people who have never known you to have the stream to flow in a new direction."

"I don't understand your strange metaphors. I don't know what to say."

"You don't have the view from above. You are severely limited by your current worldview. The only thing you have to go on is faith, faith in yourself and faith in the future."

"You are asking me to have faith?"

"Yes, faith, pure and simple."

"What am I supposed to do?"

"Do you love Zoë?"

"I love her with all my heart."

"And she loves you."

"Well, I think she does. Sometimes I'm not sure."

"Remember, you must have faith."

"Faith!" Patrick said more emphatically, still not certain where all of this was going but willing to listen further to this enigmatic man.

"When two people are in love, what is the outcome?"

"Well, they live together and often get married."

"And?"

"They usually have children."

"You and Zoë will have a child, a very important child."

"Important?"

"The child will be important in ways that are now beyond your ability to understand."

"I don't know about children. I don't even have a regular job. I haven't even asked her to marry me."

"Remember, faith? You will ask her and she will accept and you will have a child. Doesn't this seem right and natural to you?"

"Well, yes, but I don't know if I'm ready to do that just now."

"Patrick, this is not just about you and Zoë, it is about the future. It is about the future of the human race. You have had a lot of uncertainty and indecision in your life, but think about your path. You have come this far having made the choices you made. Now is the time for another choice. It is your choice, not mine. I know that your choice to be with Zoë and having a child bodes well for the future. It is absolutely crucial for the future. This is because I have a perspective you lack. Life is full of choices and paths, some better than others. Your path with Zoë is most wonderful. However, timing is an important factor."

"What do you mean, timing?"

"There is an optimum time to plant a seed. Too soon and it might not sprout because of the cold. Too late and it might wither because of heat or lack of water. The time must be right."

"I still don't know what this means about having children."

"Not children, Patrick, a child, a single child. If you and Zoë are to have this wonderful child, the seed must be planted soon."

"Soon? What do you mean, soon? I don't think I'm ready for this."

"In the next three or four months."

Patrick's head swirled. He was confused. The man kept talking and talking. His voice was melodious but Patrick couldn't understand all the words. He talked about loving Zoë and how important this all was. He talked about a crucial change that had to be made for people to survive in the future. Patrick felt warm, comfortable and peaceful as his head filled with a gentle white light as the old fellow softly spoke. Light seemed to fill the room and his thoughts soared. The talking became a humming in his ears that got increasingly louder. It was as if he were melting into a vapor and then all was quiet. He heard Zoë's loving voice in his mind and felt a wonderful closeness to her.

Suddenly, Patrick bolted upright from his stupor. Was he dreaming? He had been asleep on the couch? The table lamp was on and the old man was gone. Had this strange meeting really happened or was it a strange dream? It had seemed so real but now he could hardly remember what transpired. He looked at the clock and it was 5.40 a.m. He opened the front door and looked out at the street. A light rain was falling and the street light reflected brightly off the wet pavement. There were no cars and not a soul to be seen. Patrick breathed deeply the cold, damp air. He felt wonderfully rested and refreshed and he realized that it had not been a dream.

Chapter 44
The Annunciation

Zoë awoke before dawn, took a shower, dressed and made tea. She sat on her couch drinking the fragrant warm liquid as she gazed out the window at the coming of the light. The glowing orange sun disk slowly emerged over the horizon and a gleaming beam of light fell on her face. She thought of the millions of miles the light had traveled as the gentle warmth increased on her forehead. As she had learned early in her life, she relaxed her body and focused on her slow, deep breathing and went into a deep meditative state.

The sunlight poured into her head like a warm river and permeated her body as she visualized the light traveling into her chest and abdomen and then out into her arms and legs. Finally, her hands and feet seemed to glow as every bit of darkness left her body and there followed a sense of profound peace and love. She knew with all her being that she was greater than her physical body and could sense the whole universe filled with wondrous life and incredible creation. She sensed the infinite mind within all things. From deep within herself she whispered a thank you to the universe. A feeling of pure transcendent joy overcame her and tears of rapturous delight streamed down her cheeks. She opened her eyes, dabbed them on her sleeve and smiled from the depths of her being. This morning was the most powerful meditation she had ever experienced and it left her feeling that she was deeply loved and at peace with herself and the universe. She whispered a prayer to the spirit she felt in all of creation. "Help me to do whatever I should do in my life's journey."

She sat quietly for a few moments, savoring her experience when someone knocked at the door. She was not expecting a visitor and wondered who it could be this early in the morning. She unbolted the door, pulled it open and was pleasantly surprised to see Rachel Devane.

"Ms. Devane, what a great surprise. Please come in. It's great to see you again. I didn't realize you knew where I lived."

Rachel's countenance and wonderful smile seemed angelic. As Zoë looked at her more closely, she actually appeared to glow, almost as if there was an aura around her. Zoë was delighted to see her and strangely had thought about seeing her just before her knock at the door. She had frequently thought about Rachel since their last fascinating encounter in her beautiful garden. There was a sense of presence around her as if this aged meek-looking person was filled with great inner strength.

"Zoë, I'm sorry to barge in on you so early this morning, but I have something very important to talk to you about. May I come in and chat with you for a while?"

"Mrs Devane, I am always delighted to see you and am so very pleased to have you come visit me. I don't have to leave for several hours and you're certainly welcome to spend some time with me. Would you care for some breakfast?"

"No, I don't care for anything to eat, but I would take a cup of tea if you don't mind. Please call me Rachel. Ms. Devane makes me sound very old."

"Well, I don't want to make you feel old so I will call you Rachel. There's some tea in the next room."

"Zoë, you are an astonishingly beautiful person and being with you makes my heart glad. You are such a delight, but more than this, you are wonderfully unique in ways that you do not understand. You may think yourself meek and small, but you are very powerful. The entire universe is enfolded into you and each of us. You may not understand this now, but you will in the future."

Zoë was pleased with her flattery and as was often the case, somewhat puzzled by her comments as she invited her into the room where she had been meditating. Sunlight filled every corner of the space and everything glowed in the deep yellow light of the morning sun. She invited Rachel to sit, but she remained standing directly in front of her and seemed to be glowing even more radiantly in the light. Rachel put out her hand and touched Zoë's face as she said:

"I have been sent to you by the light and by thousands of generations who revere you. You are the mother and the hope of humanity. Within you is the ability to change the course of human history. From now into the future, you are the mother of mankind, the Earth Mother who will be known to thousands of generations to come when human beings will no longer live on this planet."

Zoë was stunned. Am I dreaming this, she thought with her mouth agape. As she gazed upon Rachel, she now seemed transformed into a radiant, almost angelic younger-looking being than the matronly, aged woman she first knew from Devane House. Zoë nervously glanced around her room, breathing deeply and squeezing her hands together as she realized that this meeting and everything Rachel said was very real.

"How can this be?" Zoë stammered, not believing what she had heard and certainly not understanding it. Zoë tried to walk away, but Rachel held her hands firmly and looked squarely into her eyes.

"I know this is very difficult for you to understand. You are involved with your life and your work and cannot see beyond that, but you are also involved in much more. You are a key figure in the great drama of the human story. Thousands of generations know of you and revere you."

"I don't understand! What you are saying frightens me. I am just an average girl from an average family and there is nothing special about me."

"Despite your protests, this is just not true. Just now, I know you don't understand and so, in many respects, it is impossible for you to understand, but you must know that I am speaking the truth. There are things you must understand about you and Patrick. Some of this you have already discerned. You will have a wonderful son and ultimately his children and their children and their offspring will be the lone survivors of human beings into the future. A time will come and there will be a great disaster and few human beings will survive. This event will forever change the future of life on earth. It will happen and there is no way to prevent it."

"How can you possibly know these things?"

"You will know in time, but for now, remember I told you that you are a spiritual being in a physical body. Your spirit is not constrained by space or time as I have also told you. So when you were in deep meditation this morning and felt yourself in the immensity of creation, that was not just your imagination. You and the universe are one. You will come to know this."

"When will these things happen?"

"Not in your lifetime but soon afterwards."

"Will everyone really die except for some of my descendants?" Zoë gasped.

"Nearly everyone will perish except for a small group including your son's children. The great cities will fall and much of the land will be wasted. Much of technology and learning will be lost and mankind will have to begin anew."

"This is terrible. I can't believe what you are saying. How can this be allowed to happen? Can't the future be changed?"

"Some things can be changed and some cannot, but it is with great fear and trepidation that any attempt at change is made. It is only after thousands of years of study and an absolute consensus of necessity before any change is made that may affect the future. That is why I am here, to ask you to affect a change," Rachel said with deep sincerity.

"What change do you want?" Zoë asked in disbelief, her face filled with concern.

"It is not only me who wants the change, but the light, the entire universe. Human beings are a delight and an enigma in creation and their preservation is an imperative. Despite all the foibles, human beings are wonderful. With humanity, there has always been a teetering balance between good and evil and over recent times, goodness has had an edge. Think of the possibilities of goodness. Imagine a world of peace with no energy or health problems, no hunger and with a dedication to peace, equality, tolerance, altruism, art, learning and the development of the human spirit. Imagine a world where everyone is aware of their spiritual being and works for communion with the universal force, with God, a world where war and strife are unknown. This is the possibility."

"So, what is the problem? I don't understand."

"The problem that must be changed is an unexpected, complex and insidious genetic mutation that has occurred in your son that has been passed onto future human beings."

"What kind of mutation are you talking about?" Zoë asked, trying to understand.

"As humans evolved, they gradually lost many violent tendencies. The expected course of evolution would be for less and less primitive aggression and increasingly more thinking, reasoning and logic. This was the expectation. However, something happened that was never imagined, this horrid genetic mutation. It undermined the progression of mankind to a God- conscious level. This new gene from an unknown source, quite simply stated, is evil."

"Evil?"

"Yes. It affects the brain and the psyche in such a way that many who had the gene become terrible self-serving sociopaths, paranoid, belligerent, angry and domineering individuals. Each subsequent generation seemed to be worse than the previous. This produced a future of wars and terror that have become unbearable. The environmental, social, political and governmental structure ultimately collapsed. Every effort to stop it, eradicate it, or ameliorate its effects has failed. It has been muted in some people by means of great, sustained efforts but in the end, all human beings in the future have it and will be lost. They will literally destroy the planet and themselves. We know this to be a fact."

"Where did the gene come from?" Zoë asked.

"It came from Patrick David," Rachel said solemnly.

"Oh, my God! Patrick? How could that be? How did he get it?"

"We have no idea how or where he got it, but he doesn't have it now. In less than six months he will have it and can then pass it along to future generations as has happened. It will be a permanent change in his germ cell DNA thereafter. The rest of his cellular DNA is fine so he will not be affected but all of his offspring will be. This can be due to any number of things that cause mutations such as carcinogens, radiation, various environmental chemicals, certain viral infections, and genetically engineered pathogens."

"I'm beginning to understand the issue. This is like a disease that must be stopped before it spreads to everyone. How can we stop it?"

"Zoë, what we are asking you to do is to conceive your son before Patrick acquires this terrible gene."

"If it has already happened and people have already lived and died and the future is in shambles, how can a change be made now that will help those poor bastards in the future? Will preventing the spread of that gene alter what has already happened in the future?" Zoë asked flatly, obviously deep in thought and perplexed by the proposed solution.

"The answer is both yes and no. In a sense, the future I have told you about has already happened. Mankind will go extinct in that future. If a change is made now, there will be a different pathway, a second future, a second chance for mankind to survive without a heart of evil and evolve into God Conscious Beings."

Zoë's mind reeled with the information given to her. How could all of this fall on her shoulders? How could one obscure medical student be the mother of mankind? Are we all just pawns in some cosmic chess match? She had to think. She had to talk to Patrick.

"Zoë, it all comes down to you and Patrick. You have three months, possibly four at the most. Everything needs to be as close to the original event as possible except for the timing. Timing is everything."

"I don't know. This is so much. This is more than anyone should have to bear. What if it doesn't work?" Zoë contemplated the incredible message she had been given.

"We will never know until we know. This is our best chance. It will be our only chance. You are our hope."

"There is one more thing."

"What is that? I don't think I can handle much more."

"Patrick can have only one child. After three months, another child would have the gene. If that child had children, I can't imagine what would happen if they survived."

"I have so many more things I need to ask you. This is all overwhelming."

"Zoë, you are strong. Mankind and the earth need your help."

Rachel once again smiled at Zoë and after a soft and affectionate embrace, she left as quickly and mysteriously as she had come.

Zoë was stunned. The sun shone brightly through the window and she went out into the yard. She faced the sun, closed her eyes and held her hands open at her sides.

"I will do what you want me to do," she whispered.

Zoë stood there for a long time pondering all these things in her heart and then she knew what her decision would be. The air was fresh and clear and the birds sang their ancient songs as a dove flew over her head touching its wing to her brow.

Chapter 45
Creating a New Life

Patrick drove onto the street to the house where Zoë lived with her housemates. Her friends were away that weekend and Zoë had not yet arrived home. Patrick got out of his car carrying a bag containing wine and candles and walked up to the porch. There was still no sign of Zoë as the sun moved closer to the horizon. He placed his hand in his pocket and felt for a small box from Perry's Jewelers. He carefully touched all six sides and smiled as he thought about the contents. He hoped that Zoë would say "yes" but he also knew that she could be very stubborn about her plans. He had often taken a back seat to Zoë's wishes. He was not uncomfortable with this at all, but loved her and supported her as she forged ahead deciding her path in life. They had always been very good friends but during the past year they were increasingly drawn to each other and when they were apart, longed for each other's presence. They were very comfortable in bearing their souls and confiding their hearts to one another, and the hours they spent discussing the Asterman enigma and the many strange pieces of the puzzle had served to bond them further. What did all of these things mean and how did he and Zoë fit into the puzzle?

In the previous weeks, both he and Zoë had experienced strange visits with even stranger revelations that had dismantled their fragile world view and even how they viewed themselves. These encounters had begun to blur as if their minds could not accept what they heard. They both knew that they must write down everything they could remember that had been said to them by Rachel Devane and the strange old man, because the memories were fast fading. Their notes had been an anchor for them as their minds insidiously rejected the reality of what had happened to them.

When Patrick was told that he would marry Zoë and they would have a child, this was not a surprise but rather an affirmation of what he believed would ultimately happen. He believed that their relationship had grown deeper and he knew that if he persisted, Zoë would come around eventually. But there was always some uncertainty in his mind since she did not approve of many aspects of his life. She was proud that he now seemed to have some focus and determination with his new job and seemed to have finally gotten his act together.

Zoë had been searching for her path all of her life. She now more than ever firmly believed that every event in her life was for a purpose and that the purpose would be revealed in time. She had little patience with people who lacked purpose and this was her greatest hang-up with Patrick. Recent events seemed to indicate that both of them were involved in the same purpose of life and that this was an incredibly significant purpose indeed.

Patrick's view of life was that everything is interesting and that he should try as many things as possible to decide what he would ultimately do. Maybe he would never find one thing that he could consider his life's work, but he would certainly enjoy the quest. Patrick never felt that there was a path or mission for him but rather, he would decide his own path and purpose. He certainly did not have a sense of spirituality that Zoë had shown recently. Most things Patrick tried could not hold his interest even when he was very good at the endeavor. He certainly lacked the sense of purpose Zoë had, but he sincerely believed that he would find a worthwhile endeavor before he died. All of the recent revelations had seriously shaken Patrick and for the first time in his life, he had begun to look beyond the obvious side of the world he encountered every day.

Zoë's Honda turned onto her street and Patrick's heart soared like a hawk as the most loved person in his life approached. He smiled broadly as she pulled up to the curb in front of the house. She greeted him with a large white bag marked with red Chinese characters. As Zoë bolted out of the car, Patrick took the bag and gave her a passionate kiss.

"You're a dear. Thank you. I hope you don't mind if we have Chinese at home tonight. I just didn't want to go out. Maybe we can go to Guytano's Restaurant some other night. Do you mind terribly?" Zoë said with her cute, little smile.

This was not exactly what Patrick had planned but it would work. So much for a romantic evening out, he thought. Once again, Zoë changed his plans.

"Not at all. As long as I am with you, Chinese at home is fine. I got a good, rich Syrah and brought some candles so we can still have a nice, romantic dinner."

"Welcome to the Chateau Hovel. May I take your coat?" Zoë kidded.

"By all means. Let me wipe the crumbs off the table and I will grab some plates and glasses."

"I'll go freshen up a bit and be right back," Zoë said, giving him a quick kiss.

Zoë went upstairs and Patrick took the small box out of his coat and put it in his pants pocket. He then set the table and dumped the food into bowls. After opening the wine, he turned down the lights, lit a candle, placed it on the table and turned on some soft music. Zoë returned looking refreshed and lovely in a new blue sweater and jeans.

"Hey, what is going on here? You could have left the Chinese in the boxes. Now there are a lot of dishes to wash. It's dark in here," she said as she turned up the lights.

"Zoë, I really want us to have a nice, romantic dinner tonight and I'll be happy to wash the dishes," Patrick said, on the verge of exasperation as he dimmed the lights again.

"Okay, let's eat. I'm starved. I had to work through lunch today and I've been thinking about that Chinese all day." Zoë smiled as she rubbed her hands together.

They both heartily ate multiple portions and quickly consumed the wine. Zoë pointed to an unopened wine bottle as she vented her list of toils and troubles of the day. Patrick uncorked the wine and poured more for them while he listened patiently. He had come to understand that Zoë needed to blow off steam when she got home each day. His role was not necessarily to help her solve problems but to simply listen and allow her to work problems through for herself. Zoë gradually became relaxed and happy and finally changed the subject.

"So how was your day?" she asked.

"It was very good and I got a lot of jobs finished that have been bugging me for weeks, but the very best part was thinking about being with you this evening," Patrick said softly.

"Patrick, you are so sweet," Zoë said, leaning over and kissing his cheek. "I thought about you a lot today too."

"Bring your wine and let's go over to the couch," Patrick said, taking Zoë by the hand. "It's a lot more comfortable and we can be closer. There, that's better."

The old, overstuffed couch was soft and comfortable, and Zoë snuggled up to him and kissed him once again, this time on the lips.

Zoë looked at Patrick's face, almost transfixed as if she were gazing deeply into his soul and seeing his love.

"I love you, Patrick."

"And I love you too."

"I don't know what I would have done if you hadn't been with me."

"Oh, you're very resourceful, you'd manage."

"Patrick! Sometimes I could just punch you!"

"Go ahead, right here," he said, pointing to his chin.

"It's very tempting," Zoë snarled and she made a fist and shot him steely daggers with her eyes. Instead, she grabbed his chin and kissed him passionately. "You are such a clown but, you know, you are my knight in shining armor. You have always been at my side and I know I couldn't have done it without you. Thank you for being here and thank you for being my friend."

"I will always be your friend, Zoë, but I want our relationship to be more than that. There is nowhere I'd rather be than with you. I think about you every day and yearn for you all the time. You are beautiful, kind and caring and your heart is pure love. You say that you are afraid and weak, but you are truly brave and tough as steel. All of these things that have happened to us have only drawn me closer to you. I want to always be at your side no matter what the future holds.

Patrick then awkwardly fumbled for the treasure in his pocket and finally produced the little green box. He extended the tiny box to Zoë.

"Zoë, will you marry me?"

Tears of joy filled Zoë's eyes as she whispered: "You know I will."

She opened the box and found a diamond ring set in white gold. Two light blue sapphires flanked the sparkling round-cut stone.

Patrick was apologetic: "It is not very big, but it sparkled more than any of the others."

"Oh, Patrick, it is beautiful. I love you so much. I know you worked very hard to get this."

She kissed and embraced him again and again as a wonderful smile spread across her face. They sat together for several minutes smiling brightly with their arms intertwined. Then Zoë stood up, took Patrick by the hand, picked up the candle and walked upstairs to the bedroom. She placed the candle on the dresser, kicked off her shoes and put her arms around Patrick once again and hugged him tightly. She kissed his eyes, nose and mouth as she unbuttoned his shirt. She pulled off her blouse and jeans and removed Patrick's shirt and pants. She kissed him deeply and caressed his back. Very slowly, she removed his shorts and let them drop to the floor. His hardness was wonderful against her as she touched his face and neck and down his back to his hips. His muscles twitched involuntarily beneath her delicate touch. She removed her undergarments and nothing separated them as they stood in the flickering candlelight. He kissed her eyes, tasted her ears and neck and deeply explored her mouth. His hands moved across her shoulders and down the curve of her back and hips. They gently swayed side to side allowing their skin to touch ever so delicately. Small goosebumps appeared as the hair on their skin became erect at the sensuous touch. Their hands came together outstretched at their sides and their fingers barely touched as they moved to the soundless dance within them. Then they tightly embraced each other and became aware of the cold air in the room. Patrick pulled her over to the bed, jerked back the covers and slid a sheet up over them. They kissed deeply and explored each other's bodies as if for the first time. As their passionate warmth increased, they threw back the sheet and kissed every inch of each other, delighting in pleasures they had never before explored.

Patrick caressed her breasts and kissed her neck as she caressed his intense hardness. Zoë took his hand and slowly moved it down her body. His touch produced an undulating wave of pleasure erupting into sounds of ecstasy. They kissed and caressed and the wave returned even more intense than before. As her muscles relaxed, Zoë rolled Patrick on his back and sat astride him so that he could see her fully and touch her at his pleasure. As she gently moved on top of him, she watched his every expression and responded in turn with her erotic rhythm. Patrick looked as if he were going to explode as she stopped and smiled. She continued to tease him and then leaned down, touching her breasts to his chest and kissed him passionately, deeply.

She whispered softly in his ear: "Your turn." Sitting upright, she slowly and vigorously filled herself with him as a spasm of pleasure moved from his toes throughout his body and up to his neck. As Zoë watched Patrick, her deep pleasure returned like an unstoppable tide. Soon Patrick lay quietly, unmoving.

"Are you okay?" Zoë whispered.

"I think I died and went to Heaven," Patrick said with a silly expression coming over his face.

"There is a lot more Heaven where that came from, big boy," Zoë kidded. "I think I'm going to have you forever."

"I'll never recover. You will have to find someone else," Patrick smiled.

"Never? I think I can rejuvenate you." Zoë smiled as she covered him with kisses. Her prediction was correct as they both enjoyed the rejuvenation process.

They lay in bed, transfixed on each other in the faint glow of the flickering candlelight. Patrick studied Zoë's face, the subtle colors of her irises, her eyebrows, her eyelashes, her dimples, her nose and every curve of her body. She gazed at Patrick's boyish face, his dark eyes, long eyelashes, cheekbones and the stubble on his chin. Against his muscular body she felt safe in his arms. Like two mated birds that had bonded for life, their minds fused at an unknown level. No pronouncement, ceremony or legal paper could make them one, but now they were one by the intent of their hearts.

Chapter 46
The Little Bloodsuckers

Patrick was returning to Nicaragua at least once a month and bringing back continually increasing numbers of artifacts and data. Professor Horowitz had insisted on staying during the last trip and had now been absent for eight weeks. Patrick had been working in the lab for at least fourteen hours each day and often longer, cataloging and photographing the new specimens. He had made what he believed to be a number of very significant observations and had recorded these for Horowitz's perusal when he returned. But for now, Patrick had to prepare for his next trip in two days. In addition to the usual items, he had been instructed to bring a number of special pieces of equipment and a camera for infrared photography for something Horowitz wanted to try. There was no lack to the man's imagination. A final message was to bring more mosquito repellant since the site was now swarming with the pests. After due preparation, Patrick was again ready for his journey.

Upon arrival, a message was waiting for him requesting that he pick up more supplies and drive to the site in a vehicle that would be designated for him. The vehicle looked like an army transport truck and was filled with burlap and ropes and a portable winch. Horowitz was obviously planning to lift something heavy. The map to the site was in the glove compartment of the huge vehicle. Patrick had never driven anything larger than his Volkswagen and was quite intimidated at the prospect of driving the truck into the jungle. The gears crunched and scraped and he was off to his destination. The truck would not go as fast as he liked, so it was over four hours until he got to his first turn-off. It had been raining heavily and the road was a mess of ponds and potholes and would surely worsen before he got to his destination.

At the next turn, the road looked like a small river and he had second thoughts about proceeding. However, Horowitz would be furious if he didn't get there today, so he knew he had to forge on. At least if he got stranded, he had food and would be found eventually when the other workers came out to the site the following day. One final turn remained but nothing looked familiar. The brush had overgrown considerably and a small marker that had been placed to show where to turn was nowhere to be seen. Everything looked the same. Patrick kept driving and came to an elevated clearing that he had not seen before. He knew he had gone too far and missed the turn. He stopped and got out of the truck after positioning it so he could turn around. He needed to stop and this appeared to be a good place. He stretched and walked to the edge of the clearing to relieve himself. The jungle was amazingly quiet. He remembered the serenade of birds and monkeys from his previous trips but now there was dead silence.

As he zipped up his pants, he looked to the side and saw something strange, a pile of fur in the distance. He hiked over the rise and was startled as he saw at least thirty howler monkeys lying dead on the ground, surrounded by hundreds of birds all covered with ants quickly recycling the dead carcasses. Suddenly he felt the ants crawling on his legs and he turned and ran down the hill wildly beating them off.

At the truck he dispatched the last fierce biter and thought to himself, what the hell is going on? What has happened to all these animals? He drank some water as he leaned against the truck, considering what he should do next. At least the rain had stopped for now. Gradually he began to hear the sound of motors from the direction he had just driven. Some of the workers must be leaving the camp. Now was the time to find the hidden turn. He quickly cranked the truck and began driving back down the decrepit road. Within half a mile, he saw the tail lights of one of the university vehicles heading back to the main road. Fortunately, the tire ruts had marked the place where he needed to turn. Once again, he was on track for the site.

The mud and undergrowth were thick, but the large truck was able to forge ahead. Patrick was now glad he had this tank of a vehicle. As he pulled into the clearing, he noticed that there were no other vehicles in the camp and Horowitz was standing alone by the tent. He waved at Patrick as he stopped the truck and got out.

"You just missed them. They all have headed back." Horowitz was quite displeased.

"I couldn't find the turn. I was lucky to see them coming out so I could even find the road in. What's happening? Why did everybody leave?"

"It's those damned mosquitoes. They have gotten really bad the last few days. Nobody wanted to work. This morning I did get them to load up most of the new artifacts and they took them and left. You can pick up two boxes for me at the warehouse near the airport on your way back home and take them along."

"Aren't you going back with me?"

"No! You can do it. No concern. I've got to stay here; there is just too much going on and I'm worried about looters. The men told me that they have already heard rumors that we were working on a very valuable site. I wouldn't be surprised to see a truckload of treasure hunters show up here tomorrow."

"You really need to come back with me. Conditions are not good at this dig site and you have been here too long and you are missed in the lab. There is a lot going on and we need your direction. I'm directing everything right now and that is a scary thought, me being in charge."

Patrick's try at humor was unsuccessful and he was quite troubled that Horowitz wanted to stay longer when so much had to be done in the lab and his guidance was desperately needed. It had turned into a huge responsibility for him and Horowitz kept adding to his workload unaware of all that needed to be done. He now wanted Patrick to write up an abstract for the anthropology meeting in the spring.

"Patrick, we are onto something phenomenal here and I just can't leave it now. It really upsets me that a few mosquitoes have run everyone off. I need their help and those bastards have just abandoned me. They say they will be back next week but I'm not leaving because there is just too much at stake."

"What have you found that can't wait?"

"Come with me!"

Patrick grabbed his backpack and water bag and they walked into the forest.

"Here is some mosquito repellent I brought. There is a lot more in the truck. I've already put some on."

"Well, put on more. You'll need it."

When they reached the site, Patrick was surprised at how much of the foliage had been removed and how beautiful the exposed structures were. Horowitz took him to the trench that was now both wider and deeper than when he had last seen it. On the ground by the trench was a large marble slab with intricate carving quite different from those of other sites.

"This we thought was the main slab covering the burial chamber. We struggled like dogs getting it off but we found a second cover beneath this one. Here, follow me."

Horowitz then went into the trench and motioned for Patrick to follow. There at the end of the trench was the second cover still in place.

"There is a definite undisturbed burial chamber beneath this. We have the acoustic imaging that shows the hollow chamber with multiple objects inside. Look closely at the images on the surface."

Horowitz brushed aside the dirt clinging to the ancient surface. There again was the Asterman-like image Patrick had first seen on the wall by the pyramid.

"This has to be a new deity. It is closely associated with the dead, but remarkably different from Kukulkan, Quetzalcoatl, Chac, or any of the pantheons of Aztec or Mayan gods. Where did this one come from? How old is this site? There are similarities but many differences from other sites in this area. This is completely new in Mayan history. Look at this image. It doesn't even look Mayan. It looks like something from the Middle East, not Mayan. This is an incredible find. This tomb may hold the answers. Regardless, it is untouched as far as we can tell and may put King Tutankhamen's tomb to shame. I will stay here until it is opened.

This is the find of a lifetime. This is my destiny." Horowitz nearly choked with emotion.

Later that night, the outside of the tent literally hummed with the persistent blood-hungry mosquitoes. Patrick sprayed the inside of the tent and carefully checked the netting to keep them out. If there was even one small hole, the little bloodsuckers would find it.

"The horde of mosquitos is awful. I can see why the workers got out of here," Patrick noted as he swatted two that had invaded the tent.

"Everyone was really doing okay with them until they found a dead monkey. Two of the Indian workers said that was a bad omen and we should leave. Then they found another one and then they all started leaving. Superstitious primitives!"

"You know, when I was coming in, I came across a field of dead birds and a lot of dead monkeys with them. That makes me wonder if the mosquitoes are carrying some kind of disease."

"There are mosquitoes and dead monkeys here all the time. There is nothing to worry about. We just have to get that tomb excavated but it will take more than the two of us to do it. There are plenty of other things to do until they come back next week. A few insects are not stopping me. There is a lot we have to do tomorrow so let's get some sleep for now."

Chapter 47
The Scourge

Zoë was afraid. Patrick had not returned from Guatemala yesterday as scheduled. It was not unusual for him to be late, but it was very unusual for him not to call. Zoë kept thinking that her fears were irrational and that there was probably a good explanation. After all, things often did not go as planned on these archaeological digs and the work was slow at best with all the rain and primitive conditions. She knew that he had been in the jungle excavating a Mayan burial site that Professor Horowitz had found using Landstat and other satellite images and remote sensing equipment. Patrick had shown her the photographs and was very excited that this appeared to be a pristine site untouched by looters. These digs always take a lot of time she kept telling herself. He will call soon. Finally, Zoë called Professor Horowitz's office but his secretary had not heard from him either.

About six hours later, Zoë's phone rang shortly after she had returned home from her day at the hospital.

"Zoë, this is Patrick," the strange voice said.

"Patrick, you sound terrible! What is wrong?" Zoë was very concerned.

"I've been in the hospital in Belize for three days and terribly sick."

"Please tell me you are going to be okay. You don't sound well at all."

"I still feel like hell but I am actually a lot better. I had been completely out of it until this morning when I started getting my mind back. Zoë, Professor Horowitz is here in intensive care and I don't think he is going to make it. The doctor taking care of us said he is unconscious and getting worse and they had to put him on a ventilator to keep him breathing. Please call his office and let them know what is going on. His wife died some time ago, but I know he has a son who needs to be notified."

"I'll call his secretary right away. What in Heaven's name has happened to you?"

"I'm not really sure. We were working the new site and finding some really neat stuff, but the mosquitoes just became intolerable. All the other workers left but Horowitz wouldn't leave. We were using a lot of insect repellant, but it didn't help much and we both just got eaten. Then we developed a rash and started having chills and fever. We tried to keep working but couldn't even stand up because we got so weak. By evening I ached all over and started having lymph node swelling in my neck and groin and even my testicles got swollen. I couldn't wake up Horowitz and got on the radio and called for help. That is the last thing I remember until I woke up today in the hospital. I don't know how they got us out of there. Horowitz is in really bad shape, Zoë."

"Is it malaria?"

"No, but the doctors here do think we had some kind of viral infection, possibly from the mosquito bites. They sent some blood to the CDC in Atlanta, but it may be weeks before they give a report. We have been in isolation as a precaution and I hope they will let me out of here soon. This has been horrendous, whatever it is."

"Patrick, I am so very sorry. I was really worried when your plane didn't come back yesterday and no one called. I kept thinking you had crashed in the jungle. I love you and I'm so glad you are okay!"

"I am feeling a lot better now that the fever has gone and I think I'll live but for a while, I had my doubts. I'm still very tired and washed out and ache all over. It may take me a little while to get home."

"Please call me this evening and let me know how you are. I love you so much and I need you back safe and sound. I'll come and be with you as soon as I can catch a plane."

"You stay right where you are. I love you, Zoë, and you shouldn't be exposed to this. It could be dangerous. Don't worry. I'm going to be all right and will keep you posted every day."

Zoë was relieved by Patrick's call, but she could think of nothing else the rest of the day and would not be comforted until she saw him again. When Patrick called back the next day, Zoë learned that Professor Horowitz had died, probably from encephalitis. Patrick assured her that he no longer had fever and was feeling much better. The doctors had examined him again and assured him that he had no signs of encephalitis and that his swollen glands were improving. They anticipated that he would recover completely. The nature of the virus, or whatever it was, was still unknown but they were betting on the mosquito being the transmission agent, possibly from monkeys. Patrick again assured her that he would call her daily until he came home and told her how much he loved her.

Zoë hung up the phone and stood looking out the window, contemplating her situation. She put her hands on the barely discernable bulge in her abdomen as she remembered what Rachel Devane had told her nearly three months earlier. Then she thought that this must be when Patrick picked up the virus that produces the evil mutation.

Chapter 48
Watching and Waiting

The trail along the Hudson River was always a pleasant walk and was used by many for recreation and exercise. This portion of the trail was smooth and several benches were scattered along the way at strategic vista points. At a stop ahead, an elderly man with shaggy white hair and mustache sat watching the view. At closer approach, he was noted to have on a straw hat, jeans, a plaid shirt and hiking boots. Several hikers had passed him by when a woman hiker stopped where he was sitting.

"May I join you?" she asked.

"Certainly. Nice day today. I love the view of the river from here."

"My knees aren't as limber as they once were."

"I wish it was just my knees. I don't have a good joint left in my body."

"The river is magnificent today," she said.

"Always changing yet always the same."

"Yes, it is."

"Have you planted any seeds this season?"

"I finally did. Nearly missed doing it in time. Timing is everything."

"It certainly is."

"How about you, Ms. D? Did you plant anything?"

A young couple with their backpacks walked past as they chatted. There was a brief pause in their conversation until the hikers passed.

"Oh, yes. I was able to plant several seeds and one that was exceptional."

"Do you think our seeds will grow?"

"Well, the conditions are right and the soil is good."

"And no varmints."

"No varmints that we know about. I have a feeling there may be a varmint hiding in the bushes."

"That's true and it pays to keep watch."

"There is a lot to worry about when you plant."

"Yes, but we do what we can and then have to have faith."

"We definitely need to have faith, this is true. When you have done everything you can do, it will unfold as it's supposed to."

"Morris, I worry. There is a danger. I can feel it."

"I sense it too, Rachel. Everything depends on the seeds growing."

"We've done all we can do for now. We can only wait."

"Be careful and don't let your guard down. We need to watch the garden without being obtrusive. We have to be there for them in case we're needed and I think we will be needed."

"It would be good if we weren't needed any more, but I have a feeling that we will have to act quickly before it is all over."

As another hiker passed, they said their casual goodbyes and left in different directions.

Chapter 49
Time and the River

The misty dew on the ferns, drips slowly to the moss-covered earth saturated with heavy moisture. Slowly, the collecting dew seeps into the organic, rich earth and wet leaves becoming tiny trickles across the rocky ground. Trickles become rivulets and meld into diminutive streams that coalesce into a cascade flowing into the great glacial valley.

Atoms of hydrogen and oxygen combined into the simplest of molecules, the universal solvent, dissolving that which would be dissolved, polishing away solid rock one tiny bit at a time, moving everything down to the sea. Yet all the parts are not the river but yet are the river. The river is here. The river is there. There is no beginning and no end. It is the simple combined atoms, the dew, the trickles, the river and the sea in an unending cyclical dance. It forever changes and is always the same. Look into the river, for it is your life and being, and see that there is no time, there is only now. The river transcends all things. Serenity is hearing the voice of the river and accepting one's destiny to be forever one with its flow.

Chapter 50
The Nativity

This is the day that will be remembered and celebrated for thousands of generations. This is the beginning of the great redemption of human beings from the clutches of evil. I was there, looking down and am witness to it all. It is my duty to record all things in regard to the birth of this child. This is what I see as it is happening:

Orion and his dogs, shimmer in the cold black New England sky. In the crystal air, the blood-red Betelgeuse, the sapphire-blue Rigel and the incandescent white Sirius are brilliant jewels. The Pleiades hang high in the sky like fireflies caught in a glowing gossamer web. A bright meteor streaks toward Earth as the great winter stars beam down their long-traveled lights. The brilliant sky of stars overwhelms the landscape as if the gods are gazing down from the heavens at the earth below.

As the moon slowly emerges above the eastern horizon, a magical transformation begins unfolding. A thin layer of new fallen snow covers the rooftops and withered grass, and the flocked fir trees seem to be images from a sentimental Christmas card from a bygone era. The moonlight pierces the darkness and glares its reflection from the icy snowflakes as the scene is slowly filled with a soft white glow.

The first breaths of a baby's cry cut through the silence, objecting to the cold air filling his lungs and the rough fabric against his skin. Silence once again returns as his mother caresses him and draws him to her breast. The child is born.

As the moon rises higher in the sky, a small group of lights move through the stars from the east across the river and the farmlands toward the meager house at the edge of town. The lights do not go unnoticed. Several farmers, who are caring for their livestock tonight see the lights, stop their work and watch the colorful spectacle move across the sky.

They look at each other and know that something remarkable is happening that they must observe. They secure the gate and get into their truck looking toward the direction the lights are drifting.

Three young boys bundled in thick winter gear stand in a nearby field looking at the stars with binoculars and a small telescope. The Great Nebula in Orion is a beautiful sight and they are observing the tiny cluster of new stars in its center when they hear the baby cry. They have anxiously awaited the baby's coming since they had seen the young man and his very pregnant wife move into the house about two weeks before. They know in their hearts they must see this wondrous sight. With great excitement they run to the house for they know the baby is there.

Zoë and Patrick have done everything they were told to do regarding the birth of the child. They are filled with a great sense of purpose and know that everything is unfolding as it should. Zoë was certain of her due date and insisted the birth would be at a remote and secure place. Jennifer's new small, yet comfortable house had been prepared at the edge of town for almost a month. Deirdre and Jenna had volunteered to help with the delivery but in the end everyone had come. They all knew that they had to be there for Zoë, Patrick and the baby. But there was more than a sense of duty, like some primal urge, they knew they must be there when the baby was born. And so, the group of friends had all put aside everything and came together for one more time: Deirdre, Jenna, Martine, Erin and Scott. All of them knew that something very important was happening here, perhaps the most important event of their lives. No one told them this but all of them could not escape the wonder of the event.

As the three young astronomers approach the house where the new child sleeps, they also notice the bright lights in the sky. The lights are moving to a position just above the dwelling. One stops to look with his binoculars, but the others urge him on, encouraging him that they will look after they see the baby.

José, Joseph, and Asher Gonzales, the brother farmers who followed the lights in their pickup truck, stop near the front of the house and gaze at the wondrous sight when they see the young boys excitedly going toward the house. The boys run toward the door and the farmers jump from their truck and follow closely behind, knowing they are all there for the same reason.

The doorbell rings and soon Rachel Devane opens the door. She smiles broadly as the boys announce that they have come to see the new baby. She sees the farmers close behind and motions for them to come in as well. As the boys enter, Rachel smiles and gently pats their heads. The farmers take off their boots at the door and one says that they have followed the lights to the house.

They move into a large central room and find Zoë, Patrick and the baby. The baby sleeps soundly in a bed made for him on a chair. They all gather around and there are many "oohs" and "ahs" for the beautiful new baby boy. Others are there in several small groups, sipping warm beverages and talking softly including Jack Adams, Roger Morris, Marcus Newel and Jennifer Wells. Two tall foreign-looking people wearing long robes stand quietly in the corner. No one is surprised by any of the visitors who came here to witness the event. There is a soft, scintillating, warm glow to the house and a sense of great joy, peace and serenity.

The young boys whisper to each other that they must give the baby a present since it is his birthday. After a moment's thought, each gives a present that is of great value to them: a penlight, a pair of binoculars and a star map. They place the gifts at his bedside with great delight. They pat Webster's head as he sits quietly by the baby.

Everyone gazes at the sleeping child, knowing that he is very special and yet wondering what his birth actually means. Zoë looks around the room at everyone gathered there and is filled with deep gratitude for the love and kindness that comes from each of them. She smiles as she looks at her baby, bundled in a blanket and lying quietly on his makeshift bed. Everyone's eyes are on him as she picks him up and holds him close to her with Patrick coming to her side and kissing them both. She knows that the baby must be protected and that the future depends on him. She says a soft prayer for him and for the trials and tribulations he will face.

As everyone savors the warm moment, the carolers from St. Mary's Church can be heard in the distance singing:

O holy night

The stars were brightly shining.

It was the night of our Dear Savior's birth.

Long lay the world in sin and error pining,

But he appeared and the soul felt its worth.

A thrill of hope, the weary world rejoices.

For yonder breaks a new and glorious morn.

Fall on your knees and hear the angel voices.

Oh night, Oh night divine...

The carol fades away into the night and it is once again quiet. Everyone hears and contemplates the irony of the moment.

The three young boys go to Zoë and thank her for letting them see the baby. It is getting late and they have to leave before their parents become alarmed. They all ask in unison: "What's his name?"

Zoë looks at their bright, young faces and softly says: "Joshua."

"Josh! That's good. We like it!" the boys say almost in unison. They smile broadly and were quite pleased with his name.

"And what are your names?" Zoë asks.

"I'm Lucas," says the youngest boy.

"I'm Matt," says the second.

"And I'm Mark," says the third and oldest. "This has been great, but we really have to go. Our parents will be worried about us."

"Boys, you really need to stay awhile longer. I don't want to worry you, but I think we need to take care of a little problem before you go," Jack said as he looked around at everyone in the room. "Everyone, please remain here for a few moments while we take care of an issue that has come up. This won't take long so please be patient with us."

Chapter 51
Standing in the Light

Outside the house, the large object hovering over the house in the cold night air begins emitting a rainbow of colored lights. An almost imperceptible distant drone is heard off to the east, almost imperceptible at first but then most definitely becoming increasingly louder. Six bright lights come into view, traveling near the ground as the noise of the helicopter rotor blades increases to a deafening roar. The heavily armed aircraft fly in a direct path toward the small house where the wondrous new child sleeps surrounded by his family, friends and adoring strangers. Following the helicopters, a convoy of military trucks and a single black sedan move rapidly down the highway. The soldiers know there will be no survivors.

The large object begins to glow and a cone-shaped beam of bright white light slowly descends from the bottom of the mysterious, radiant mass. The light completely engulfs the house, and every board, window and shingle, becomes crystal-clear. Suddenly the light and its source are gone and the house stands empty of all who were there only seconds earlier. Three rockets from the helicopters find their mark and explode the house into an intense bright yellow-white ball of fire. The intensity of the fire is beyond expectation and when the soldiers arrive there is nothing left but ash. The electrical wiring and the metal pipes in the house have even vaporized. In the months that follow, people remember the story of the airplane that had gone off course and crashed into a small house at the edge of town and how the army unit that came there that night was unable to save anyone. Who was in the house? No one seemed to know.

Jack Adams is the first to speak. "Is everyone okay? We are going to be all right, so please don't be frightened. Take a few slow, deep breaths and everyone hold hands here in a circle."

"I'm not afraid," the apprehensive Lucas said as he quickly grabs Mark's and Matt's hands.

Jack's soft, melodic voice speaks with authority and confidence and he quickly has the complete control and confidence of the group. Everyone follows orders and gathers into a circle holding hands which greatly eases the tension and disbelief that everyone is experiencing. Zoë holds baby Joshua closely and looks at Patrick with a worried and perplexed expression. The farmers are trembling as they cross themselves and look with wide eyes around the strange enclosure. Everyone is in a state of dumbfounded silence.

The place where they are has smooth, sloping walls and a flat floor. There are no angles or corners and the walls and floor glow with a cool, soft light. Everyone feels comfortable and safe, but no one knows where they are and there seems to be no one else with them.

Jack continues. "I don't want anyone to be afraid. You are very safe here and you will soon be back to where you belong in familiar surroundings but just now, we need to wait and I will talk to you in detail about what has occurred."

"Please explain what is going on. What has happened?" Jenna tearfully asks with her voice quivering in fear.

This question seems to break the ice and almost everyone begins talking at once. Still, no one is comfortable in releasing the hand of the person next to them. Jack raises his hands to calm them and assures them their questions will be answered. His voice is now less commanding but rather soft, soothing and almost hypnotic. The tension in the room subsides somewhat as he speaks with a slow and comforting, melodious voice.

"Remember this day, for we have seen something wondrous. The birth of this beautiful baby Joshua is the beginning of a new age for mankind. Because of his birth, the human species now has the hope of a wonderful future of peace and prosperity, a future that expands to the stars and even throughout the universe. The legacy of mankind without this newborn child is fear, hatred, war, evil and ultimately extinction. His birth gives our species another chance. Another chance for us to grow and evolve into intelligent, compassionate, loving people who will eventually be one with the source of all creation. You were there at his birth. You are exceptional people beyond all others. Your names will be remembered for the ages. Remember all that you have seen and everything that has happened. Please record what you have seen however you can for future generations to know." Jack is ecstatic as he speaks these words.

The group listens to his every word and affirms their understanding of why they are there this night. A sense of joy and wonder fills them with ecstasy.

"Regrettably, there are those who do not want this to happen. They are evil, greedy, self-serving, mean and angry people. If somehow, they could receive anything they ever wanted they could not be happy because others are happy with their open, unbounded and free lives and not under their control. They want absolute power to force their will upon others for they believe that they are right and all others are wrong. They will eventually destroy themselves, but for now they are here and they are a menace. They want to destroy you, me, Joshua, all of us and just now tried to do that very thing. But they failed because goodness triumphs over evil and all of you are part of the great goodness of creation. You were brought here by friends who love you and want to protect you. Have you heard of angels? We have hidden friends who are angels for all of us who do the will of the cosmic being. There is so much we do not know nor can understand and that is all I can tell you about them just now, but you will come to know much more in the future."

"I want to go home," Matt says with sadness in his voice.

"Me too!" Lucas and Mark plead in unison.

"You will be going home very soon. You are wonderful, little boys to have followed your hearts and come on your own to see the new baby. You were not asked, but you knew to come so you were definitely supposed to be here. I want to tell you something very important. In a few minutes you will be home. Your parents are very worried about you and will be so glad to see you. There was a fire in the house where we were staying and they are concerned that you may have been in the fire. Let them know that the house burned down after you left and that you are okay. Tell them that everyone in the house had already gone and they are in a safe place. Sometime in the future, we want each of you to write a story about what happened tonight. It will be very special and important for all times. I think you will meet baby Joshua in the future, and it will be a very special treat. Some of what has happened tonight you will forget for now but will remember later. You are going to be safe and happy and soon at home. Now, I want the three of you to stand over here and hold each other's hands very tightly. In just a minute you will be in Matt's backyard. When you get there, go quickly to your parents and let them know you are all right. Okay?"

"We are ready to go home," they each say together.

A scintillating light in the room seems to surround them and they become transparent and disappear. Very soon, three sets of parents are rejoicing for finding their children safe and sound.

The remaining group looks astounded and stands in utter silence. The baby begins to cry but soon is quiet as Zoë nurses him.

Jack smiles at them all, knowing their fears and concerns, and again reassures them.

"The reason we are here is that, seconds after our departure, the house we were in was attacked by a special military task force. Nothing is left of the house. They think we are dead. They want us dead. José, you, Asher and Joseph are unknown to them. They know nothing about you so you can safely return now. We were concerned about your truck, so it was moved to a rest stop on the highway where you will go shortly. You are also very special people. You were drawn here tonight and you don't know why but you thought it very important. This child and maybe this group of people is your destiny and you will eventually find out a special purpose for yourselves and why this happened."

"Señor, we don't know why we were compelled to come tonight but we know that God is in this place and in this child. We have been blessed," José responds as Joseph and Asher voice concurrence.

"Tell everyone that there is hope for the world and hope for human beings. You have within your power to make life better. This is our goal. You have our blessings," Jack replied.

Jack then takes them aside and thanks and encourages them.

"Now, it's time for you to go. Your truck is low on gas, by the way, but you should make it home all right. Via con dios amigos."

The light again appears and they are gone.

"Zoë and Patrick, your homes are not safe any more. Joshua, the wonderful gift you brought us is in danger at every turn. You must go far away, at least for a time, to a safe haven where no one knows and no one cares about you or where you're from. There is a lush island with kind and enlightened people where we want you to go. It will be safe and secure for many years to come until your destinies can be fulfilled. There is much you will have to give up; family, friends, possessions, and even your profession at least for now, but the future depends on it." Jack is not really asking but telling them how it must be.

Erin held Webster and hesitantly says: "I want to go with them too." She looks at Scott who smiles and tries to hide the tears in his eyes as he nods concurrence.

"I go where Erin goes." Scott beams. "She is my love and best friend. We are supposed to help Zoë, Patrick and Joshua. I have seen this and know it to be true. We have to be there for our best friends."

"Thank you so much. You are both wonderful." Zoë is delighted.

Jack again counsels them about the commitment they are making: "Remember, you will be burning bridges for at least several years and there is no going back. No family contacts, no communication. It is a lot to require. You also need friends on the outside for when you can resurface. Those who remain will be here for you."

Erin continues: "Scott and I sincerely want to go. We know that our place is with you. We have all been this wonderful family since the beginning and it is only now that we have this awesome sense of purpose.

It feels right. It is just the right thing to do. We have to go. We are committed to each other and to you."

Patrick and Zoë beam and thank them both. So much is happening that everyone's minds are spinning. They had no idea that they were in such danger.

"You have all spoken from your hearts and this is how it must be. The place you go to is safe, and your needs will be provided. You will know when it is time to return. Go in peace and joy."

Jack is about to dispatch them when Zoë approaches him. Webster follows and is at her feet. She leans and whispers into his ear.

"I have known Jack Adams and John Asterman and I know that you are not Jack Adams. You cannot hide your loving kindness."

"We use the vessels we must use to achieve our goals."

They both look down at Webster sitting at her feet. He looks up at them and barks once with his gruff, little voice.

"Vessels. Webster has to stay, though. We have great plans for him — something Macey would be happy with."

Jack picks up the little white dog and hands him to Rachel as everyone smiles.

"Zoë, there is one other thing. In time, you will understand more and more and all of this will make sense. Be patient. Remember, the creator is in us all. There is something I want to give you to take on your journey." He gives her a single red rose and she remembers her dream.

After the departure of Scott, Erin, and the young family, there is a sense of relief for their safety, but everyone's mind is again spinning with uncertainty and concern. Will they be safe or will someone come after them in the night? What can they do to help Zoë, Patrick and the baby? Martine, Deirdre, Jenna, Jennifer Wells and Marcus Newell move in to fill the circle and each expresses their love and caring for the young family and their concern for their own personal safety.

Jack speaks to them individually and as a group, giving them advice and recommendations. He assures them that they will have protection of which they will not be aware. He encourages them to meditate daily and remember each other in their prayers and meditations and always ask for guidance.

"The primary goal of this attack was to destroy the participants in what the government agents thought to be an unauthorized and dangerous encounter with an alien presence. They think they have accomplished this, but they don't know who else was in the house. Jennifer, since you bought the house, they may come asking you questions and you have to convince them that you just left the house when it blew up and the only occupants were Zoë, Patrick and Joshua. It will be difficult and you have to act very emotional and devastated by what you saw. Also, you may be pressured about your 'alien connection'. Don't deny it but convince them that you are a bit kooky and believe that almost everyone you meet is an extraterrestrial and this will deflect their interest in you."

"I can do it. I can also convince them that I allowed them to use the house because Zoë was having problems and needed to be near her doctor. Also, it's easy for me to act as if I'm nuts. I'm a natural," Jennifer assures him.

"Be certain to be consistent with your story. They may question the rest of you also and I would encourage you to give minimal information. You will be protected. Lastly, if you need to contact each other for any reason, don't use a phone or computer. Be careful what you put into writing. I would recommend putting a personals advertisement in the *Boston Globe* on the first of the month announcing a B&B reunion on a specific date and time and then meet someplace that is open and very public like the Boston Common."

Jack makes additional suggestions to help them through what might be difficult times. He also gave them non-verbal information as well, some of which will come to their minds at a later time if they need it.

Everyone discusses the plans and agrees. There are hugs and thanks all around and they return home in a flash of light like the others who had departed earlier.

"Well, here we are again, just the three of us and thankfully everyone is safe. Now we again watch and wait," Jack sighs.

Rachel Devane and Roger Morris smile broadly and kiss each other. Each places a hand on Jack's arms and gives him an affectionate hug. Jack acknowledges their affection with a nod and a kind smile. They close their eyes and a warm flow of energy courses through their bodies as their minds commune in profound renewing harmony.

Rachel looks into Jack's eyes and says, "You have achieved the unbelievable once again, John. We all on the council are in deepest gratitude to you. There is now another chance for an unending future for mankind and our destiny of goodness and light. An incredible intervention has been accomplished. It almost didn't happen but now there is hope once again for the future, real hope. Maybe this time goodness will prevail and mankind will once and for all break the shackles of evil and tyranny and find the path to the creator."

"Yes, there is hope and another chance for everyone in Zoë, our dear, young mother, our earth mother and her son. We must do everything to ascertain the pathway is secure. Joshua will need our continuing support to survive the cataclysm so that his offspring become as countless as the stars as we move to a wonderfully bright future."

Chapter 52
The Sanctuary

This is another perfect day as the crystal-clear azure sky merges with the pastel blue-green of the tropical sea. The lagoon and beach are peaceful and quiet except for the delighted squeals of Joshua as he splashes at the edge of the water. He smiles and calls, "Look, Mommy!" as he jumps up and down. Zoë sits in her wooden recliner chair in the shade of a group of palm trees, waves and encourages her son. He now amuses himself by throwing buckets of water into the air and dancing around.

Zoë sees several small boats come into view from the rim of the atoll. Erin, Scott, and Patrick have gone out fishing with some of the local residents and are hopefully bringing dinner. The island is truly a tropical paradise with abundant food, sunshine and an easy lifestyle. No hurry and no worry to bother them on a perpetual vacation. It all seems unreal in its dreamlike splendor. They have been treated well and have made many good friends who seemed to have expected them and have never questioned why they are there. It is more than obvious that the islanders seem to know they are to be protected. They have more than ample seafood, fruit and vegetables and a boat with additional provisions and supplies comes by every several weeks. They have no physical needs whatsoever and have discussed feeling guilty after all that has occurred and their current life of leisure.

Zoë remembers her previous life with the nightmares that have never returned and the anguished feeling of dying alone without any hope or purpose. She remembers her feelings of inadequacy and anger toward God with the death of her mother. Now she has a sense of purpose and direction and a knowing that things are happening as they should. It is ironic that we as human beings can evolve into God-like beings that can alter our course in history. We have the ability within us to make our lives and our world Heaven or Hell. We are all part of the great mind of God, and Zoë has come to understand and know with certainty that all things within the universe are interrelated and the universe itself is spirit connecting us all in time and space. Rather than being lost and alone in a cold and unloving universe, we are all part of the universal spirit that flows like a river through everything. As we give ourselves to the universe and each other, we remarkably take control of our own destinies.

As the boats approach the beach, Scott and Patrick lift a string of fish and wave their arms in a cheer. Everyone is beaming smiles as they unload their catch and start preparing the fish. Zoë waves to Erin and notices that she is now beginning to show the new life growing in her belly.

How long will this surreal shortcut from the troubled world last? Zoë doesn't know. She ponders in her heart the wonderful things that have happened and the truths she has learned. There are so many questions remaining but for now, she can only think and wonder what the remarkable future will hold. A cold shudder breaks through the warm, tropical air as she remembers what she was told about the destiny of the world as the next event begins to unfold unseen far away but yet there is hope despite all the dreadfulness to come. Zoë knows she and her son are that very hope and she will be the new mother of all mankind.

The End

Author's Notes

Within this novel is a compilation of many thoughts and concepts interspersed with epiphanies that I have had over my many years of spiritual growth, knowledge acquisition, and both personal and shared experiences with the paranormal and unusual aspects of life. I have long been intrigued by the paranormal and UFO phenomena which continue to generate deep mystery for everyone who has experienced things that simply should not happen and could not happen by any rational means. Once I established the basic theme of this work, which is we as human beings can move in time and change our destiny, the story seemed to write itself taking me down paths I never previously considered. In this section are some comments on various themes that have been introduced into the book.

The Hudson River Valley Setting

The Hudson River that was found in the new world by Henry Hudson in 1609 extends nearly three hundred miles north in an ancient glacial valley from Long Island and has been home to both Native Americans and European settlers. People came here because of the beauty and bounty of the land and water. Grand estates were built along the banks of the river by the early American aristocracy who pioneered new businesses and trades. The area is rife with many stories that are strongly rooted in the history of our democracy as depicted in local art and literature. The river is more than just a waterway and draws people to itself, evoking a sense of wonder and inspiration for artists, writers, and city-weary travelers. This is home to legends of enchanted woods and strange stories like Rip van Winkle who was intoxicated by dwarfs and then slept twenty years while life and the American Revolution passed him by and the Headless Horseman of haunted Sleepy Hollow, roaming the area with his head tucked under his arm in a tale that still fascinates children and adults alike. In the valley there is a sense of a pervasive, ancient, hidden mystery throughout the area and the river reflects our personal lives in its coming and going and kindles thoughts about the deeper meaning of life. This milieu is a perfect setting for this story of conflicted characters touched by other worldliness who are looking for a new and better life and, in their quest become part of a greater plan for humanity.

The Hudson Valley Lights

The stories told by Jennifer Wells and Marcus Newell about the mysterious lights are consistent with multiple true accounts by hundreds of eyewitnesses in the area of the Hudson River in the 1980s. The underlying stories of this series of events are taken from a book by Dr J. Allen Hynek and others who investigated the sightings in detail. It is interesting that there was a major effort to discredit this work by the FAA and USAF, which was and continues to be their basic modus operandi for anything dealing with UFOs or unidentified arial phenomena (UAP) that has become the new designation. I remember seeing the news on TV about the lights that initially revealed a lot of information and interest but when the official debunking started, the story was dropped by the media and nothing else followed. I have found that this is usually how the government and military works with UFO reports: denial and repression, ridicule and sometimes worse. Many others have written about these sightings as well and some references are cited below. This story of strange, glowing unearthly craft seemed to be the perfect mechanism to get John Asterman into the story with some degree of realism.

The late Dr J. Allen Hynek was one of the investigators who seriously studied the UFO situation. Hynek was an astronomer who joined the Air Force Project Blue Book to evaluate the increasingly numerous UFO reports. As a scientist he was skeptical about what people were seeing but ultimately through his personal research, he became

264

convinced that the public was having real encounters with strange, unearthly objects and non-human beings. His book about investigating the Hudson Valley Lights, *Night Siege* is an excellent reference for anyone wanting to read more about this most unusual phenomenon and the emotional and physical effects it had on the observers. Investigators such as Linda Zimmerman and others have published reports of multiple people's experiences with the Hudson Valley Lights.

Suggested reading:

Hynek, J. A., et al. (1987). Night siege: the Hudson Valley UFO sightings. New York, Ballantine Books.

Hynek, J. A. (1998). The UFO experience: a scientific inquiry. New York, Marlowe.

Zimmerman, L. (2013). In the Night Sky. Eagle Press.

UFOs and ETs and the Paranormal

The extent of belief in the paranormal by the general population is difficult to determine because of multiple conflicting factors including fear of ridicule, deeply ingrained religious beliefs, concerns about mental illness and negative topics such as witchcraft, evil spirits and demons. Also, many people believe that anything paranormal by definition is pseudoscience and therefore untrue.

People are actually more likely to talk about UFOs. In a recent Gallop poll (2019), 33% of U.S. adults believe that some UFO sightings over the years have in fact been alien spacecraft visiting Earth from other planets or galaxies. The majority, 60%, are skeptical, saying that all UFO sightings can be explained by human activity or natural phenomenon, while another 7% are unsure. Sixteen percent of Americans say they have personally witnessed something they thought was a UFO while the vast majority (84%) have not. Even as most Americans are skeptical that aliens have visited Earth, the majority (56%) believe that those who spot UFOs are seeing something real, not just imagining it. This is up from 47% in 1996, possibly reflecting public awareness of military testing and the proliferation of drones and artificial satellites which people may think can be mistaken for UFOs. About half of Americans, 49% think that people somewhat like ourselves exist elsewhere in the universe. Even more, 75%, believe that some form of life exists on other planets.

As previously noted, belief in UFOs and ETs has been officially squelched in this country and other parts of the world for many years. The universal response to such reports is ridicule and as a result, many people will not report such things even to family and friends. The character, Sarah Wells in the novel describes the almost devastating effect of such encounters for her and her boyfriend. The fear factor has also been fueled by years of invading monster books and movies and our xenophobia of anything strange or weird to which we cannot relate.

We once believed that planets were rare and that perhaps we on Earth are the only life in the universe and are a unique creation. With increasingly sophisticated technologies we have found that planetary systems around most stars are the usual finding rather than the exception. New research from data from the Kepler space telescope reveals estimates of as many as three hundred million potential planets that could be inhabited in our own Milky Way galaxy. A recent estimate of the size of our universe is that it contains two trillion galaxies with an average of one hundred billion stars per galaxy, a number that is incomprehensible to us. Furthermore, the basic building blocks of life, carbon, nitrogen, oxygen, hydrogen, as well as complex organic compounds attributed to living things such as amino acids etc., are found throughout the universe. Many astrobiologists, who are scientists who study these things, believe that the development of life throughout the universe is not only common but inevitable. Recently, over two hundred stars with planets have been noted to have complex radio signals suggesting that advanced life may be there. There are even suggestions of possible life on Mars, and some of the moons of Jupiter and Saturn and the atmosphere of Venus. Some of this life is likely not intelligent, but the most interesting point is that it may have occurred spontaneously and has the capacity to evolve to intelligent beings. I think the possibilities are certainly there and with proof, this finding will be an overwhelming discovery that will radically shake up our worldview.

Another consideration is that many scientists claim that ETs can't get here from distant stars or galaxies because of the constraint of the speed of light (186,000 miles/second). For beings that are one thousand or ten thousand or one hundred thousand years ahead of us in technology, they are likely to be able to warp or manipulate space/time in such a way to travel through time and the universe with impunity. The knowledge and abilities of any such beings would exceed anything we can imagine, and it would not be surprising that they may function with one singular mind and exist in states of reality that we do not know, including pure energy.

Some authors, including Dr Steven Greer, have speculated that if greatly advanced civilizations of highly evolved beings exist throughout the cosmos, then they, through necessity, must have solved the many problems that are the nemesis of the human race such as inequity, xenophobia, armed conflict, racism, bigotry, hatred, intolerance and moral depravity to name a few. This implies that they must have evolved at a deep spiritual level to understand the interrelationship of all life in the universe and each being has much more in common than we have differences, and we share a common origin from our unique mother universe creator.

I believe that our government continues to keep many secrets from us about UFOs and ETs out of fear that such knowledge would disrupt society because they think we are incapable of handling the truth. Also, there is fear of our anger with them about lying about the most significant finding in human history and keeping earth-saving technology from us that could literally save the world. I believe that the secrecy is about money and control and not about truth or doing what is right for humanity. I look forward to a time of truth, transparency and major changes in our society. Recent news stories show that some in government and the military are acknowledging the veracity of many reports and are beginning to take the phenomenon seriously. I will continue to hope that we learn more.

Suggested reading:

Blumenthal, Ralph and Kean, Leslie. No longer in shadows, Pentagon UFO unit will make some finds public. New York Times. July 23, 2020.

Fox, James, Producer. The Phenomenon October 6, 2020 NETFLIX.

Greer, Steven. (2017). Unacknowledged: an expose of the world's greatest secret. West Palm Beach, FL, A&M Publishing. LLC

Time Travel

The concept of time travel has fascinated humankind for many years. We have all had the feeling that if we could only go back and change what we did, things would be better. Also, going back in time we could witness the great events of our history and find out the truth of what actually happened. Despite our desires, it seems that time only moves in one direction, like an arrow shot into the air, and the past seems to be frozen forever unchanging and it is only in the future that we have many options for paths to take. The possibility of moving backward or forward in time is a simple concept that is actually exceedingly complex and has been the subject of numerous books of fiction and motion pictures, as well as scientific research papers and advanced theories. As of now, time travel is only a theory that awaits proof.

In this novel, the extraterrestrial represented by John Asterman is actually our advanced descendant from the future who comes to create a change that will produce a better future for mankind. Of course, this is beyond anything our current knowledge of physics can allow so the possible reality of something like this awaits further knowledge. Interestingly, a recent book by Penniston regarding a UFO landing in the Rendlesham Forest in England in December, 1980, purports that the UFO occupants were human time travelers from the future.

Recommended Reading:

Greene, B. (2004). The fabric of the cosmos: space, time, and the texture of reality. New York, A.A. Knopf.

Kaku, M. (1995). Hyperspace: a scientific odyssey through parallel universes, time warps, and the tenth dimension. New York, Anchor Books.

Penniston, J. W., Osborn, Gary (2019). The Rendelsham Enigma. Independently published.

Wells, H. G. (1895). The time machine, an invention. London, W. Heinemann.

Zemeckis, Robert, Director. Back to the Future. Universal Pictures. 1985

Fractals and Chaos

Rachel Devane is fascinated with fractals and has many books about the subject, beautiful paintings and artwork of them and a gadget in her garden that projects changing images of their remarkable design (Manus Deoru). She is convinced that fractals are the basic structure of the universe. Since she obviously has advanced thought processes, she may be on to something.

A fractal is a natural phenomenon of a never-ending pattern. Fractals are infinitely complex patterns that are self-similar across different scales. They are created by repeating a simple process over and over in an ongoing feedback loop. Driven by recursion, fractals are images of dynamic systems and the pictures of chaos. The behavior of chaos seems to be random but is created by non-random deterministic processes of dynamic evolution. Geometrically, fractals exist in between our familiar dimensions. Fractal patterns are extremely familiar, since nature is full of them and we see them in trees, rivers, coastlines, mountains, clouds, seashells, hurricanes, and in places we would not expect. Abstract fractals, such as the Mandelbrot and other sets can be generated by a computer calculating a simple equation over and over. For Rachel, the huge complexity of the universe is actually quite simple. For me, not being a math whiz, it seems quite complicated and certainly takes a mathematical mind to grasp sufficiently.

Suggested Reading:

Gleick, J. (2008). Chaos: making a new science. New York, N.Y., Penguin Books.

Jurgens, H. P., Heinz-Otto; Saupe, Dietmer (1990). "The Language of Fractals." Scientific American.

Mandelbrot, B. B. (1983). The fractal geometry of nature. New York, W.H. Freeman.

Mass Extinction

One of the terrible revelations that Rachel Devane told Zoë was that most of humanity would die in a natural catastrophe. Because of this, Joshua's offspring would survive and assure a new and good future for mankind. In considering this scenario, I looked closely at the natural history of the earth as revealed by geologists studying the fossil record and found that mass extinctions are an expected and relatively frequent event affecting the evolution of life on our planet.

Each of the major geologic ages of the earth appears to be punctuated by some great natural disaster such as climatic change, often a result of a great meteor collision or major volcanic activity. These events are so devastating that multiple species often die, both plants and animals. Examples include the largest known mass extinction, the destruction of over 90% of plant and animal species at the end of the Devonian period some two hundred million years ago. This was probably due to extensive volcanic activity. Better known is the extinction of the dinosaurs at the end of the Cretaceous period sixty-five million years ago that appears to be due to a large meteor impact in the Yucatan region of Mexico. There is growing evidence of similar and other catastrophic events marking the end of other major periods. Each geologic period is characterized by the fossils contained within the rocks of that period. In fact, the fossils themselves define the geologic periods with the older rock layers (strata) containing the simpler life forms and newer strata tending to contain increasingly complex and diverse forms. It is only the most well-adapted species that have been able to survive and evolve into other species through the ages. The result of the cataclysmic destruction at the end of each geologic period sets the stage for the rapid development of new species that filled the niches previously occupied by the extinct victims of disaster. Even in the several million years that man and his ancestors have been around, natural disasters, volcanic activity and climate changes have killed off many of our kin and affected who we are today. Seventy thousand to eighty thousand years ago, there was a super volcano named Toba that erupted in a major cataclysm in a catastrophic blast that devastated much of the life on Earth. It is suggested by human studies that only several thousand human beings survived. Studies of human DNA show considerable homogeneity in the genetic make-up of modern human beings which support the concept that we arose from a small group of ancestors who survived this event.

In the last few thousand years of our existence, we have lived in relatively uneventful times. This gives us a false sense of security that we will not be subject to geologic disasters that have occurred in the past. This, of course, is wishful thinking. The same forces that affected our ancestors in the past are still at work and unfortunately great disasters will come again. We need to focus on the reality of our tenuous situation and be prepared for what will eventually come our way. It is simply a fact of life that we will sustain a disaster such as a human-induced ecological catastrophe, large meteor impact, giant volcanic eruption or massive earthquake that could destroy our civilization or even us as a species. Currently the greatest risk for human beings is the destructive effects of human activity on the environment, producing devastating climate changes that are wiping out many species. Many scientists believe that the sixth mass extinction is underway due to our rapid destruction of many natural habitats and the current accelerating extinction of many of Earth's plants and animals. The question is not if another mass extinction could happen, but when in the relatively near future it will happen and will it include the human species. The survival of Zoë's family is anticipated in this work and provides food for thought about our future pathway.

Suggested Reading:

Attenborough, D. (1979). Life on earth: a natural history. Boston, Little, Brown and Company.

Biello, D. (2014). "Fact or Fiction? The sixth mass extinction can be stopped." Scientific American.

Kolbert, E. (2014). The sixth extinction: an unnatural history. New York, Henry Holt and Company.

Wilson, E. O. (2002). The future of life. New York, Alfred A. Knopf: Distributed by Random House.

Halloween and Other Ghostly Tales

I am impressed with the number of people I have encountered that have on occasion experienced strange and seemingly inexplicable events in their lives. People have to be specifically questioned about unusual experiences as they would not normally discuss such things. Often, they are reluctant to talk freely for fear of ridicule or simply because they are trying to forget something that simply cannot make sense. Our brains actually seem programmed to block out such events because it is a reality that does not make sense and therefore cannot be accepted. The acknowledgement of the true reality of bizarrely strange events will radically change one's worldview. The stories from the Halloween party chapter are some of the ones I have collected over the years from people I trust and believe to have had genuine unexplainable experiences. It is interesting to me that most people under the appropriate circumstances can recall at least one so-called paranormal event in their lives. Sure, there will be tall tales, but truth can be found from trustworthy people. In my years of growing up in North Carolina, it was always a joy to me to talk to the older folks about things that had happened in their lives. Most of the people that I knew here were strongly rooted in a fundamentalist Christian faith and sincerely believed in spirits, angels and the hand of God intervening in the world on a regular basis to serve his will and take care of his people. These basic simple beliefs were the foundation of their lives and this seemed to allow their minds to accept fairly incredible concepts without any doubts. As I became increasingly analytical, I still pondered their simple yet profound beliefs that were quite paranormal in nature that they accepted with minimal questions. Seeing a ghost or strange lights was no big deal with them because paranormal was only one aspect of what we consider normal. I am a reasonably sane and sober, overly educated individual, but it is without a doubt that I have repeatedly experienced things for which there is no logical explanation that could easily fill a book.

The group that calls themselves the Bold and the Beautiful came together like a group of magnets during their first year of medical school. Not only were they delighted with each other's presence, they felt a long-standing kinship as if they had been together before and were reuniting. Each of the people in the group had one or more paranormal circumstance in their lives that they shared at Halloween. My oldest daughter, Jane, was a member of such a group dedicated in support of each other during her medical school training and this fact was used as a model for the group in the story. However, to my knowledge, they did not espouse any paranormal experiences.

My selection of the stories also comes from experiences at Halloween and other celebrations in the past where my friends and I would tell stories of strange occurrences that we sincerely believed were true. There is occasionally some embellishment, of course, but the basic stories are as told by my family and friends. Jenna's haunted house story is personal and pretty much accurate from experiences my wife, Fran and I had in a house in Charlotte, NC (1998–1999). The story of the English village is from my daughter's friend. The story of the ghostly, little children is from my brother-in-law. The story of the UFO in the desert is from one of my fellow residents at Duke. The story of the leprechaun is from another friend. Scott's story of the surfing injury and out-of-body experience is from an acquaintance of mine from a meditation conference several years ago.

Religion and Faith

Many of us over the years and certainly in modern times have struggled with basic questions of our existence and questions about our universe and is our being a serendipitous coincidence or the result of some omnipotent controlling force or plan. Religious faith is a powerful force that has shaped our history in wonderful positive ways and also with horrific cruelty and destruction. Zoë struggled with her Catholic faith and its almost glib assertion that the prolonged, painful death of her mother and her personal crisis of faith was God's will she must accept. When afterwards she realized the creation of her future was in her own hands, mysterious doors opened and pathways emerged that she never anticipated.

The spiritual principles espoused by Rachel Devane are Buddhist in nature but touch on other faiths including Christianity. Reincarnation is basic to Buddhist belief and is the basis for several souls moving from one body to another in the book. Many of Rachel's thoughts fall under what most people would call New Age ideology that incorporates the concept of all of us being a part of the universal mind.

The visitations of Zoë and Patrick are inspired by the New Testament accounts of angelic visits to Mary and Joseph and also by the strange visitor in Whitley Strieber's book, *The Key*.

Readers will notice that there is a strong correlation between Zoë's story and the New Testament narratives about the annunciation and birth of Christ and the subsequent fleeing from the enemies into Egypt. Joshua is Christ-like in many ways in that he is born free of the dreaded mutation and has the capacity to save the future of mankind from certain destruction. There is a strong sense of direct intervention from the god-like John Asterman, who mysteriously comes from the future and yet free will is present at every step of the story and the ultimate choice for the future lies with Zoë and her friends and with us all.

Suggested Reading:

Collins, F. S. (2006). The language of God: a scientist presents evidence for belief. New York, Free Press.

Conze, E. (1951). Buddhism; its essence and development. New York, Philosophical Library.

Frankl, V. E., et al. (1997). Man's search for ultimate meaning. New York, Insight Books.

Goswami, A., et al. (1993). The self-aware universe: how consciousness creates the material world. New York, Putnam's Sons.

Mackenzie, Vicki. (1995). Reborn in the West Reincarnation Masters. Trafalgar Square Publishers.

New Testament. Matthew, Chapter 2; Luke, Chapters 1 and 2.

Streiber, Whitley. (2011). The Key. Penguin Publishing Group.

Trapped minds and mental powers

As a physician, I have had patients who no longer could be cared for at home and ultimately became residents of nursing care facilities and retirement homes. In an age when we are seeing increasing numbers of patients with severe, disabling diseases, there are still many individuals who, like Macey Grabel and the initial John Asterman, are intellectually intact but live in the crumbling houses of their declining bodies.

A wonderful nurse I knew many years ago, after whom I portrayed Freida Harrison, told me as a student to always treat patients with respect and as if they knew everything I was saying since sometimes they are quite aware, despite their physical and mental limitations. I continue to follow this advice and find myself reminding other physicians, nurses and families the importance of treating patients with respect regardless of the circumstances. The fact that someone cannot smile, speak or acknowledge our presence does mean their intellect is inadequate or lacking. The power of the mind to affect aspects of the physical universe are not in question any longer. Consciousness affects the physical world and the power of our minds is much greater than we have been programmed to believe. Scientists have struggled with the 'spooky effects' of consciousness on quantum physics and much has been written on the subject without definitive understanding. Many scientists who study the paranormal have been marginalized by mainstream science, but much interesting and significant work has been done.

Suggested reading:

Alexander, E. and K. Newell (2017). Living in a mindful universe: a neurosurgeon's journey into the heart of consciousness. Emmaus, Pennsylvania, Rodale.

Kaku, M. (2014). The future of the mind: the scientific quest to understand, enhance, and empower the mind. New York, Doubleday.

Radin, D. I. (1997). The conscious universe: the scientific truth of psychic phenomena. New York, N.Y., Harper Edge.

Targ, R. (2004). Limitless mind: a guide to remote viewing and transformation of consciousness. Novato, Calif., New World Library.

Wilber, K. (2001). Quantum questions: mystical writings of the world's great physicists. Boston

New York, Shambhala; Distributed in the U.S. by Random House.

Guatemala Archeology

The story of Horowitz's finding of a new deity on his archeological dig is fictitious. However, the stories about the Q site and Tikal are based on published research. While Horowitz used satellite photography to help him locate new finds in the Guatemalan jungle, the recent use of LiDAR (Light Detection and Ranging) scanning has revitalized jungle archeology by digitally removing the canopy of trees and brush from densely covered ancient sites. Recently vast areas of Guatemala have yielded evidence of extensive cities ruled by rulers designated as snake kings.

Suggested reading:

(2018). Lost Treasure of the Maya Snake Kings. National Geographic, National Geographic.

Clynes, T. (2018). Exclusive: Laser scans reveal Maya "Megalopolis" below Guatemalan jungle. National Geographic.

Physics

The concepts of entanglement that are both predicted and measured products of quantum mechanical theory are indeed stranger than can be imagined. There are several excellent books dealing with these ideas. Greene and Hawkin have excellent popular books expounding on relativity, quantum mechanics and string theory. Dean Radin has written about extrasensory experiences in quantum reality providing an interesting explanation for psi phenomena. This entire field continues to evolve and has taken on almost mystical qualities. Readers wanting a good explanation of the more unusual findings of quantum mechanics will be disappointed since the best minds in physics still consider it a mystery.

Suggested reading:

Greene, B. (1999). The elegant universe: superstrings, hidden dimensions, and the quest for the ultimate theory. New York, W.W. Norton.

Greene, B. (2004). The fabric of the cosmos: space, time, and the texture of reality. New York, A.A. Knopf.

Hawking, S. (2002). The theory of everything: the origin and fate of the universe. Beverly Hills, CA, New Millennium Press.

Kaku, M. (1995). Hyperspace: a scientific odyssey through parallel universes, time warps, and the tenth dimension. New York, Anchor Books.

Radin, D. I. (1997). The conscious universe: the scientific truth of psychic phenomena. New York, N.Y., Harper Edge.

Genetics and Virus-Induced Mutations

The DNA techniques referred to in the book are established methods for studying evolution, genetic relationships, lineages, mutations and genetic-based diseases. Each person's genetic make-up is unique unless they are identical twins or otherwise came from the same fertilized egg, and this has become the basis for modern identification as well documented by entertaining programs such as *CSI*. Genetic evaluation has become the keystone for certain cancer diagnostic treatments as well as other genetic diseases.

The idea for a genetic mutation creating havoc for our future stemmed from an interest I have had for many years. When I was doing research with the Public Health Service at the National Cancer Institute in the Viral Biology Branch in 1972–1974, many researchers were looking for viruses (particularly retroviruses known as RNA tumor viruses) associated with cancer. These viruses could insert their genetic material into normal cells and alter them in such a way as to produce cancer. There are many animal models, certain particular inbred mice, that have tumors caused by viruses that insert their genetic material into normal cells and at some point, transforms them into tumor cells. Subsequently, with the advent of increasingly more sophisticated genetic studies, scientists have found segments of inherited viral genetic material in human beings and genes that may be related to human cancer.

The DNA of ancient viruses first spotted in the Neanderthal genome have now been identified in modern humans, although is not yet clear if they cause disease in humans. Additional genetic studies suggest that the virus genetic material was first introduced into our ancestors one hundred thousand years ago. These retroviral gene sequences make up about eight per cent of the human genome, and are part of what is sometimes called 'junk' or non-coding DNA because they don't contain genetic instructions to make proteins.

A retrovirus that infected our ancestors one hundred million years ago became a human gene that is expressed in embryos and cancers, and can be detected in the blood of pregnant women. Accumulating evidence suggests potential roles for endogenous retroviruses in early life events, which may affect adult health. In 2010, researchers unveiled the genomes of two extinct groups of humans — the Neanderthals and the Denisovans. This research revealed that some humans share a few per cent of their DNA with their extinct cousins. Recent findings suggest that the viruses probably infected our ancestors roughly four hundred thousand years ago.

This information is presented to you to help you understand how genes can be manipulated through viral infections to lend some credence to the idea that Patrick David's acquired mutation could occur. However, please note that most viral infections damage or destroy cells and do not just alter their genetic material. Also, for the gene to be passed to other generations, the germ cell (eggs or sperm) must be infected with incorporation of the genetic material. For the average reader this is probably too much information, but for science geeks like me, some references are listed here for you.

Johnson, Welkin. Endogenous Retroviruses in the Genomics Era. Annual Review of Virology, Vol. 2: 135–159, 2015 Barbulescue, M. et al. Many human endogenous retrovirus K (HERV-K) proviruses are unique to humans. Current Biology, Volume 9, Issue 16, 1999.

Nagiorkinis, G. et al. *Roles of Endogenous Retroviruses in Early Life Events. Trends in Microbiology, Volume 25, Issue 11, Page 876–877, 2017.*

Temin, H. M. (1972). "RNA-Directed DNA Synthesis." Scientific American.

Walter Holder, MD
Winston-Salem, NC
December 22, 2021

CPSIA information can be obtained
at www.ICGtesting.com
Printed in the USA
BVHW030924070422
633675BV00007B/184